Caine, Leslie

Manor of death

DUE DATE 0906 29.95

28c 7/13			

CORNWALL PUBLIC LIBRARY
335 Hudson Street
Cornwall, NY 12518
(845) 534-8282
DISCARD

MANOR OF DEATH

Center Point
Large Print

This Large Print Book carries the
Seal of Approval of N.A.V.H.

MANOR OF DEATH

a domestic bliss mystery

Leslie Caine

CENTER POINT PUBLISHING
THORNDIKE, MAINE

To my brilliant editor, Kate Miciak

This Center Point Large Print edition
is published in the year 2006 by arrangement with
Bantam Dell, a division of Random House, Inc.

Copyright © 2006 by Leslie Caine.

All rights reserved.

The text of this Large Print edition is unabridged. In other aspects, this book may vary from the original edition. Printed in Thailand. Set in 16-point Times New Roman type.

ISBN 1-58547-799-0

Library of Congress Cataloging-in-Publication Data

Caine, Leslie.
Manor of death / Leslie Caine.--Center Point large print ed.
p. cm.
ISBN 1-58547-799-0 (lib. bdg. : alk. paper)
1. Interior decorators--Fiction. 2. Haunted houses--Fiction. 3. Murder--Investigations--Fiction. 4. Large type books. I. Title.

PS3603.A39M36 2006
813'.6--dc22

200600282

chapter 1

A ghost was on Francine Findley's roof!

That was my first thought at spotting the figure in white—luminescent in the moonlight outside my bedroom window.

My second thought was that the stress I'd been under lately was finally getting to me. It was not a ghost. Just a girl, wearing a white nightgown, her long red tresses ruffled in the breeze. Could that be Lisa, up on her mother's roof at this hour? Who else had long red hair like that?

No, this girl was taller and older than twelve-year-old Lisa. It was too dark and, with our houses separated by Francine's and my own backyards, too distant for me to be certain, but the girl looked a lot like Willow McAndrews, the college student who was renting a room in the house next door to Francine's. Willow had short blond hair, though.

Still staring out the window, I brushed aside my sheet and comforter, sat up, and struggled to rouse myself from my brain fog. Why would Willow McAndrews don a red wig and climb out onto a neighbor's roof? And how could she or anyone else get onto the roof of the third-floor tower room in the first place?

As an interior designer, I was intimately familiar with Francine Findley's octagonal-shaped room. Francine had hired me recently to renovate her Victorian mansion in preparation for Crestview's annual tour of historic homes. Contrary to my advice, Francine had insisted on keeping the wall that sealed off the only staircase to the roof. Decades ago, previous owners had built that wall after their daughter Abby had fallen to her death, a tragedy that later inspired the rumor that the ghost of Abby haunted the "widow's walk"—a flat roof encircled by banisters. The architectural feature was modeled after homes along New England shores where wives of fishermen stood to watch for their husbands' boats.

This afternoon, Francine had mentioned that she was exhausted and planned to "have an early dinner and collapse in bed." Had she suddenly needed to leave home, however, and asked Willow to stay overnight to watch Lisa? That would at least explain Willow's presence *in* the house, just not *on* it. All the windows were dark. Should I call Francine's cell phone? I looked at my clock on my nightstand. The red digital numbers read 1:06 a.m.—a horrid hour to call a single mother who might be in the midst of a real emergency—to report that her sitter was strolling around on the roof.

I looked outside again, but the girl had vanished. She couldn't possibly have eased herself over the railing and climbed down a ladder that fast. She must have dashed down the stairs and was now in the three-by-twelve-foot walled-off space, getting in and out through the window. That window had been boarded up the last time I'd looked, though. Yawning, I rubbed at my eyes as I lay back down, cursing my insomnia, which had left me addled for a full month now. In desperation, I'd poured a small fortune into my bed: Egyptian-cotton sheets with an obscenely high thread count, a silk comforter as light and soft as angel wings, and—

Wait! I bolted upright. There was a second—and horrible—means for someone to vanish from a rooftop in an instant!

I gasped as my cracked door creaked further open. Framed by the doorway, I could make out my black cat's silhouette and see her amber eyes. My heart thudding, I looked out the window again. No one was on the roof. "Oh, Hildi, I have to go check my neighbor's yard!" I informed my cat.

I clicked on the small Tiffany lamp atop my nightstand, sprang from my bed, jammed my arms into the sleeves of my dusty-rose bathrobe to cover my silk teddy, and grabbed the first shoes I could find—black stilettos. If I did have to run to assist some badly injured girl, I'd probably trip on the two-inch heels. I started for the door, then whirled to grab the flashlight by my bed. I raced down the stairs, my confused cat darting out of my path. I threw open the back door, crammed my feet into my shoes, and tore across the lawn. My heels sank into the wet grass, but I didn't slow my pace until I reached the landscape rocks and the row of rosebushes that rimmed the property line.

With the stones crunching beneath my feet, I trotted across the hard-packed dirt alley, stepped over Francine's low wrought-iron fence, and swept my dim beam across her back lawn. "Hello? Is anybody out here?" I asked the silent darkness, my voice barely above a whisper.

No groans. No crumpled bodies clad in white nightgowns. No maniacal cackles, either. My presence did, however, set off Francine's neighbor's dog to barking—Diana Durst's beagle. Diana's attic window was aglow with a yellow light. Was that lamp on earlier, or had I wakened her? Or could that be the room that Willow McAndrews was renting from Diana? Diana had once told me that Willow was a rock climber. Willow was *also* self-absorbed and immature; perhaps pretending to be the red-haired ghost of some long-dead soul was her idea of humor.

Hildi joined me, her soft fur now brushing against my bare shins. "Let's go back home," I told her over Bugle's ruckus. At least it was reassuring to realize that if anyone had fallen off Francine's roof, Bugle would *already* have been barking.

Come to think of it, his shrill barks were what had originally awakened me.

Though typically hot and dry in mid-July, Crestview was doing its best impression of Seattle the next afternoon as I walked to Francine's home. I held my London Fog overcoat closed, careful not to crush the rolled-up lengths of wallpaper angled into my inner pockets, and luxuriated in the soothing, steady patter of raindrops on my umbrella. When I'd called Francine this morning and reported last night's disturbance, Francine insisted she'd been home all night and that "it is absolutely impossible that anyone was on my roof." She sounded as though she thought I was as flaky as old paint on a picnic table.

Could I have dreamt the whole thing? If so, I'd never had such a vivid dream. Maybe my struggles with the neighborhood association and with my beloved landlady, Audrey Munroe, were wreaking havoc with me, even during my sleep.

While stepping over a puddle, I silently repeated my personal mantra: *confidence and optimism.* In so many ways, this was my all-time dream assignment—an interior-design job within my own astonishingly lovely neighborhood of Maplewood Hill, at the Victorian mansion that I'd lusted over for two years now, ever since I'd first moved to Colorado. Granted, my work to date at the mansion had met with a series of snags and brick walls, but that goes with the territory—the better the job, the bigger thc challenges. And my optimism was already being affirmed; just last week Audrey had told me she understood and supported my decision to accept this assignment at Francine's—that I couldn't very well give up a major career opportunity without as much as knowing *why* Audrey didn't "wish to associate with Francine." (Nor was Audrey willing to elaborate on the matter, even now.)

Soon the neighborhood association would approve of our plans to install three picture windows within the octagonal tower room. Better yet, if they rejected them, I'd have more ammunition to convince Francine to remove that awful inner wall, which not only blocked the staircase but made the room lopsided. Her sole argument was that she had "a severe fear of heights" and didn't want young Lisa to be able to get onto the roof. For the life of me, I couldn't understand why she refused to remove both the wall *and* the staircase to the roof. Be that as it may, when it comes to interior design, the customer *is always* right; after all, she or he is the one who must live with the final results. However, some customers need more nudges than others to discover their own good taste and sound decision-making skills. Francine Findley required a nice, firm shove, and fortunately for her, she'd hired just the right designer to give her one.

Speaking of shoves, a chilly blast of wind encouraged me to increase my pace. Francine's and my landlady's backyards bordered each other, so it was a thirty-second walk between our back doors. Today, with the lawns drenched, I'd taken the more formal front-door route, which required me to circle to the opposite side of our block. Even as I picked my way across a veritable river forming alongside Francine's walkway, I was so taken by the looming presence of the tower room that I tilted my umbrella and looked up through the raindrops. The curtains were quivering, as though someone had spotted me and ducked out of sight—Francine's daughter Lisa, no doubt.

Protected by the roof over the Findleys' stoop, I shook off my umbrella and closed it, enjoying the wonderful damp air, a delectable pine scent wafting from the majestic evergreen in the front yard. I rang the old-fashioned twist-key doorbell. After a brief wait, Francine, a pretty woman in her late forties with auburn hair like mine, threw open the door. "Good afternoon, Erin," she said with gusto.

"Hi, Francine." My heart danced as I stepped inside her marvelous foyer. The maple parquet floor, ivory-colored walls, and carved archway had such a regal grace. For me, it felt as magical as being able to walk into a Fabergé egg. I grinned at Francine. "We're having quite the rainstorm today."

"We sure are. Let me take your coat."

"Thanks. Just let me empty my pockets. I've got the wallpaper samples with me." I extracted the samples and some double-sided sticky tape.

"I *thought* you looked a little stiff—and wide—around the waistline," she teased.

Handing her my coat, I wondered what could have caused such a deep rift between my affable landlady and Francine in the three short years since Francine had moved to Crestview. The latter had always been unfailingly charming and gracious to me, although I'd only been in the neighborhood for eight months or so and hadn't known her for long.

She slid open a pair of paneled pocket doors. As she grabbed a hanger out of the coat closet, her hand brushed against a Halloween costume. It was a cheap, department-store purchase—a skeleton painted on thin polyester black fabric and a plastic mask for the skull, its elastic cord looped over the hanger hook.

"Oh, look, Francine," I said with a smile, "it seems

as though you've got a skeleton in your closet."

Francine chuckled. "Well, I suppose we *all* have skeletons in our closets. But this one in particular must be Lisa's doing. She must be trying to give us a message about the lack of closet space in her bedroom."

Francine's twelve-year-old had been the friendliest of all my neighbors—up until she learned that I had been hired to turn her would-be bedroom into a studio for her mom. Now, along with my landlady and the homeowners' association, Lisa was a third source of contention. It was my job to ensure that *all* members of the family were satisfied (and preferably thrilled) with the transformation of their living spaces. "I can design a wonderful, spacious closet for her," I said.

"Oh, that won't do the trick," Francine scoffed. "Believe me."

"She's still hinting that she wants to have the third-floor room as her bedroom?"

"She sure is. And Lisa's 'hints' have all the delicacy of a bull in a china shop. I'm not budging, though. I've told her all along that I was eventually going to convert that room into my music studio." A professional musician, Francine played an electric organ. "But now, after we've lived here for almost three years, she seems to think—"

Francine broke off as a door above us slammed, followed by the sound of footsteps tromping down the stairs. Lisa, Francine's only child, sneered at me as she rounded the corner. She wore cutoffs and a black camisole underneath an unbuttoned denim jacket and dragged a black backpack along the gorgeous maple floorboards, making me inwardly shudder. She was a freckle-faced redhead, and I couldn't help but study her now to see if that could have been Lisa on the roof, after all. I was even more certain, however, that the girl I'd seen was a young woman and not Lisa. She lowered the earphones on her iPod and grumbled, "Oh. *You're* here."

"Yes, Erin just arrived," her mother replied breezily. "Which you would have realized if you weren't always pumping rap music into your ears." Lisa rolled her eyes and slung a strap of her backpack over one shoulder. Francine explained to me, "Lisa is off to a sleepover before her best friend leaves town for three weeks."

Lisa shrugged off her mother's attempt to hug her, muttering, "You don't need to tell the whole world my private business, Mom."

"I'm only mentioning it becausc, at somc point soon, the three of us need to sit down together. We need to discuss what we want done with your bedroom."

"Jeez! I already *told* you! I *want* the tower room as my bedroom! If I can't have that, you might as well do whatever *you* want to *my* room!" Lisa stepped into a pair of fire-engine-red flip-flops on the closet floor.

"We noticed your Halloween costume, by the way, dear."

"*What* costume?"

"This skeleton." Francine removed the costume on its hanger to show Lisa.

In a voice rancid with disdain, Lisa replied, "That's not mine. I've never seen it before."

"Well, it certainly isn't *mine*. It's six sizes too small, for one thing." Francine examined the tag inside the costume neckline before she stashed it back in the closet. She added, "It must be one of your friends' costumes, then."

"Nope. Not possible. I'd remember. Bet it's Abby's."

"Lisa!" her mother admonished.

"Abby's our ghost," Lisa informed me, one hand on her hip, which she jutted in my general direction. "Our house has been haunted ever since some kid jumped off the roof fifty years ago. Abby lives in the room that you're remodeling. And, I can tell you right now, she is *not* going to approve of the way you plan to destroy her bedroom."

"Lisa! That's enough!"

In spite of the girl's undisguised disdain toward me, I liked Lisa and I understood all too well her frustration at losing out on her favorite space. I smiled at her and replied, "Then we'll just have to put all our heads together to come up with a fabulous room that we *all* approve of."

"Yeah. Like *that's* gonna happen." She returned her headphones to her ears. "I gotta go, Mom. We're riding our bikes and meeting halfway."

"But . . . it's pouring outside."

"I know. That's why we're riding our bikes."

"Wait!" Francine followed her out to the stoop. "You shouldn't be wearing sandals while you're riding your bike. Put *both* straps of your backpack on. And take those headphones off!"

The flip-flops stayed put, but Francine managed to pantomime the safer position of the backpack and the removal of her headphones and, although Lisa grumbled something to herself in the process, she complied. Francine sighed and held up a hand, calling, "See you tomorrow," as Lisa straddled her bike and rode off.

Francine shut the door and turned back to me. "Sorry about that, Erin. Lisa's social skills have been plummeting ever since her father's and my divorce."

"Oh, it's truly not a problem. Lisa's a total sweetheart, most of the time. My half-sister's roughly Lisa's age, and she's equally moody." The fact that I rarely got the chance to see my sister, who lived in California with my semi-estranged father, brought an unexpected lump to my throat.

Francine rolled her eyes. "I'm just hoping she grows out of this soon."

I decided to give the matter of last night's nocturnal visit one last mention. "It's funny that Lisa happened to bring up Abby. Last night when I saw someone on—"

"Oh, heavens! Is this about the prowler you think you saw on my roof? Erin, you don't actually believe that ghost nonsense, do you?"

"No, of course not. I was going to suggest that Willow McAndrews might be doing this as a practical joke, making people think that they'd seen Abby."

"What possible reason would Willow have to pull a

stunt like that?" Francine chuckled and shook her head. "Honestly, Erin! You're letting your imagination run wild. You must have been dreaming last night. That's the only rational explanation."

If forced to choose, I'd rather believe that I saw a ghost than worry that I was now unable to distinguish my dreams from reality. I held my tongue and studied my client's green eyes, curious as to why she was so resolute; from her second-floor bedroom, would she have heard someone on the tower roof?

The doorbell rang. Francine grinned. "Watch. This'll be Lisa's friend. They'll have taken different routes and missed each other." She swung the door open.

It was Diana Durst, Francine's next-door neighbor. Diana, a real estate agent who ran the historic-homes tour, was in her late thirties, plump but attractive, with dark brown hair and eyes. She wore one of her customary pastel skirt suits—now slightly rain-spattered—and her ever-present broad smile.

"Brrrr," she exclaimed to Francine. "Goodness! It's raining cats and dogs out there!" She craned her neck to smile at me. "Hello, Erin. I spotted you on the sidewalk a minute ago and hoped you'd be here."

"Hi, Diana." I couldn't help but return her smile. The woman was always so upbeat that to do anything else would feel like scowling at a puppy. Which reminded me: Should I admit that I had caused Diana's dog to bark at one o'clock in the morning?

"Did you hear any weird noises last night, Francine? Coming from the tower room, maybe?"

"Oh, no!" Francine clicked her tongue and put her hands on her hips. "You *too?*"

"Pardon?"

"Erin thought she saw someone on my roof last night."

"Oh! Oh!" Diana hopped up and down. She'd once told me she was a former cheerleader, and it was easy to envision her with pompoms now. "Thank goodness someone other than just me saw her! Did you show Audrey, too, by any chance?"

"No, I didn't want to wake her, but—"

"This is amazing!" In her excitement, Diana grabbed Francine's wrist. "We'll be able to sell *twice* as many tickets to the tour, once the word gets out."

"*What* word?" Francine asked, in no way sharing Diana's perky optimism.

"Why, that the ghost is back, of course . . . the ghost that haunts your tower room!"

Francine's brow furrowed. "There is no ghost in my house! Nor on my roof! That's just a silly rumor started by silly people who obviously don't have enough to talk about." She peered at the two of us as though weighing the notion that we were in a "silly" league together.

I too was growing more skeptical by the moment. Diana could have hired her renter to waltz around on Francine's roof as a publicity stunt. Perhaps she'd even encouraged Bugle to bark once Willow was in place, to increase the possibility that their immediate neighbors would look out their windows. "Diana, I've got to say that it didn't look like a ghost to me. It looked like a young woman . . . flesh and blood."

"No, no, Erin. Believe me. That's how this particular ghost always appears . . . solid as a rock, then she vanishes into thin air." She giggled. "Isn't this just *wonderful* news, ladies? Couldn't you just *die?*"

Not willingly, no, I said to myself.

"It's quite a coincidence that, according to everything I've ever heard, nobody's seen this ghost in more than ten years, then it reappears right when we're about to show the house on *your* tour of homes," Francine pointed out tartly.

"Coincidence?" Diana cried happily. "Puh-leeze! This is no coincidence. Abby's been haunting the very room you two are now redecorating. She doesn't like anybody to touch that room. Whenever anyone does, she creates mayhem."

"Does she?" I asked, amused at the notion of an interior-design-vigilante ghost.

"Yes," Diana replied firmly. "*Always*. And I should know. I took over the real estate company from my mother, who inherited it from *her* mother, and we've been handling the sale of this house back before it was even haunted."

"I'm really very certain that this was a girl I saw. Not a ghost."

"Oh, it was a ghost, all right," Diana chirped. "And any talk of its just being a run-of-the-mill girl will nip my publicity right in the bud . . . so that's quite enough of that."

"In fact, I thought she looked a lot like your renter," I persisted.

"That isn't possible," Diana countered. "Willow was home with me all of last night. It *had* to have been the ghost. As a matter of fact, I've heard from more than one source that Willow was the spitting image of Abby Chambers."

"Well, Erin," Francine said, an eyebrow cocked. "Maybe you were right, after all. I'm going to ask Willow about all of this. If she *is* climbing onto my roof, I'm never going to hire her to watch Lisa again."

"Don't be ridiculous, Francine," Diana objected. "Why would Willow do something like that?"

"Maybe she thought it'd help you and your tour," Francine replied.

"It's hardly *my* tour. It's not as though I'm making a bundle of money for running it every year. I don't even get a cut of the ticket sales."

"No, but it doesn't hurt your real estate business to offer your card to everyone on the tour, either."

Diana's smile faded at last. Rose-colored splotches formed on her round cheeks. "I saw the ghost myself, and I assure you, it was *not* Willow!"

"Frankly, I'm surprised you can even see onto my roof from your little house."

There was a sharp edge to Francine's comments that made me realize what might make Audrey dislike the woman. But Diana replied evenly, "I can see. Easily. From my attic office. I happened to be up there working very late." She cleared her throat. "Anyway,

Erin: Thank you for verifying my ghost-sighting. I was going to ask if you'd mind if I send someone over from the Crestview *Sentinel* to interview you, but maybe I shouldn't."

"No!" Francine said before I could even open my mouth. "This is my house, my roof, and I do *not* want reporters nosing around my property!"

Diana started to object, then forced a smile, and said sweetly, "Mum's the word. Have a nice evening."

The moment the door was shut behind Diana, Francine sighed. "Well. I hope Diana doesn't turn out to be on this secret committee that our illustrious neighbors elected." She was referring to the group that would decide whether or not we could proceed with the remodel as planned. "She'd probably vote to have us turn my room into a gift shop."

"Oh, I think she just gets a little caught up in bringing lots of people to the tour. She doesn't mean any harm."

"No, nor does Bob Stanley. But you know what they say about the road to hell being paved with good intentions."

The situation with Bob, my next-door neighbor, was indeed a bit hellish. Bob manned the architectural-review function of our association and, I was told, rubber-stamped his approval of everyone's remodels. Mere hours after he'd hinted to me that he would give a few words of praise to my "truly stunning design," he instead announced at the homeowners' meeting that my plans to install picture windows would "not maintain the original integrity of a historic home." Caught off-guard and armed with insider information (we'd been discussing ideas for *his* house when he'd complimented me over Francine's design), I'd blurted out, "Why is it that Francine Findley's picture windows would damage the house's 'historical integrity,' whereas the bay window you're planning on installing in *your* historic home is fine?"

A massive blowup ensued. The homeowners sided with either Francine or Bob, and the debate grew so contentious that a private committee was formed by a secret ballot. Until a decision was reached, "no architectural changes are to be permitted by either party."

Francine's brow was creased with worry lines. I told her, "I'm confident and optimistic that the committee will approve of our plans as is. But if they don't, we'll make some revisions that can work every bit as well." *Better,* even.

"You mean, removing the wall and the staircase?" She scoffed, "Maybe I *should* do that. Just to see if 'Abby' "—she drew finger quotes—"can still levitate onto my roof."

I ignored her crabby tone and said happily, "Whether or not we go with the picture windows, removing that one elongated wall would be a major improvement."

She shot a glare at me.

"Actually, Francine, according to"—I hesitated, realizing I shouldn't mention Audrey's name to her enemy—"the grapevine, we'll hear the decision no later than tomorrow. That's why I want us to go ahead and select the wall treatments. Once we know our square footage, we can place our order and go from there."

"Sounds like a plan to me. And you're going to hang the sample pieces now?"

I told her I was and explained that I was going to use easy-to-remove double-sided tape, and she excused herself to make some phone calls while I did so. I climbed the stairs with growing energy; seeing the empty canvas of a room and envisioning how it would soon look was one of my favorite phases of my job. I hurried past the four upstairs bedrooms to the second staircase, which led to a small attic where my work would begin.

This windowless attic was illuminated solely by an unremarkable pendant light fixture centered over the stairwell. The white plaster ceilings were so steeply slanted that, at five foot eight, I had to duck as I rounded the banister to reach the tower room. Francine had balked at the expense of rebuilding the attic roof to eliminate this neck-craning approach, but my minor improvements would work wonders toward revitalizing the space. I would upgrade the banisters and the ceiling fixture, install an octagonal window in the opposite wall, paint the walls a buttery yellow, refinish the heart-pine flooring to restore its warm red hues—and *presto!* An entrance worthy of a magnificent room. I turned the boring doorknob that would soon be replaced with octagonal antique glass and strode into the center of the room.

I indulged myself with a slow twirl. In my mind's eye, the black base color and Pollockesque paint splatters were gone from the floor and the heart-pine floorboards were polished to a natural warm sheen. The dirty lavender walls were papered over in a delicate primrose-yellow floral print, perfectly accentuated with snow-white trim. The baby-blue curtains were gone, and the too-small and too-boxy windows were replaced with fabulous large arched ones on each of the seven outer walls. Oh, what I could do with the planes of the ceiling in such a room—if only I could remove the inner wall and restore this space to its original dimensions! Francine was a musician, for heaven's sake! Why couldn't she see what an ethereal symphony of light the sunbeams would make as they slanted through glorious windows?

Forced to honor my client's wishes, I scowled at the eyesore of a wall, which, in an architectural nightmare, butted against the two windows to either side of it. Those off-center windows would be removed, and three of the five remaining walls would become picture windows. "And it will look terrific that way," I assured myself aloud.

The inner wall with its relatively smooth surface was where I would now hang the wallpaper. Its surface was oddly warm to the touch, considering that there had been so little sunlight today. I chuckled at the notion that my adversarial wall had read my mind and was now simmering at the prospect of being demolished. Humming, I hung the four pieces of the wall coverings.

Wallpaper fades in direct sunlight, so all of these patterns featured subtle, light hues that would work well in the room. Even so, I had a clear favorite and had hedged my bets by taking down all the curtains and strategically placing the best pattern in the prime spot—likeliest to show the best in the natural lighting and the first piece that Francine would see as she entered the room.

Francine came upstairs to check on my progress just as I'd finished. Her eyes widened. "Oh. You put the paper over the wall that blocks the staircase."

"Is that a problem?"

"No, not really. Not necessarily. It should be fine." She didn't sound convincing, though, but I couldn't fathom why she objected. She smiled as she studied my favorite pattern. "Ooh, that looks really nice."

"Doesn't it?" I replied with a grin. "I'm going to leave you with a second color copy of my furniture plans. That will help you visualize the room in its completed state."

"Could you hang your plans on the walls, too? If you don't mind."

"Not at all. It'll be inspiring."

"Or depressing, if the vote goes against us and we have to go back to the drawing board." She sighed as she left.

The woman could clearly use my confidence-and-optimism mantra.

I quickly hung up my drawings and happened to glance out the window. The rain had stopped and the sun was making an appearance. To my surprise, my landlady was standing next to her one-car garage, a hand shading her eyes as she stared up at Francine's house. I waved, and Audrey gestured for me to come home.

Curious as to why Audrey was beckoning, I left soon afterward and dashed across the soggy lawns. Audrey was pacing near the back door in the kitchen when I arrived. "Oh, Erin," she said by way of greeting. "I got the most exasperating news today. Hugh is back in town."

"Hugh?"

"Hugh Black. Husband number four-and-a-quarter." She opened her refrigerator, saying over her shoulder, "I desperately need a glass of wine. Anyway. Hugh claims to be a changed man. He wants to reconcile with me."

"I thought you were only married four times total."

"We weren't married long enough to warrant my designating Hugh a whole ordinal number just to himself."

"I'm sorry you're exasperated, but . . . is he on his way over here or something? Is that why you wanted me to come straight home?"

"No. It's not an emergency." She poured herself a glass of chardonnay, holding out the bottle to me in an unspoken offer to pour me a glass, but I shook my head.

"Then why did—"

"I was merely waving hello to you."

Audrey was up to something, which, based on previous experience, would no doubt be revealed to me soon enough. I got such a kick out of her that I couldn't help but smile, and I slipped onto the white slat-back barstool at her kitchen island, watching as she appreciatively took her first sip of the chardonnay. I took a deep breath, gaining sustenance from this magnificent space, so bright and airy with its copper accessories and white trim against the maize-tile and butter-cream-yellow walls. "So tell me about Hugh."

"There's not much to tell. We were married, very briefly, three years ago. I dumped him because he was a skirt chaser."

Aha! Francine and her soon-to-be-divorced husband had also moved in three years ago. "By any chance, was Francine Findley wearing the skirt that Hugh was chasing?"

Audrey arched an eyebrow, held my gaze, and said evenly, "Now that you mention it, I believe she was." She took another sip of wine. "As I was saying . . . or would have been, had I not gotten distracted, I've been trying to get a feel for which direction the wind is blowing regarding the committee's decision on your design, and it appears that they're going to announce some sort of compromise."

"A *compromise?* Such as: Francine can install one and a half picture windows, and the Stanleys can install half of a bay window?"

"There's really no point in speculating if you're going to be facetious, Erin." Audrey continued, "I had a long talk with the Stanleys this afternoon about your rift. Bob now admits that he acted rashly in not hiring you in favor of your handsome friend Mr. Sullivan. Cassandra felt—"

"Wait. You talked to Bob and Cassandra about this? After I *specifically* asked you *not* to?" Hildi trotted into the room and greeted me with a meow. I took that as a feline reminder that I needed to watch my tone of voice with Audrey; although all was forgiven, I didn't want to touch off another quarrel.

Audrey flicked her wrist and replied, "It came up in conversation."

"I see," I muttered, unhappy. Immediately following the association meeting at which Bob had rejected my plans for Francine's house, he also reneged on our verbal agreement and hired someone else to spruce up his house for the tour. Out of the dozens of designers in this picturesque college town, he'd chosen Steve Sullivan, my fiercest professional rival. The man was supremely talented and sexy as hell, but Sullivan always brought out the worst in me.

The doorbell rang.

Audrey glanced at the clock and announced blithely, "Ah. That will be Mr. Sullivan, right on time."

chapter 2

And why is Steve Sullivan paying us a visit?" I stayed in my seat and kept my voice pleasant.

"Steve was next door, working with the Stanleys on their design, when I was visiting with them. He happened to mention that he would be stopping by to try to reach a détente of sorts with you." She took a quick sip of wine.

"A 'détente'? What's going on, Audrey? Please tell me you're not playing matchmaker!"

She put a hand to her chest, the picture of innocence. "Perish the thought! If I wanted to pair you with someone, it would be with my own soon-to-be-divorced son, not Mr. Sullivan. You're the one who keeps telling me that a person's home should be their haven. What with your squabbling with our neighbors *plus* the designer working right next door, the very least—" She broke off as the doorbell rang a second time. "Hadn't you better get that, dear?" she asked, sugary-sweet.

"I suppose so." I left the glorious kitchen and made my way through the disaster of the parlor. Judging by the mess, Audrey was set to embark on yet another arts-and-crafts project, but as for the exact nature of that project, I was hoping for a don't-ask-don't-tell policy this time; in lieu of paying rent, I consulted for Audrey's local Martha Stewart–like TV show and redesigned her marvelous house. Audrey redecorated with mind-boggling abandon, so my success rate was roughly comparable to that of a Colorado lottery ticket, but even *she* was unwilling to mess with the foyer I'd designed.

I paused and struggled to compose myself. Sullivan and I had argued bitterly when we last saw each other almost a week ago; he'd even made a couple of asinine remarks about my troubles with my neighbors.

I threw open the carved oak door. Steve Sullivan was dazzlingly backlit by the late afternoon sunlight; his athletic, six-foot frame cut a dashing figure. He wore an unbuttoned raincoat over black jeans and an emerald-green sweater that brought out the green in his hazel eyes. His light brown hair was, as always, arranged in its sexy state of disarray. He flashed his perfect smile. "Hey, Gilbert," he said, greeting me by my last name.

"Sullivan." I gritted my teeth. I hated the fact that the man was so freakin' handsome that my heart sometimes fluttered when I bumped into him unexpectedly. Or, apparently, when I hadn't seen him in several days, like now. My reaction was no doubt a simple case of adrenaline as I steeled myself for the conflict that invariably erupted within five seconds of our getting into conversation.

"Audrey said you wanted to talk things out."

"Did she?" I glanced over my shoulder in the direction of the kitchen: Audrey was nowhere in sight. Probably listening at the doorway. Despite denials about playing matchmaker, Audrey openly disagreed with my assessment that Sullivan's and my constant squabbles made us a terrible fit. (This from a woman who'd been divorced *four* times, as it turns out, plus widowed once.) I would much rather remain single than become half of a habitually bickering couple.

"If you hadn't taken the first step, I would have

anyway," Sullivan added gently.

He was making nice. Unlike during our *last* meeting. It was possible, though, that I'd been a bit overly sensitive then and had taken his remarks the wrong way. I grabbed my overcoat from the closet. "Let's take a little walk. Okay?"

"Sure."

We strolled side by side along the wet sidewalk, my treacherous heart still not behaving itself. "You were out of town for a few days, I hear." My voice, I was relieved to discover, sounded perfectly disinterested.

He nodded. "Northern California. On business. Missed quite a bit of action in the neighborhood, from what Bob Stanley tells me."

"Yeah. Things have been pretty wild."

"Bob told me that some of your neighbors were starting a petition drive to disband the homeowners' association. And that another group wanted to ban all remodeling projects entirely."

"Yep. Nothing like the threat of adding a couple of windows to really incite the masses."

"That *is* a political hotbed, all right. It was a nasty disagreement over picture windows that led directly to the fall of the Roman Empire, you know."

I laughed in spite of myself. "Really? They had transparent glass way back then?"

"No, which was part of the problem. It caused the famous battle of 350 A.D., known to history students as Why Installeth a Window Thoust Canst Nada See Throughst?"

"Hmm. I must have been absent the day that particular lesson was taught. But those ancient Romans had interesting accents, I must say."

He chuckled. Sullivan had adorable laugh lines that only made his hazel eyes all the more mesmerizing. "Indeed," he agreed, "however, we digresseth." At the corner, he stopped. "Audrey told you about the decision of the homeowners' association, right?"

My eyes widened. So much for Audrey's "seeing which way the wind was blowing." This was like getting the wind sock jammed down my throat. She'd told Sullivan the results before she'd told me! "From the clandestine committee, you mean?" In my attempt to sound nonchalant, my voice came out in a raspy squeak.

"Right. Here's what I'm thinking, Gilbert. If we accept each other's designs as is, Bob will be impossible for me to work with. So we'll say that you insisted I move the bay window to—"

"Stop, Sullivan. I'm not following any of this. Why would either of us have any say whatsoever in each other's designs?"

"Audrey didn't tell you? That's what the committee decided—that I'm your boss on this project, and you're mine."

"Come again?"

"We both have to get one another's approval of our plans before we can proceed."

"What? That's ludicrous!"

"What did you expect? A logical decision reached by a *committee?*"

"Good point. Still . . . if they want to leave it up to us, why not simply do just that . . . butt out and let us both proceed with our plans as they are?"

"Because then they'd have ignored Bob's concerns entirely. That tower room is the tallest structure on Maplewood Hill. Bob doesn't want it to be this modern, all-glass mini-skyscraper."

"It *wouldn't* be a—"

He lifted his palms. "Gilbert, you're preaching to the choir. I loved your plans, just not for a hundred-year-old home in a traditional neighborhood."

That was close to my precise wording when Francine had suggested picture windows, which only made Sullivan's observation all the more grating. "Hey! I'm modernizing a *fifty*-year-old addition at the request of the homeowner! One who handcuffed me by *refusing* to remove a wall that's stuck there just to block *access* to a staircase!"

"Yeah," Sullivan said calmly, meeting my eyes. "I noticed that funky inner wall on your plans. Figured it had to be a stubborn homeowner . . . that she didn't want roof access because of her kid, or something. I'm sure you suggested removing the stairs and redoing the ceiling."

"Of *course* I did!"

"Huh. So she'd rather pay for picture windows installed on a third floor."

I nodded and held my tongue, unwilling to talk about a client behind her back. Yet I was dying to vent with him, or with someone, about how contradictory it was that Francine's "severe fear of heights" hadn't prevented her from requesting that floor-to-ceiling windows be installed in her third-floor room.

"No accounting for taste, I guess." Sullivan gave me a wink, instantly winning me back to his side, even while I knew full well that he was deliberately playing me—establishing camaraderie against a common foe.

"I still can't believe a subcommittee from our homeowners' association would decide something as bizarre as making us oversee each other's plans," I muttered.

"They must be making special compensations because you live here . . . figuring they could trust your judgment."

I arched an eyebrow at him; the man was being downright obsequious. It was *my* design that sparked the controversy, so obviously they *didn't* trust my judgment.

"By the way," Sullivan added, "I had a strange message on my machine. From John Norton. Said something like how, now that he was 'single again,' we should go shoot some pool. Did you two call it quits?"

"Yes. Last week."

"Huh," he said again. His inscrutable expression masked his reaction to learning that I was no longer dating his longtime friend. Before Steve and I had accepted these new assignments—and promptly began butting heads about our respective designs—the news that I was now available might have been an enticement to him. In some alternate universe, Gilbert and Sullivan fit together like a teacup and saucer. In this one, however, we were destined to be forever in disharmony—op-art wallpaper in an ornate rococo room.

Out of the corner of my eye, I spotted Willow McAndrews making a beeline toward us. She was wearing heels and a particularly revealing black dress, and there was little doubt as to whose eye she hoped to catch with the sudden upgrade in wardrobe. Never before had she crossed the street merely to say hello to me.

She started to lift a hand in greeting, but then affected a blasé demeanor and sunk her hands deep into the pockets of her oh-so-carefully unbuttoned black jacket. "Oh, hey, Steve. How's it going?"

To my immense—and inexplicable—satisfaction, a hint of annoyance passed across Sullivan's features as he turned to face her. "Fine, Willow. How are you?"

"I'm great. Thanks."

She stood there, giddily drinking in his eyes, but said nothing further. I decided to end the awkward silence. "Hello, Willow."

"Hi, Erin."

How long would social etiquette demand me to wait before asking her what she'd been doing on our neighbor's roof, wearing a wig?

While tucking her hair behind her ear, an obvious attempt to draw Sullivan's attention to the elegant pearl earring that had suddenly replaced her usual bangles and bobbles, she asked, "So, aren't you guys kinda consulting with the enemy right now?"

Consorting, I silently corrected.

"Actually, Erin and I will be working together on both homes."

"Oh, really?" She struggled to keep her face from falling. Her eyes remained fixed on Sullivan's as though he were cool, crystal-clear water after a desert sojourn. "So do you two know each other? Before you started working next door to her, I mean?"

"For a couple of years now," he answered.

She forced a smile, but gave no reply.

"By the way, Willow," I began, "I have a clear view of Francine's roof through my bedroom window, and last night—"

She held up both palms and shook her head. "Diana already told me about what you saw. That wasn't me. It was Abby."

"Do you really believe that—"

"Wait a minute," Sullivan said, his eyes sparkling and a bemused smile on his lips as he turned to me. " 'Abby'? Isn't that the ghost Cassandra Stanley claims is haunting your client's place?"

"Yes," I replied, but quickly returned my attention to Willow. Playing dumb, I asked, "So you saw her, too?"

She shook her head a second time. "I was asleep."

"I'm surprised Diana didn't wake you up. She seemed so eager to find a fellow witness."

Willow was looking so uncomfortable—her cheeks turning crimson as she fidgeted with her hair—that I took pity on her. "Then again, I've got to admit it didn't occur to me to rouse Audrey from her sleep last night, either." Willow's embarrassment convinced me that it *had* indeed been her I'd seen on the roof, but Diana could have forced her to go along with the crazy idea. "I love your dress, by the way, Willow."

"Thanks. I just now got home from work . . . thought I'd take a little jaunt around the block to clear my head."

"Work" for her was in Cassandra Stanley's downtown store, a retro-sixties shop, where a tie-dyed muumuu would have been more appropriate than her current upscale outfit.

Again, she shifted her hungry eyes to Sullivan. "Then I decided to stop by and see your sketches for the Stanleys' house. The way you were describing your ideas to me last week sounded so . . . impressive, you know?"

Steve glanced over his shoulder and replied, "I'm sure Bob would be happy to show them to you."

"You're going back there soon to finish up for the day, aren't you?" she asked.

He shook his head. "Already done."

"Oh, so . . . where are you off to next?" she asked, fidgeting with her short blond hair behind both ears now, doubling her earlier efforts.

"Home. Next time we bump into each other, be sure and let me know if you liked the design."

Sullivan's brush-off deflated her, and she sighed. "Actually, it's getting pretty chilly. I think I'd better head on back now, but I'll catch you some other time. Have a nice evening."

"Thanks, Willow," I interjected over Steve's "You too."

We shared another awkward silence as Willow turned on a high heel and walked away. I didn't feel up to joshing Sullivan about her obvious crush on him. She was twenty-three, eight years younger than he was, but that wouldn't be robbing the cradle. The *sandbox,* maybe, but not the cradle.

"So. Ghost sightings, huh?" Sullivan asked me, grinning.

"In a manner of speaking. My guess is that Diana Durst wants to drum up publicity by hiring her renter to pose as the ghost of the Findleys' widow's walk."

"Sounds kind of desperate. You really think Diana would do all that just to generate more business for the tour?"

"Either that or Willow did it all on her own. As a joke."

He grimaced and nodded. The reaction made me wonder just how persistent Willow was being in her pursuit of him, but the moment the thought was in my head, I inwardly chastised myself: Willow McAndrews's crush on him was none of my business. I said, "It *is* getting a bit chilly out. I'm going to head back inside."

We started walking back toward Audrey's, which was in the direction of Sullivan's van, as well. "So, Gilbert, like I was saying, let's both go back to our respective drawing boards. We'll come up with new plans that maintain the traditional appearances of the homes from the street, but meet our clients' needs for the interiors."

"Fine. I can do that."

We stopped in front of Audrey's slate walkway. "Let's meet Friday night."

I peered up at him. Rather presumptuous, I thought, suggesting we meet on "date" night. . . .

He continued casually, "We'll have dinner, hash out our plans for both houses, and sign off on them. Okay?"

"No, Sullivan."

His eyes widened. "You're busy?"

"I'm free, but I hate business dinners . . . having to spread out floor plans on tiny tables . . . trying not to spill things on the drawings." Fully expecting Sullivan to take a potshot at me, I added brazenly, "Either this is a dinner date, or it's a business meeting. Not both."

He shrugged slightly. "Fine. I could pick you up around eight."

"Okay." I hesitated and studied his inscrutable expression. "So . . . should I *eat* first?"

"Not unless you want to save me money that badly. As for me, *I* plan on eating at the restaurant."

"So . . . it's a date, then."

He took a backward step toward his van, but smiled a little. "See you Friday night."

A smile had found its way to my own lips as I negotiated Audrey's slate walkway, but a moment later sanity prevailed. *What have I just gotten myself into?* I thought as I opened the door. This was *not* good. In fact, it was a disaster. Sullivan and I were fundamentally incapable of being together without arguing. If I didn't watch myself, I'd do something insane, like picture the two of us as a couple. Then, a day or two later, we'd be fighting again, and I'd be shredding that imaginary picture in disgust. Life was too short!

The next morning, following a heavenly night of uninterrupted sleep, I felt a pang when I spotted Bob Stanley through the parlor window, fetching his newspaper. A short, trim, handsome man in his late fifties, Bob Stanley was the prototypical good neighbor, always the first to offer a helping hand. He was retired, having inherited his home and his father's business, the latter of which he'd sold for a small fortune. Prior to our spat, we would always chat whenever we retrieved our papers at the same time, which happened so frequently I was sure Bob watched for me out his front window. Sometimes we'd even decide to desert our papers and stroll through the neighborhood, Bob telling me anecdotal histories of the houses that we passed. Today, however, I'd risen early and had already read the parts of the paper that interested me. Maybe my mood colored my perceptions, but Bob's shoulders seemed to sag, his movements seemed slow and reluctant. Impulsively I decided to pay him and Cassandra a visit. I'd impress on them that I bore them no hard feelings. *Bruised* feelings, yes, but not hard.

Resolved, I locked up behind me. Audrey had already left to tape one of her shows at the TV studio in Denver; her local program, *Domestic Bliss with Audrey Munroe*, aired three times a week. I trotted next door and used the Stanleys' traditional-style brass door knocker, admiring the astonishing artistry of the etching in their sidelight.

Bob promptly swung the door open. The relief on his features upon seeing me was evident. "Hey there. It's little Erin. My favorite designer." He grabbed my elbow and ushered me into the living room.

At five-eight and wearing heels, I was a couple of inches taller than him, but "little Erin" was the joke, and it made me laugh every time. "Thanks, Bob. But if I'm your favorite, how come you hired Steve Sullivan?"

He mugged comically and pantomimed pulling an arrow out of his chest. "What can I say, Erin? Sometimes ya just gotta go with the cherry pie, even when you prefer the apple. You know?"

Not really, but I gave him a lame smile. Why *not* stick with apple, if you like it better than cherry? In this case the "cherry" was more expensive, less convenient . . . and he and the apple were friends. Plus, he'd already agreed to *buy* the apple!

Bob explained, "You'd have been working on two big projects at once, both of which need to be complete in time for the historic-homes tour in the fall."

"True." Though I'd have managed the feat. This was one apple pie that was an accomplished multitasker.

"There you are, Erin!" Cassandra, an attractive, buxom woman with a mop of curly light brown hair, swept toward us. "I knew you'd be coming over this morning, and I'm so glad you did."

"Thanks. Did Audrey say something yesterday about my coming over here?"

"No, no. I had a premonition."

Bob's eyes twinkled. "One that was inspired by the sight of Erin heading up our driveway."

"Bob!" his wife scolded, "I did *not* see her approaching . . . I *sensed* it!" She turned back to me, perched on the edge of the sage-and-maroon floral-print sofa, and patted a cushion for me to join her. I complied, enjoying this warm and cozy (if a bit busy) room, even though its occupants were acting less than warm and cozy at the moment.

Bob was right; Cassandra fancied herself as a medium, yet her predictions always seemed to come a bit after the fact, the I-knew-this-would-happen style of prophecy. She had an unobstructed view of the roof herself from her and Bob's bedroom window; my designs are influenced by a space's exterior views, so I'd noted them during my inspection of their house. While I was making a bid for their decorating job. The bid that they'd accepted and for which I'd waived the standard deposit, because of our friendship. I found myself grinding my teeth. Time to employ my backup mantra: *Let it go, Erin. Let it go*.

"So, Erin. You saw the ghost of Abby the night before last!" Cassandra gushed. "Tell us all about it. Abby hasn't been around much lately."

"Here we go again," Bob grumbled, dropping into the smoke-gray velvet bergère chair opposite us. "No one will let that poor girl rest in peace."

"Well, Abby's the one who took it on herself to return. It isn't every day you get a visit from someone who left this earth fifty years ago."

"Fifty?" Bob released a bark of surprise. "It was nowhere near that long ago! I went to high school with Abby Chambers!" He waggled his thumb in his wife's direction. "Cassie likes to play up the fact that she's younger than me. But it's only by ten years. *Not* twenty."

"You never told me you went to school with Abby!" she protested.

"I did too! Many times."

"But . . . I got the impression that she was a little girl back then."

He shook his head. "She was just three years younger than me."

"Then why have you been telling everyone it was fifty years ago?" Cassandra glowered at him.

"I haven't. *You* have. Apparently Abby has given you some misinformation about how long she's been on the Other Side." The twinkle back in his eye, he turned to me. "Cassandra hosts weekly chat sessions with those who've crossed over. Kind of like low-tech, supernatural blogging, only without the Internet."

Cassandra remained silent, but was now scowling at the Persian rug.

"Ever notice how often women lie about their ages, Erin?" Bob asked.

Sensing he was asking me to choose sides, I shrugged. "Men do, too."

"True. But both men and women *subtract* years.

Whereas ghosts *add* years to their age. Apparently." He chuckled.

Cassandra said in a low voice, "It's amazing to me that you can joke about the tragic death of a girl you went to high school with."

Bob instantly grew somber. He smoothed down his thinning gray hair and focused strictly on me as if to avoid his wife's eyes. "Abby Chambers had a problem with drugs and alcohol. Got suspended from school for showing up high, more 'n once. You believe that? Fourteen years old, and already addicted. Course, this was the sixties, though, when drugs were rampant. The police investigated her death. They concluded she was depressed and committed suicide."

"Her parents must have been devastated," I said. "She was an only child, right?"

"Yes. I remember the exact date she died, because it was her fifteenth birthday on July fifteenth."

"She died on her birthday?" I asked, trying not to wonder why Cassandra was beet red and grinding her teeth.

He frowned and nodded. "One of the saddest days this neighborhood's ever seen. It'll be precisely forty years ago this Saturday that Abby died."

"No wonder she's back," Cassandra replied with a bitter laugh, rising. "She's probably here to collect on the birthday present that you owe her."

He groaned and lifted his arms heavenward. "*This* again! I forgot Cassandra's birthday last week. Now she won't let me stop paying for it."

"You've never paid the price for one single thing, Bob Stanley! And that's your biggest problem, if you ask me."

"Nobody *did* ask you!"

She stomped from the room.

The remains of that conversation lingered with me an hour later as I took the shortcut to Francine's house through our backyards. The tension between the Stanleys had been palpable, yet in previous conversations they'd always seemed so happy and relaxed, as though they had an exemplary marriage. The stress of the neighborhood squabbles must be getting to them, too.

I veered off course and paused to study the tower window closest to Diana Durst's home. One of its panes was broken. With Willow's reported penchant for climbing mountains, she would have had no trouble scaling the stone siding of the house.

I spotted Francine watching me through the kitchen window and waved, then proceeded to the French doors. She let me in and, with no greeting or preamble, said, "I saw you looking up at the tower just now. Still think that someone climbed up there the night before last?"

"Yes. There's a trellis, and the stones on the east side are almost like a climbing wall."

She shook her head. "Even so, that window is boarded up, and the wood siding on the tower is too smooth to climb."

"True, but the window doesn't appear to be boarded

up anymore. And one of its panes is broken."

"Must have been a tree branch that broke the pane. And it has to be a trick of the lighting that makes it look like the boards are down. The space is *walled off,* Erin. There's no way anyone could reach that window in order to remove the boards."

Except by breaking a pane and knocking down the boards from the outside. I was perplexed as to why she didn't want to simply go and see for herself.

"In any case"—she rubbed her hands together as if to wash away the subject matter—"let's talk about the *inside* of the tower room, shall we?"

"Certainly." I took a calming breath, reminding myself that my job was not to enlighten her about broken windows or roof walkers. She'd hired me to redesign the third floor and her daughter's bedroom, period.

She ushered me up the stairs, saying, "Last night, I took a good, long look at the wallpaper, and I've made my choice."

"Excellent. Did you look at the colors in the morning light, as well?"

"No. I should really do that, shouldn't I?"

"It would be a good idea, yes. Just to be absolutely certain."

"Unless it strikes me as totally different during the day, I'd like to go with that light-yellow floral print."

I grinned. "That was my favorite, too."

She opened the door and stepped inside. "I just love the way—" She gasped and froze.

The floor was littered with shredded bits of paper. The wallpaper samples had been yanked down and crumpled. A relatively smooth piece, lying facedown, fully captured my attention, however. On the back of that sheet of wallpaper something was written in block letters with a shaky hand:

SHE WILL DIE.

chapter 3

I stared at the torn and mangled paper. "Francine? What's going on? Who did this?"

She peeled her eyes from the scrawls, tossed her hair back with trembling hands, and forced a chuckle. "Another of Lisa's silly pranks," she declared.

"But . . . why would Lisa write 'She will die'?"

"She means Abby, I'm sure . . . that if we renovate the room, Abby will disappear."

So a *ghost* would *die?* "That doesn't make—"

A door slammed downstairs. A moment later, a teenage voice hollered, "Mom! I'm home!"

Francine whirled around, her features suddenly taut with fury. "Come upstairs this instant, young lady!"

"Jeez, Mom! What'd I do now? I haven't even *been* here!" Lisa tromped up the stairs and into the room. During her "sleepover" she'd gained dozens of braids in her long red hair. The beads in her braids clacked with each step she took. "Jeez," she exclaimed as she scanned the room with a cocky grin on her face. I balled my fists, then noticed that the death threat was no longer visible; Francine had folded over the piece of wallpaper with her foot and was now standing on it.

"Well?" her mother said. "What do you have to say about this?"

"Wow! Abby really *is* back!"

"Drop this nonsense right this minute, young lady!" Francine stabbed a finger in her daughter's direction. "You rode your bike back home last night and snuck in here!"

"Mom! I did *not!* I swear to God!"

Lisa was all wide-eyed innocence, but I didn't know her well enough to judge if she was telling the truth. In any case, it would be professional suicide to choose sides in my clients' private matters, and the space between a mother and her daughter is definitely the proverbial rock and hard place.

"You were—" Francine broke off when the doorbell rang, then demanded in a shrill voice, "Is that Jenny now, ringing our doorbell? Is she the one who put you up to this?"

"Mom! I didn't do anything! Neither did Jenny!"

"Ha! It's a good thing I hired Willow to *baby*sit you this summer." She bent and grabbed the sheet of wallpaper on which SHE WILL DIE was written, wadding it into a ball as she left the room. Heading down the stairs, she called, "I'm coming!"

Gently, I asked Lisa, "Could one of your classmates have done this?"

She whirled to face me, her cheeks blazing beneath her freckles. She glared at me with a look of abject hatred. "I told you Abby was going to freak! Now my mom thinks I'm a liar! This is all *your* fault!"

She tore out of the room and down the flight of stairs, and I heard her bedroom door slam. I too descended the stairs, but quietly. I needed to tell Francine that I was going to let myself out and would call her shortly.

As usual, all the doors on the second floor were shut tight. I'd only seen these rooms once, when she'd first hired me. I'd had to explain that I needed to see them to be sure that my design for Lisa's bedroom felt integrated with the whole house, or the effect might be jarring. I'd discovered then that the furnishings in Francine's guest room, master bedroom, and "temporary music room" were sparse and unexceptional, in sharp contrast to the main level, where her tasteful use of antiques and the occasional whimsical piece was utterly charming. She'd probably equated showing a designer three more rooms that also needed work to giving a car salesman a ride in a dented jalopy with a sputtering engine.

When I reached the bottom stairs, which, atypically for a historic home, faced the back door and not the front, I could hear Francine in the foyer telling her visitor in a hushed, anxious voice, "You need to leave. Immediately. Erin Gilbert is here. She *lives* with Audrey."

A male voice I didn't recognize replied, "Oh, cripes! I'll call you tonight."

I rounded the corner and caught a glimpse of a man's large, retreating form as Francine shut the door. He was a bit paunchy and had black hair, which featured the unnatural sheen of a bad dye job. Doing my best to act as though I hadn't overheard the embarrassing snippet of conversation, I said, "I'm going to head home for the—"

"No, Erin. There's no need for you to leave. Like you said yourself yesterday, Lisa's just going through a little phase, that's all. She'll be fine."

She was misquoting me, but that was beside the point. "Even so, she's pretty upset right now, and it's probably not a good time for someone outside the family to be here. How about if I just dash home for a few minutes, return some phone calls, then come back?"

"No. That won't work for me. The carpenter will be here any minute to talk to you, and I'll need you—"

The doorbell rang, and Francine turned to answer. "That's probably him now."

Indeed, Ralph Appleby had arrived, right on the heels of Francine's mysterious visitor. Ralph specialized in restoring old homes and had worked in the neighborhood for many years, though we'd only spoken once or twice. He was short—five-eight or so—and was bald except for a partial ring of dark hair. Something about his stocky build and short neck reminded me of a tortoise and, with his ever-present scowl, a snapping turtle. Audrey had assured me that Ralph's skill was unparalleled, however, so I was thrilled to have him on my team, despite his crabbiness.

"You're right on time," Francine said, her voice remarkably cheerful considering the turmoil she'd endured in the last few minutes. "Come on in. You know Erin Gilbert, I presume?"

"Erin." Ralph had a deep, gravelly, smoker's voice. "Couple things we need to get straight right away. I do all woodworking myself. I bring in my own crew of drywallers and workmen. They take orders from me alone." He brushed past us. "So let's go over your finalized plans for the third floor now so I can get started." His demeanor was downright hostile. The man could give scary lessons to a troll, though, so there was no sense in my taking his behavior personally.

"Sure. I'll have to go get the original plans from my house, but that'll just take me a minute—"

"Don't bother, Erin," Francine cut in, touching my shoulder. "This last bit of business regarding the tower room has finally broken my resolve. We're switching to your original idea."

"To remove the interior wall?" I asked, floored by her pronouncement. Ralph, meanwhile, pivoted and glared at us.

"That's right."

"What changed your mind?" I asked, bewildered.

"Oh, well, I'm obviously fighting a losing battle, what with Bob Stanley and the homeowners against me . . . and all the angst it caused Lisa when you tried to hang up the samples. She's wanted me to tear down that wall all along."

Her explanation made no sense. Last night I'd called her to report that the homeowners had decided to allow Steve Sullivan and me to serve as "each other's overseers" (the concept of Sullivan being my "boss" was just too appalling to say out loud), so we were *winning* our battle. Furthermore, Francine struck me as the type of parent who would never cave in to her daughter's wishes due to a tantrum—if Francine truly believed Lisa had ripped up my drawings and wallpaper samples.

Ralph's frown changed to a gape. He stormed back toward the two of us in the foyer. "Wait. You mean you're opening up the roof access again?" He seemed to be as incredulous as if Francine had just announced that she wanted him to turn her home into an ice cream parlor.

"That's right, Ralph." She looked me in the eye. "You'll have to change your design quite a bit, Erin, now that you'll have more square footage and a staircase to incorporate."

"So you want to keep the staircase intact?" I asked in surprise.

"Well, as long as it's reasonably attractive, I do. We'll install a lock on the door to the roof, and I'll keep hold of the key. I just hope this doesn't set you back too far in terms of your time."

"It's no problem at all." A true statement on my part, but what on earth was going on here? Could the visitor she'd sent away have had something to do with her baffling reversal? Or with the SHE WILL DIE message on the wallpaper? "What about the picture windows? Are we still incorporating them into this design?"

She shook her head. "I want to go with larger windows, but more in keeping with the classic look of the ones in the original house."

Yippee! Regardless of her reasons, my client was suddenly parroting precisely what I'd urged her to do all along. "That will look fantastic. In fact, I already have a drawing of that very idea." Technically, I needed Sullivan's approval before we could begin, but he would give it to me; any designer worth his measuring tape would know at once how superior that design was to the picture windows and the inner wall that dissected the room. Unable to stop smiling, I turned my attention fearlessly to Ralph, who was all but guaranteed to toss a wet blanket on me. "Let me go get it now."

He swatted at the air in my direction. "Don't need to see plans yet. Ain't like there's anything complicated or artsy-craftsy about knocking down a wall. Lemme go get the tools." He brushed past me and shuffled out the front door.

My mood suitably dampened, I knew I needed to be darned certain Francine wasn't one of those nightmarish clients who flip-flopped interminably. "Are you sure about this, Francine?" I asked pointedly. If Ralph proceeded, and she changed her mind . . .

"Absolutely. This is the only way I'll be able to function in that room."

"How so?" Now I was really confused.

"Oh, some of my neighbors are already complaining to me about the picture windows. I'd be sitting there, trying to practice, but feeling guilty about my remodel."

I still could not swallow her explanations. Much as I didn't want to argue with success, my inability to get a read on my client's frame of mind was frustrating. Her features appeared to be set into forced blankness, reminiscent of someone who was anticipating a slap but was determined not to flinch at the blow. She'd borne that same expression when she'd been hiding the writing on the wallpaper from Lisa.

Ralph trudged past us carrying a sledgehammer and a toolbox, and went upstairs without a word. We followed him. He'd closed the door behind him, but Francine cracked it open, and we watched from the attic. As many times as I've had walls removed from clients' homes, I've never gotten the chance to attack a wall with a sledgehammer and I've always wanted to do so. I've always suspected that my clients would look askance at me if, while sitting there in my apricot Chanel skirt suit, I explained that I would personally handle the demolition, but would hire my team of experts to rebuild their rooms afterward.

Ralph had donned protective goggles and a carpenter's mask and had begun to knock down the plaster between studs. Even as a mere spectator, there was something immensely satisfying about the thud and the cloud of white dust that grew with each blow.

Less than a minute into the job, the doorbell rang again and Francine moaned, "Nobody ever visits, except when I'm on the third floor."

"You should install an intercom," Ralph said, lowering the sledgehammer to peer at her through the three-inch gap in the doorway. He yanked off his goggles and moved his white molded-paper mask so that the elastic held it in place atop his bald pate like a misshapen party hat. "Long as I'm tearing down walls anyway, you should pay me to put one in for you."

"Could you?" Francine beamed. "That would be wonderful!"

Not to be overly sensitive, but I'd suggested an intercom to Francine just last week. She'd described *my* idea as "silly."

A woman's voice trilled from below. "Francine? It's just me, Diana. Could I come up for a minute?"

I was surprised that Diana had been so bold as to let herself into Francine's house and I assumed that meant the two women were close friends. Francine, however, grimaced but answered, "Sure. We're in the tower room."

As Diana came up the stairs, she called, "I saw Ralph's truck out front. I'm just dying to see how things are going. Hi, Erin!" she announced with that wonderful cheeriness of hers. Her dark brown hair was fastened in a perky ponytail.

"Hi." I returned her grin.

"Good morning, Diana," Francine said. We moved over so that Diana could squeeze beside us. "Ralph's removing the wall that the previous owners built."

She gasped happily, pushed the door fully open, and said to him, "You are?"

"Soon as I can get you gals to shut the door so's the whole house isn't caked in dust." He returned his mask and goggles to their proper place. In a muffled voice he grumbled, "Then you'll go complaining to everyone 'bout the mess I make when I work. And it ain't like I wanted an audience in the first place!"

Ignoring him, Diana cried, "Oh, Francine! This is so exciting!" She shook her fists over her head as though Team Diana was celebrating a major victory. "My mother would have been so thrilled about this! It's like you're unveiling a whole new chapter in the house!"

"More like revealing an old one," Francine said under her breath. She looked anxious and as ready to snap as a mousetrap, furthering my suspicion that she'd relented about removing the wall for reasons she wasn't willing to share.

Diana entered the room and instantly pounced. "Oh, my. What happened here?" She picked up the shredded drawings and tried to match them together. "Isn't this your floor plan, Erin? Did you actually rip it to bitty bits once you decided to remove that wall?"

"Nothing of the sort," Francine said hastily as we both followed her into the room, despite Ralph's "why me?" gestures to the heavens. "Lisa played a prank on us last night. She crumpled Erin's wallpaper samples as well. She's currently sulking in her room."

"No, she isn't," Diana said. "I saw her outside, riding her bike, when I was on my way over here."

"She must have snuck out the back." Francine stomped her foot, setting up a small cloud of dust in the process. "That kid is going to be the death of me! If only her father weren't in Europe all this month. The one time I'd actually have loved to grant him custody for a couple of weeks."

Ralph seemed poised to commence swinging his sledgehammer despite our presence, but Diana gasped again and cried, "Just a second, Ralph," and stepped toward him, her attention drawn by something near his boots. She squatted down and examined two pieces of Sheetrock. "Look! Someone's drawn a big X on the back side of the wall!"

She held up the broken section of gypsum so that we could all see the unfinished side. There was indeed an X that extended beyond the edges. I scanned the floor. A couple of additional chunks of gypsum boasted dark ink lines that probably were continuations of a giant X on the back side of the wall.

Diana was giddy with excitement. "I've heard about this! My mother told me that all *three* previous owners had complained that someone had mysteriously drawn a big X on this wall!"

I glanced at Francine, who had visibly paled.

"Back then, of course, the X was marked on *this* side of the wall, where everyone could see it," Diana went on happily. "But Abby must have known you were about to finally tear down the wall." She set the Sheetrock back down, spanking her hands together. "Don't you see, Francine? X marks the spot! This isn't Lisa's doing; it's *Abby's!*"

"Don't be silly," Francine said, rolling her eyes, her color and confidence returning.

"No, no, I know I'm right about this, Francine," Diana insisted. "Lisa would have no way of knowing that Abby used to draw an X on this wall whenever she visited. I think you're doing exactly what Abby wants. She wants the wall taken down." She clapped her hands. "This is wonderful! Don't you think?"

"Don't sound so damned wonderful to me," Ralph mumbled, lifting his mask to its less-than-jaunty-looking perch once more. His bald head was covered with a fine dusting of white powder, reminiscent of a floured cake pan.

"Oh, but it *is,*" Diana replied. "It will be a *huge* boon for the historic-homes tour. A whole lot more people will see your completed work on the house, Ralph."

He merely grimaced, but maybe that was his idea of an agreeable smile. Diana hugged Francine, then excused herself and departed cheerily, the wheels obviously spinning in her head at the possibility of turning a haunted-house rumor into a splendid personal bonanza.

"It's those damned Stanleys," Ralph told us. "They're the ones that got everyone to believing in the ghost in the first place."

"How so?" I asked.

"I'm getting back to work now. If you two gals want to get your clothes all dirty, that's your choice." He centered his goggles and his mask.

"He means due to Cassandra's claims that she's clairvoyant," Francine interpreted for him.

Ralph swung his hammer with great force, and an enormous section of gypsum broke free. He stood back, waiting for the dust to settle from the gaping hole he'd created.

Unable to keep my curiosity at bay any longer, I stepped close.

"Let me see," Francine cried. Suddenly we were acting like schoolchildren, on the verge of elbowing each other to gain the best view.

My heart sank. Illuminated by the window that, as I'd realized this morning, was no longer boarded up, the staircase wasn't nearly as nice as I'd hoped it would be. It appeared to be merely functional: straight gray-painted stairs that formed a switchback halfway up, with unadorned wood-dowel rails. The aesthetics were dreadful. Talk about throwing a room out of harmony! These straight, bold lines were all wrong—a veritable slash through the space; the octagonal room cried for the curved lines of a spiral. I had been envisioning maple stairs and handrails, polished to a glossy sheen, and ivory-painted posts.

"Well," Francine said. "There it is. The infamous staircase. I certainly hope Bob Stanley is happy now."

"Stanley *wanted* you to remove the wall?" Ralph's bullfrog voice was incredulous. He removed his mask again. "You sure about that?"

"We never discussed the wall itself, but Bob certainly hated my idea to modernize the room." She did a double take. "What happened there?" Her eyes narrowed. She'd apparently just noticed the broken pane in the window behind the staircase.

"Boards are down," Ralph said. "Someone must've knocked 'em out."

"Huh," Francine muttered, eyeing me. "Looks like you were right once again, Erin."

" 'Bout what?" Ralph wanted to know.

"She noticed that the window was no longer boarded up. And she saw someone who looked a lot like Willow, the girl who rents a room at Diana Durst's, on my roof the night before last."

It could have been my imagination, but Ralph's scowl seemed to deepen with Francine's every word.

She continued, "All I know is, six weeks ago, which was the last time I checked for ccrtain, that window was definitely still boarded up. Which means Willow, or someone who looks like her, broke that windowpane and climbed onto my roof. And probably drew the silly X on the back side of the wall." She puffed indignantly. "Those boards must have been in place for fifty years till she knocked them down." They were now neatly stacked beside it.

"Window was boarded up *forty* years ago," Ralph stated flatly.

"How do you know that?" I asked, surprised that he'd apparently been chatting with his enemy, Bob

Stanley, who'd told me some ninety minutes earlier that the wall was only forty years old.

"I grew up in Crestview. I remember when Abby died, right after my junior year of high school. Not the kind of thing a person forgets."

Though momentarily nonplussed at his statement, I asked quietly, "How did you know how soon after the accident the staircase was closed off?"

" 'Cuz I built the damn wall," he snapped.

"You *did?*" I asked, astonished. He'd certainly begun his carpentry career at a young age.

"Also sealed off that window and padlocked the door to the roof."

"So you knew the previous owners?" Francine asked.

He made no reply, and the firm set of his jaw made it clear he had no intention of ever doing so.

I brushed past him. "Let's see if we can get the padlock off."

"No!" Ralph shouted, but I was already squeezing between a pair of studs.

Surprised, I turned to face him from the other side. Ralph hurled his mask and goggles to the floor and glared at me with his fists on his hips, looking like an ugly—and dusty—Yul Brynner. "Nobody's been up there or on those stairs for forty years. If anybody's gonna risk falling through some rotted-out board, it's going to be me." He tried to follow me, but had more difficulty getting through the narrow opening. More the dragon than the Sir Galahad type, Ralph clearly wanted the honor of being first to stand on the widow's walk after all these years. Not counting the resident "ghost," that is.

"I weigh less than you do, Ralph," I said. "And I'll be careful."

"No! *I* go up first!"

Surprised at his tone, I stepped back down and peered through the wall opening at Francine, expecting her to cast the deciding vote, but she was staring out a window on the opposite side of the room. She said, "Oh, good. Here comes Lisa now. She's with Willow."

Ralph pushed past me to climb the stairs. "Dang," he muttered. "The padlock's missing, too." He opened the door at the top with ease, and firmly shut it behind him, making a strong unspoken statement that I was not to follow.

Leaving the room, Francine said, "Erin, since Lisa's got Willow to entertain her for a while, I may as well get back to my music. I need to calm my nerves. It looks like you've got everything under control here."

This is what she calls "under control"? I silently mused. I could tell by the footsteps over my head that Ralph was walking around and not crashing through the ceiling. That much was good.

I eased myself back through the opening between the studs. A moment later, Lisa and Willow raced into the room, Lisa in the lead. Ignoring me, Lisa called, "Cool! Look, Willow! They're taking the wall down! We can see the stairs to the roof!"

"Hi, Erin," Willow said, suddenly—and suspiciously—friendly. She'd reverted to her borderline-slutty look and was wearing a spaghetti-strap top in a Windex turquoise and cutoffs short enough to reveal a bluebird tattoo at the top of her outer thigh. "How's it going?"

"Fine, thanks, Willow. How goes everything for you?"

"Oh, you know." She shrugged, then frowned at the partially demolished wall. "Are you, like, excited about the wall being removed? Is that what *Steve* wanted you to do?"

"I wouldn't know. It's *my* design, not his." Her question raised a good point, however; Sullivan and I were supposed to serve as each other's *overseers,* and I probably should have checked with him before I unleashed Ralph's demolition skills. I continued, "We only agreed to consult each other regarding the exteriors of our homes." To my delight, I realized that, though I'd spoken off the cuff, my statement was accurate. I would tell Sullivan as much, too, when he pitched a fit about my making architectural changes without his approval.

Willow scrutinized me from head to foot, as though trying to decide if I was attractive enough to deserve Sullivan. In a forced casual tone, she exclaimed, "I didn't realize you two were a couple."

I gave her a smile, but held my tongue.

"Willow, let's go up!" Lisa urged, still intent on the staircase.

"You can't just yet," I told them. "Ralph Appleby is

inspecting the roof right now to see if it's safe."

"*He's* here?" Willow cried over Lisa's groan of disappointment. "Yuck! That guy gives me the creeps." Willow circled the room, peering out each of the windows. "I've never spent much time up here. It's got great views. You can see Audrey's whole property. Diana's, too. Wow. Her place is so tiny! It looks like the servants' quarters in comparison to all the other homes." She paused and, again, gave me a visual once-over. "You're lucky, Erin. You've got the coolest landlady around. It's not much fun at Diana's."

Willow and Diana had always struck me as fairly compatible. "Diana seems to be full of energy to me," I replied mildly.

Willow grimaced. "She's, like, totally different when she's home, though. She just puts on a happy face when others are around." She shot a deliberate glance at Lisa as if to signal that she couldn't elaborate in Lisa's presence. "To tell you the truth, I'm not so crazy about the Stanleys, either. Cassandra is, like, a *slave driver* at her shop."

The door above us creaked open, and Ralph started thumping down the steps. "Leave that open," Lisa commanded him. "Willow and I are going to go up."

"No, you're not," he answered, clicking the latch shut behind him. "Flooring's a mess. Railing's not steady. Nobody's going up there. Not till I've got it all restored."

I needed to see the widow's walk for the sake of my design, but once again I held my tongue, not wanting to embarrass Ralph in front of the girls.

"Let's go, Lisa," Willow said, suddenly anxious. She probably just wanted to keep her distance from Ralph, and who could blame her? "There's a sidewalk sale downtown with some really fab clothes." She and Lisa made a hasty exit.

Once they were out of earshot, I announced, "I'm taking a look for myself, Ralph. Don't worry. I'll be very careful."

He showered me with grumpy objections as I went up the stairs. A cool breeze kissed my face and ruffled my hair as I stepped onto the small, octagonal widow's walk, and I was instantly seduced by the glorious view of the Front Range. From here I could see the upstairs bedroom windows of the other homes as well, including mine, Audrey's, and the Stanleys', along with Diana's attic window.

Ralph was waiting for me, pacing fretfully at the bottom of the stairs when I returned. "That's redwood decking up there," he said. "Too difficult to maintain. Whole thing needs to be replaced with composite boards."

"It's strong enough to support a few hundred pounds without giving way, though."

He made a derisive noise. "You're just a decorator. *I'm* the one who's been working with wood near every day of my life. I'm gonna go tell Francine it's all gotta go."

Knowing that I couldn't win this argument, I resisted the urge to inform him that my degree in design included architectural studies, which covered such matters as the weight-bearing capabilities of wood. Instead, I followed him downstairs.

We found Francine in her quasi "music room"—the spare bedroom directly below the tower room. Like every level of her extraordinary home, the second floor featured high, twelve-foot ceilings. This medium-sized beige room was dominated by an enormous Waterford chandelier, suitable for a ballroom. Francine said the light fixture "inspires my music." I planned to move it upstairs during the final install of her permanent music room, where its new setting would be in scale and would do the chandelier much better justice. She'd also been forced to keep her Steinway grand piano in the main-floor parlor but, while the windows were being replaced, a crane would move it into the tower room. There it would become the room's focal piece.

Not counting the piano bench and the electric organ itself, which looked like a small upright piano, the only furnishings in this second-floor room were a mohair loveseat and three mismatched wood chairs. Francine was practicing with her earphones plugged in, silencing the instrument entirely. Already, she was so absorbed in her music that she didn't notice us until Ralph cleared his throat twice. Then she removed her earphones and gave us a wan smile.

"The roof is off-limits," Ralph stated repressively, giving me a sideways glare. "Everyone needs to keep off till I've got those boards replaced. I'm not going to have an accident on my conscience, so I'm making that my top priority."

"The widow's walk is your top priority?" Francine asked. "Why don't I just put another padlock on it for the time being, and we'll make it the *lowest* priority?"

He shook his head. "Weather's perfect for doing it now, and I like to work from top to bottom anyways. I'll go get the lumber. Already made the measurements."

He stomped off.

"Is it really that precarious up there?" Francine asked me.

"No, but the wood does need to be replaced in the next year or two."

She frowned. "May as well get it done now, then."

"Francine, I've got to leave for an appointment at another client's home, but if it's okay with you I'll be back this evening to take some measurements and redraw my plans for the room. Now that the wall's down, I'm like a kid with a brand-new box of crayons. I can't wait to get started!"

Ralph was pulling away in his pickup truck by the time I returned that evening. He didn't even bother to acknowledge my wave. Francine let me inside, but explained that she was busy making dinner. Willow and Lisa came running into the house from the backyard, Willow admitting that she too was eager to see the staircase and roof. Francine grudgingly gave them permission, "but only if Erin says it's safe."

The girls rushed ahead of me. I hesitated before

climbing the flight of ugly stairs onto the roof, envisioning myself ascending a dramatic spiral staircase.

Willow and Lisa were goofing around on the widow's walk when I joined them. Ralph had obviously brought in a whole crew in my absence, because the work was already about two-thirds finished. Only one section of old boards remained. Willow was waving her arms and saying "Whoa" as though she were being knocked over backward. Lisa was pretending to have her foot stuck through the floor.

"Okay," I said, "time to go back down. I'll get the door."

Willow paused and stared at something at her feet. She reached underneath the old section of boards and pocketed something.

"What did you find?" I asked.

"Oh, it was just a quarter that Ralph must have dropped." She grinned triumphantly and added happily, "Finders keepcrs."

As I had long suspected, Willow and Lisa were at the same level of maturity. I ushered them off the roof and shut the door, then told the girls that I needed to concentrate on making some precise measurements.

Willow looked at her watch and cried, "Oh, jeez! I'm going to be late for work!" As the two of them crossed the room, I couldn't help but notice that Lisa was taking on Willow's every nuance and gesture. I wished she'd chosen a better role model.

Shortly after I returned home, there was a knock on the

door, and I opened it to discover a tall, handsome man in his late fifties to early sixties standing on the front porch bearing an armful of long-stemmed red roses.

"Evening, miss. My name is Hugh Black."

"Good evening," I said, trying not to stare at his black hair. Audrey's ex-husband was Francine's mysterious visitor.

Audrey joined me in the foyer, saying with a gracious smile, "Hello, Hugh."

"Hi, Audrey. These are for you." He beamed at her and held out the lavish bouquet.

"That's nice. Thank you, my dear. Knowing you, I'm quite sure you'll have no problem finding another recipient for them."

She shut the door in Hugh Black's face.

chapter 4

Consuming alcohol is highly unlikely to solve one's problems. However, used in moderation, it's highly unlikely to worsen them, either.

—Audrey Munroe

DOMESTIC BLISS

As she turned from the still-vibrating door, Audrey brushed her hands together as though she'd just completed a messy task. Smoothing her ash-blond hair into place, she said complacently, "*That* was most unpleasant. I think I'll go spend an inordinate amount of time in the wine cellar, in case he has the audacity to ring the doorbell again."

"Your wine cellar isn't soundproof," I pointed out.

"No, but it will give me the chance to expunge some old memories. Come join me." She turned at the head of the basement stairs and added, "Oh, and bring the brie and a box of crackers."

"And wineglasses?"

"Unless we want to swig straight from the bottle," she called over her shoulder.

I quickly gathered up the snacks and a few implements, opting to grab the white-wine glasses, simply because they were closer than the red-wine glasses. Carrying the plate of cheese and crackers with one hand and the glass stems with the other, I rushed down the stairs, so delighted at Audrey's invitation that I didn't mind serving as the waitress. Audrey had recently upgraded her wine cellar, and the results were absolutely divine. She'd consulted with me on several of her choices, though she'd hired a company that specialized in custom-made wine cellars. I'd insisted on the all-heart redwood tongue-and-groove paneling on the walls and ceiling, the travertine-tile flooring, and the glorious accent lighting.

Managing a balancing act, I opened the fabulous stained-glass door and shut it behind me. The door made liberal use of the purples and greens of a vineyard without overdoing artistic renditions of grape bunches. The room was chilly, yet was so fragrant and lovely with its wonderful European ambience that it felt like walking into some quiet and thoroughly charming bistro. That had been precisely my intention when I'd selected the "seating for two" where Audrey now sat, with an opened wine bottle in front of her. The tabletop was a circular oak frame that enclosed a porcelain mosaic, awe-inspiring with its vintage glazes and old-world charm. The bentwood chairs were simple and yet quaint and authentic for a European café.

Audrey was staring off into space. I set everything down on the table and slipped quietly into the chair. I could hear the light tinkling sounds of a bubbling brook behind me. This was the waterfall-style humidifier, which not only served its all-important function but provided soothing sounds and visuals as the sheet of water cascaded down the pyramid-like sides.

I took a deep breath, luxuriating in the woodsy aroma. "I totally love this room. Don't you?"

Audrey nodded. "Absolutely. It smells like you're strolling through a Napa Valley forest at dusk . . . surrounded by live oaks and California redwoods. But here's my favorite aroma of all." She poured a splash of Beaujolais into her glass and swirled it directly below her nose as she slowly inhaled. "Ah! The bouquet of a fine wine."

She took a sip. She smiled at me, then filled both

our glasses half full. "This has become something of a tradition of mine," she said. "I buy myself a bottle of wine on the day I decide to accept a proposal of marriage, with the plan to consume it on our tenth anniversary. Or on the day the divorce is finalized. Whichever comes first. So far, the latter has won out. Except for Henry, that is. Not long after we'd split a fabulous tenth-anniversary bottle of cabernet, he died."

I grimaced sympathetically, and she held up a hand and added cheerfully, "Nothing to do with the wine. Henry'd had sky-high cholesterol and he'd already had two heart attacks. I'd *told* him that a glass of wine is good for the heart, but he refused to imbibe, till that bottle on our tenth." She clicked her tongue. "He had his fatal attack a week later. As the paramedics were rushing him into the ambulance, he grabbed my sleeve to pull me close and whispered, 'I told you the wine wouldn't help.' " She sighed. "That man just always had to have the last word!"

I examined the label of the Beaujolais. "Why haven't you already consumed *this* bottle, on the day you got your divorce from Hugh?"

"I did. More than two years ago. But I also have an emergency contingency plan for times like these . . . when the fool comes back. I always replace that bottle with the same wine."

I eyed the hundreds of bottles in their diamond-shaped racks, thinking she would be trumping Elizabeth Taylor and every other starlet if that were Audrey's *only* criterion for purchasing wine. Reading my thoughts, Audrey said, "Not that I need an excuse to buy a wonderful wine, you understand."

"Of course not." Unable to get a fix on Audrey's mood, I held up my glass and said with forced cheer, "Here's to saying 'Adieu to Hugh.' "

Though she rolled her eyes, she clinked my glass, and we both savored the spicy, rich-flavored wine. "I wish it were that easy, Erin. But Hugh's tenacious. He'll be back a dozen times, and I'll shut the door in his face each time, and he'll still fail to take the hint." Audrey helped herself to a cracker, spreading such a perfectly smooth layer of brie on it that I was reminded of applying Venetian plaster to a wall.

"How did you meet him?"

Audrey tapped her glass with her fingernail, which made a pretty, bell-like sound. "The purpose of this particular selection of wine tonight is to allow me to forget such things."

I nodded and indulged myself by scanning our yummy surroundings. I'd fastened realistic-looking plastic-and-silk grapevines along two of the walls. Although they appeared to be merely decorative, one of the vines masked a piano hinge along the corner of what looked like another floor-to-ceiling wine rack. Audrey saw me studying it now and said to me, "You'd never know a room was back there."

"No, you really wouldn't." Inside was a substantial

safe, though Audrey hadn't told me anything about the safe's contents.

"When I was in France last year," she said, "one of the men at the inn was telling us about how, as a little boy, his job was to place spiderwebs over his family's hiding space for their best bottles of wine."

"I'm glad we didn't need to go that far in hiding your safe room."

"Well, our house is unlikely to be seized and occupied by Nazi Germany anytime soon. But if it *were*, the first thing I'd want to do is move my very best bottles inside the room."

"And if that happened, I wouldn't hesitate to move spiderwebs over the seams in the secret passageway."

"So, it's agreed: I'll move the bottles; you'll move the webs. That calls for another toast." She lifted her glass toward mine. "To teamwork."

We clinked glasses.

chapter 5

How unusual," Audrey said to me the next morning as she hung up the phone, which she promptly set atop the stack of papers on the wingback chair in the parlor. Cordless phones had not been designed with people like Audrey in mind; she managed to misplace the handset two or three times a day. "That was Cassandra Stanley. She and Francine are coming over to speak to us."

"Is this about Steve's and my designs?" I was sprawled out on my favorite sofa, nursing a mug of coffee, my insomnia having returned last night. Although, thankfully, there had been no ghost sightings, I'd noticed that the windows in the tower room had been glowing yellow at midnight, then again at three a.m., which was odd, because the light fixtures had all been removed when I was there last evening.

"I don't think so," Audrey answered, pulling back the plum-colored cotton curtain to peer at the walkway. "Cassandra said it had to do with the supernatural . . . with 'our not-so-blithe spirits,' was her precise wording." She added under her breath, "This must be something along the lines of *Amityville Horror* to spur Francine into coming to my house." Though it quickly faded, I caught a hint of a smile.

A few minutes later, Audrey answered the front door and invited the two women to join us in the parlor. Their wardrobes were an interesting contrast. Though both women were wealthy and in their forties, Cassandra favored the aging-hippie look of peasant blouses and loose-fitting khakis that complemented her retro-sixties shop; Francine's idea of casual attire was perfectly tailored and coordinated designer slacks and blouses. We greeted one another, Francine jumping at the sound of Audrey shutting the door behind her.

"Can I get you some coffee?" Audrey asked.

Cassandra accepted just as Francine was declining,

saying, "This will only take a moment." She caught Cassandra's gaze and added with a touch of desperation, "And we're all very busy."

"All right then." Cassandra fluffed her sandy-colored curls. "Hold the java."

"I suppose biscotti would be out of the question, then," Audrey said. She gestured for them to take seats, which would be a challenge, because the chairs were currently littered with the materials from various art projects gone awry, not unlike a crafts store in the aftermath of an earthquake. "Don't mind the mess. I'm experimenting."

"With what?" Cassandra asked.

"I won't know until inspiration hits me."

"There's room here on the sofa. And I think that's an ottoman underneath the crepe paper," I said, pointing to a spot nearby. Audrey was fulfilling her side of the bargain that I would put up with her perpetual messy projects as long as she never touched the beloved sage-hued velvet sofa.

Both visitors gave me an appreciative smile as they picked their way through the paraphernalia and sat. Audrey cleared a space for herself in the wingback. Wearing one of her signature kaftans, she settled into the large, comfy damask chair as if it were her throne.

Her pretty features pinched with tension, Francine said into the mostly obscured Oriental rug, "I'm sure you're wondering what we're doing here. Though I guess Cassandra already told Audrey a little." She looked at me, her eyes pleading. "You see, I'm not saying it's a ghost, exactly. Just that, well, something odd is happening at my house, and I've got to put a stop to it."

Cassandra reached over from her perch on the ottoman and patted Francine on the knee. "The bottom line is, poor Francine is being driven up a wall by Abby's nightly tantrums."

"To be accurate, though, Cassandra and I are not in agreement that Abby is the source of the noises," Francine interjected.

Cassandra held up her palms. "*She* thinks Lisa's got some hoodlum friends who are behind all the noises and the shaking of the walls."

Audrey and I exchanged glances. Neither hoodlums nor ghosts made much sense to me. "What kinds of noises are you hearing, Francine?" I asked.

"Oh, just the silly 'wooo-oo-oo' type noises that little kids make when they play ghost make-believe. And old music, like from a scratchy Victrola." She met my gaze. "Actually, it's been going on for a couple of weeks now, well before you spotted that so-called *ghost* on my rooftop. You probably saw one of Lisa's classmates, pretending to be a ghost. Unfortunately, I can't figure out which classmate in particular, or I'd get her parents to ground her for life." She balled her fists. "Whoever is doing this has gone way too far."

"And the X that Diana tells me she found on the back side of the wall in the tower used to be visible on the *front* side as well," Cassandra added. "Francine has washed it off twice already this month."

Francine frowned, but nodded. "I have reason to suspect that it's a group of freshmen who are acting inappropriately," she said, waving casually to indicate the triviality of the whole matter. "But in any case, I have to take some kind of action. So . . ." She let her voice fade.

I was still certain that the roof walker had been Willow. In any case, why had Francine kept quiet about this till now?

"So we're going to host a séance tonight." Cassandra beamed at us. Just then, Hildi pranced into the room and hopped onto the cushion between Francine and me. Francine edged away from her, while Cassandra said, "Why, hello, Hildi," as though she were greeting an old friend.

Rubbing her brow, Francine said, "I don't believe for a moment that my house is haunted. But my strategy is that by humoring my daughter, I'll give her enough wiggle room to drop the ghost routine."

"You think your twelve-year-old daughter has convinced a group of fourteen- or fifteen-year-old boys to come over to your house late at night and pretend to be ghosts?" Audrey asked.

Francine's nostrils flared and her lips pursed, but she didn't reply.

"We're doing the séance in Francine's dining room at eight p.m. sharp," Cassandra said. "You're both invited."

"I wouldn't miss it," Audrey said with a gracious smile.

"Neither would I," I chimed in, stroking Hildi's soft fur. This wasn't the sort of invitation that came along every day. I hadn't been to a séance since my days of slumber parties in junior high.

Francine promptly rose. "Well, okay, then. We won't take up any more of your time."

Audrey showed Cassandra and Francine out, returning to lean on the doorjamb. "That was interesting. I wonder what on earth Francine is up to. Why would she invite me? We haven't exchanged an unnecessary word in two years."

"Maybe she's trying to change that."

"Not likely. And I don't believe a single word of her story. The woman is always willing to lie to suit her own purposes. If she were truly being harassed by a group of Lisa's little friends, or by a spirit from the other world for that matter, she'd never want me to know, let alone help her. She'd be too afraid I'd take delight in her trials." She narrowed her eyes at me. "Hmm. Maybe she needs you to be there tonight for some reason and knew that she'd have to invite me too, in order to ensure that you'd come."

"You're suggesting Francine's staging an entire séance just to get me to come to her house tonight?"

"Merely thinking out loud, Erin. All we really know is that Francine is behaving very much out of character, and she can be highly devious. It's important that we don't walk into anything tonight unawares."

"That reminds me, Audrey. I'm fairly certain Hugh Black paid Francine a brief visit while I was there working the other day."

There was the slightest hitch in her movements, which was noticeable to me only because I'd become so familiar with her natural gracefulness. Although now in her mid-sixties, my landlady had once been a dancer in the New York Ballet.

I added, "She shooed him away, so I only caught a glimpse as he was leaving."

"I shouldn't be surprised. If he's paying visits to me, he's visiting with Francine Findley as well. That man only knows how to sing one tune." She made a face. "Talk about getting an annoying tune stuck in your head."

That night, much to my surprise, Sullivan was at the séance and wound up seated next to me. Audrey sat on my other side. Willow McAndrews nearly stomped on Diana Durst's foot in the process of clambering past everyone to grab Sullivan's other hand. Lisa Findley squeezed into a chair between Willow and Diana. Francine and Bob took the two remaining seats on either side of Cassandra—our medium for the night.

Knowing that the next night Sullivan and I were heading off on our "date," I was soon battling a case of sweaty palms, despite the chilly room temperature. Francine had dimmed the lights and cranked up the air conditioner upon Cassandra's orders. She'd explained: "We need to make our world as similar to theirs as possible." Apparently rooms were shadowy and severely over-chilled on the "other side."

Cassandra launched into a long soliloquy in a funereal voice about the importance of our being respectful and told us to "focus your energy on inviting Miss Chambers to join our circle." I tried to concentrate on following Cassandra's instructions and not on the thought that it was Steve Sullivan's hand that I was holding. I didn't need to *act* like I was in junior high just because I was at a séance.

Just as the room was silent and Cassandra had officially begun the proceedings, she cried, "No, wait! Our aura is out of balance. Bob, Francine, trade places."

Though Bob grumbled and Francine grimaced as though she were in physical pain, the two complied. This placed Bob between Cassandra and Diana, and forced Francine to sit next to Audrey. The latter gave my hand a bone-crushing squeeze, as if our seating arrangements were somehow *my* fault.

Actually my aching knuckles were a distraction from the Shaker chairs, which were lovely to look at but sheer torture to sit upon. The room, with its ruby-and-black-patterned rug and long one-piece cherry table, had a lemony fresh-waxed aroma. Francine had obviously just polished the rich red grain. She had a truly lovely table runner in place that featured earth tones and a double border of navy blue and forest green.

I tried to pry my thoughts away from the furniture and onto the ghostly proceedings, only to notice that my nose was itching. With her eyes closed, Cassandra kept calling for Abby to "make your presence known."

"Yes, Abby. Fire a spitball our way," Bob interrupted, chuckling. "Oww!" he cried a moment later and broke our circle of hands. "You didn't have to kick me," he snarled at his wife.

I promptly released my grip on both Audrey's and Sullivan's hands and indulged in tending to my itchy nose.

"Did I?" Cassandra asked innocently, then added under her breath, "Maybe it was *Abby,* propelling my leg, reminding you to be respectful."

"Well, I'm sorry, Cassie, honey, but what can I say?" he asked gently. "You've been calling for her for fifteen minutes now. And she *did* used to throw spitballs, during our chemistry labs."

"With Old Man McKenna," Lisa contributed in a throaty voice.

Cassandra gasped audibly, smiled, and cried "Welcome, Abby" to Lisa, as though there were no other possible explanation for Lisa's words.

Bob paled and gaped at Lisa. "How did you know the teacher's name?"

"'Cuz I remember, that's how. You and me. We'd aim at his shiny bald head as McKenna wrote on the blackboard."

"Lisa! Quit this nonsense this instant!" Francine said, already livid.

Her daughter gave a chuckle. "Aw, get over yourself, lady. You're so scared your secret will be revealed, you can't see straight. Meanwhile, Lisa already knows all about it. So does half the neighborhood, for that matter."

Francine got to her feet, her cheeks aflame. "I'm not going to sit here and—"

"Francine, please," Cassandra urged. "Stay calm. And sit back down. It's dangerous to jar Lisa from her trance."

Lisa clutched her forehead and closed her eyes. In a small voice, she whined, "I want to go be with my mom and dad now. You have to confess. Stop holding on to me. Let me go."

"Who are you talking to, Lisa?" Cassandra asked.

Lisa's head jerked and her eyes rolled back, then she snapped forward in her seat and started to whimper. In the blink of an eye, she looked like a frightened little girl. She gasped and looked around the room. "Mom? What happened? Did I fall asleep?"

"She's just playacting," Bob explained.

"Shush!" Audrey scolded, narrowing her eyes at him.

No one else at the table made a sound, although Francine remained standing and was staring at her daughter with a look of shock mixed with anger. Steve and I exchanged glances and, ridiculously, I had to battle an urge to take his hand once again.

"What's the last thing you remember, Lisa?" Cassandra asked intently.

"I don't know." She shook her head. "Something about respect, and you calling for Abby. But then . . . I could kind of hear what people were saying, and I could hear a voice that sounded like my own, but it was like I was asleep and just dreaming."

With obvious forced humor, Bob said, "Aw, come

on, guys! This is just a practical joke! Somebody fed her the information about our chemistry teacher. All she had to do was see an old yearbook, and she'd have known McKenna's name."

Cassandra fired back, "But how would anyone but Abby herself have known that, as a freshman, she took an upper-level science class with you?"

Bob frowned and smoothed his gray hair with both palms. He didn't answer.

Lisa continued more forcefully, "I felt this . . . I don't know . . . chill, and I smelled something, kind of like cinnamon or pumpkin pie, maybe, and . . . then suddenly you were shaking me, and I was waking up."

"Okay, everybody." Francine said it firmly, pushing her chair aside. "Séance is over. Time for everyone to leave."

"Francine, please don't—"

"You too, Cassandra," Francine interrupted. "I never should have agreed to this inane idea of yours in the first place. If you've hoodwinked me into putting my own child in harm's way, there is going to be hell to pay!"

"But—"

"Time to run, everybody," Diana said, clapping her hands twice. "Out, out, out." With the subtlety of chartreuse-and-hot-pink-striped curtains, Diana began to herd us out of Francine's house. She got the Stanleys out first, closely followed by Audrey. Willow had taken the opportunity to continue to grip Steve's hand, acting as though she was too terrified to make it out the door of her own accord. With Willow and Diana flanking him, he managed to call over his shoulder at me, "I'll pick you up at eight at your place tomorrow night, Erin," as the door swung shut behind them. Lisa tugged at my sleeve as I tried to head outside with the others.

"What is it, Lisa?" I asked, keenly aware of Francine's watchful eye.

The girl's eyes were full of fright. "Erin, don't keep working at my house. All right?"

"Pardon?"

"If you don't quit right away, something really terrible's going to happen."

"She's just upset, Erin," Francine said. "Don't worry. Either of you. Nothing bad is going to happen. Good night, Erin."

I stepped onto the porch, but Lisa's eyes pleaded with me to mark her words. At least for this one moment, I believed in the supernatural and was sincerely frightened for her.

Francine said sharply, "I expect to see you here at four p.m. tomorrow, just as we've got on our schedule. Good night, Erin."

As Francine closed the door, Lisa cried in a choked voice, "Please, Erin! Stay *away!*"

chapter 6

The following afternoon, Francine apologized profusely for her daughter's behavior at the séance. "Lisa just got a little carried away, is all," she told me for the third time, again interrupting our discussion. With my design spread across the mahogany coffee table, we were sitting on the too-firm-but-lovely camelback sofa in her living room. This was an elegant space, furnished in period pieces that Francine had personalized with family photographs on the side tables and an adorable collection of porcelain figurines in an eye-catching étagère on the opposite wall. "I think she honestly believed she was possessed. But it's just the product of her fertile mind. You remember what it's like to be twelve, I'm sure . . . not an adult, but not really a child anymore. It's such a difficult age."

"Yes, I do, and that's a challenging age for all concerned." When I was twelve, my adoptive mother was gravely ill, my adoptive father had deserted us, and my "fertile mind" entertained fantasies of my biological parents swooping into town to invite us to come live with them in a mansion, not unlike this one. Instead, Mom and I had gradually transformed our tiny apartment in Albany, New York, into a warm, welcoming home, and now I desperately wanted to help Francine and Lisa manage the same feat.

Despite my reassurances, Francine continued to search my eyes. Her green eyes were now bloodshot and her skin seemed unnaturally pale. In truth, I was spooked—and, clearly, so were Francine and Lisa, along with, perhaps, the house itself. I said gently, "I don't know whether or not I believe in ghosts, Francine. Maybe somewhere between spirits and angels lies some sort of . . . existential truth that I'd just as soon not grasp. What I *do* know is that the top floor of your home is in a state of disharmony, and that's something I can fix right now."

Francine gave me a sad smile. "Do you really think my house will become peaceful just by making it look better?"

"I've learned to never underestimate the restorative powers of creating a space that you truly love."

She pursed her lips, but nodded as she stared down at my drawings. "Your design is terrific, Erin. The new staircase will look superb with what you're doing with the ceiling and the windows. Let's go for it. I'm sorry I'm not more enthusiastic. I just can't ever seem to . . . drum up that Diana Durst type of . . . peppiness. I'm just so tired."

"You didn't hear more noises last night, did you?"

She nodded. "Lisa keeps turning on the radio in the kitchen. And the television sets. Or I *think* she's the one behind their getting switched on at all hours. She swears she's not. Maybe I'm sleepwalking. Maybe I tore up the wallpaper, too, in my sleep. And drew those darned Xs."

"But you couldn't have drawn the X on the *back* of the wall."

Francine grimaced, but said nothing. I asked, "Have you been known to sleepwalk in the past?"

"Yes, when I'm really stressed. Such as now. Though I never can remember what I did. I sleep right through everything."

"But . . . would you have written 'She will die' on the wallpaper in your sleep?"

Again, she winced and didn't reply; it was a rhetorical question anyway.

Ralph Appleby lumbered down the stairs and entered through the archway. "Roof's finished," he declared. "Wall's gone. Got the framing up for the ceiling, so the plasterers can build the new fancy-dancy coved one. They'll be here tomorrow. Still got a lot to do on the floorboards. A crew of specialists will be handling the sanding and refinishing, but I'm replacing the damaged boards myself, where the wall used to be."

"Oh, that's wonderful, Ralph!" Francine said, suddenly capable of "peppiness" after all. "You're a regular wonder!"

When his dark, angry eyes shifted to me, I rose, swept up the designs, and announced, "You might need to replace the boards under the banisters and bottom step as well. We've decided to replace the staircase."

His jaw dropped. "Why? That one works fine."

"It's ugly, Ralph," Francine pointed out.

"So am I!" he shot back. "But I'm 'a regular wonder.' Remember?"

"And yet the staircase *isn't* a wonder," I interjected. "It's just harsh and bulky." Before he could again declare *So am I!*, I thrust the blueprints into his hands. "Here's what we want." Knowing what a perfectionist he was, I braced myself and explained, "This company custom-makes their staircase kits."

While Francine rose and rounded the coffee table to stand beside me, he made a big show of how put out he was to have to use his eyes to look at the drawings, as opposed to glaring in disdain at me, but he finally managed to shift his vision. Though his expression never softened, at length he said, "Huh. Nice," and thrust them back at me. "You shoulda told me right away you had this in the works."

That was true, although the man hadn't exactly set out a welcome mat for me. More important, I hadn't gotten Sullivan's approval of the plans yet. I needed to talk to him right away. Our date was tonight; maybe I should turn it into a business dinner after all.

"Also, Ralph, the window installers will start work next week," Francine told him as he walked away from us.

"I know. I'm counting on having to fix their messes afterward. Good thing I'm a *wonder.*"

With my work here also finished for the day, Francine and I followed Ralph as far as the central hallway while he let himself out. A female voice from just outside the door said, "Excuse me," and Lisa dashed inside. Some of her numerous hair braids were starting to unravel. She gave me a sheepish smile and said to her mother, "I ran into Willow on the way home. She says she needs to talk to you."

"Is she waiting *outside?*" Francine asked in obvious confusion, then promptly added, "Tell her to come in."

Lisa's cell phone rang, and she answered while gesturing for Willow, who looked more than a little flustered as she entered. Lisa squealed at something the caller was saying and left the room to chatter to her friend in privacy.

Willow said somberly, "Francine, something's come up. I can't watch Lisa tonight after all. I've got to work late at the store."

"Oh, dear." Francine explained to me, "I've got a concert in Denver tonight." Returning her attention to Willow, she said, "Well, let's see. ScentSational closes at eight." That was the name of Cassandra's downtown shop, which sold aromatherapy lines as well as retro-sixties merchandise. Francine glanced at her watch. "Lisa will be fine here by herself till you can get here at nine, or even at ten."

"Actually, I've got to work even later than that. I'm supposed to run inventory. It could take me past midnight."

"You're taking inventory on a Friday night?"

Willow rolled her eyes. " 'Fraid so. Something came up with Cassandra, so she can't do it, and I kind of promised."

Francine studied the girl's tense features and asked gently, "Willow, is everything all right?"

"Yes. Sure. It's just . . . Cassandra can be so demanding sometimes. I might have to quit, if she keeps riding me like this."

Lisa returned, her cell phone no longer pressed to her ear, and demanded, "What's up?"

"I found out I'm going to be working an extra shift, so I won't be over tonight after all."

"Hey. No prob. I'll give you a hand at the store."

"That's not a good idea."

"You were saying I could. And Cassandra said she didn't mind either. I asked her a couple of weeks ago if I could help out, and she said as long as I wasn't alone behind the cash register, it was fine."

"Not tonight." Willow shook her head. "Some other time."

"Why not?"

"Lisa, Willow doesn't have to explain her reasons," Francine scolded.

Willow said firmly, "It's not a good idea, Lisa. Just accept that, okay?"

"Don't see why I can't," Lisa grumbled.

"I'll be available any night next week, Francine, to make up for this. I've got to get to the shop now. I'm already late." Willow hesitated at the door and smiled at Lisa, who was fidgeting with her iPod. "I'll see you tomorrow."

"Whatever."

"We'll do a treasure hunt next week," Willow promised, but Lisa had already turned her back and headed up the stairs, earphones in place. Willow sighed and shifted her glance a little. Our eyes met. In that one instant, Willow looked desperate, frightened. Then the moment passed. She smirked. "Hey, Erin, hear you and

Steve have a hot date tonight. Have fun." She whirled on a heel and left.

Francine and I chatted briefly in the foyer, then, just as I excused myself to head to my downtown office, she exclaimed, "Oh, shoot! I promised to give Willow her paycheck tonight. She mentioned she really needed it right away." She grabbed her purse from the front closet and snatched up her checkbook. As she started writing, she explained, "I'd run out of checks and couldn't pay her the last couple of times she worked for me. It's gotten to be such an embarrassment! Your office is close to Cassandra's store. Would you mind dropping a check off for me to Willow sometime tonight? I'd feel so much better having someone put this directly into her hands."

Her wording made me wonder if she didn't trust Diana to pass along Willow's babysitting check. Maybe Willow was late with rent money. I merely replied, "No, I don't mind," and we both left it at that.

That evening, I had a minor catastrophe to deal with: a supplier had fouled up the drapery order for one of my most exacting clients. The next thing I knew, Steve Sullivan was climbing the flight of stairs that led to my loft-style office. He carried a beautiful mango-orange calla lily in a slender crystal bud vase.

"Oh my God," I said, totally discombobulated. "Is it time for our date already?"

He smiled, his eyes merry. "How time does fly, huh, Gilbert?"

"I wanted to run home and change first. I thought . . ." I let my voice trail off as I looked at my watch and saw that it was only ten minutes after seven. "Wait. Weren't you picking me up at Audrey's? And didn't we say eight p.m.?"

"Couldn't wait that long to see you."

I furrowed my brow and studied his handsome features. Never had I heard a less Sullivan-like phrase from the man's lips. "Pardon?"

"I was heading back from the florist's and saw that you were still here. Figured I'd bring this to you now, before I spilled the water all over the seat of my van."

"How thoughtful. Thank you."

He shrugged.

"Actually, it's just as well that you brought this to my office, rather than my home. Hildi has a nasty habit of tasting house plants, and calla lilies are toxic."

"Hildi?" he asked.

"My cat," I said a bit sharply. Good grief! It might be asking too much for the man to remember my pet's name, but did he seriously think Audrey had taken on a second tenant who routinely devoured our flowers?

"Lucky for me, then, that I happened to think of bringing it now. I'd hate it to be my legacy that I killed your cat on our first date."

First date? That implied he thought there would be a *second* date! Yikes! Sullivan was like an attractive but uncomfortable chair that didn't mesh with my décor. I was too smart and experienced to entertain notions of giving my entire life a makeover just to accommodate one nice-looking-but-wrong-for-me man. I muttered, "That would be a major downer, all right."

"If memorable."

I chuckled. "Thanks again for the flower. I'd better lock up and get home now." I set the vase on the corner of my desk.

"Looks perfect there." He rocked on his heels. Were my eyes deceiving me? Was the man truly a little nervous around me? Well, heck! If I was going to make *him* uncomfortable, it'd be worth spending an evening with him just for the ego boost. "I'll, uh, walk you to your car."

We descended the stairs and I locked up, only then remembering that I still hadn't followed through on the small favor Francine had asked of me. "Actually, I need to stop in at ScentSational for a moment. Want to walk me there instead?"

"Sure. Looking for some sensational doodads?"

"No, I just need to give Willow something . . . a babysitting check from Francine."

"*Willow* works there?" he asked stiffly.

"Willow McAndrews. Yes."

"Maybe I . . ." He hesitated. "On second thought, this'll be good."

I put two and two together. "For her to see you with me tonight, you mean?"

"Yeah, actually. Willow's been making a nuisance of herself lately," he said. "Bob complained to me about it this morning."

"She's coming over there uninvited to see you, I take it?"

He didn't answer.

"By the way, I'm planning on removing the inner wall at Francine's place and replacing a hideous staircase with a sexy spiral one." Okay, that was misleading, considering that the wall was already long gone, but hadn't he himself remarked on how "funky" it was the last time we'd spoken? "What would you say to my installing larger windows in the tower room that echo the roofline and the existing windows of the original structure?"

He raked his hand through his hair, a sure sign that he wasn't pleased. "Depends on what you'd say to my updating the Stanleys' kitchen, putting a bay window in the den, and installing a marble surround on the fireplace on the west side of the house."

Updating the kitchen? Since when? Granted, he'd been forced to pick a back room for the bay window, but why not choose the dining room, where he could capture the mountain views? And what was wrong with the redbrick fireplace? "Sounds great," I lied, with effort.

"Ditto."

After a moment of silence, he added, "You're moving Francine's grand piano upstairs, right? And you're going to furnish the room in period antiques, I assume?"

"Not really. Traditional pieces. I found a settee to die for at a place in Denver, and a burled-ash console with mahogany inlays that I just love."

He looked at me for a moment longer than he should have if he had any interest in pretending to trust my judgment. "You care to describe this 'sexy spiral staircase' to me?"

"Not really. Do you care to describe the kitchen upgrade to *me?*"

He cleared his throat in what sounded disturbingly like a growl. We walked the next block in silence. Finally Sullivan said in a strained voice, "I'm sure whatever you're doing at your client's house is just . . . *great*."

"Ditto," I said frostily.

We reached the store, and he opened the door for me. A pretty brass bell jingled above our heads. I was surprised to see that Cassandra Stanley stood behind the counter. Hadn't Willow said that *she* would be at the store at this time?

Cassandra's store was a fun mishmash of New Age and sixties-retro merchandise—a jumble of colorful and imaginative candles and mobiles, lava lamps, massage oils and perfumes, and books on spiritualism. Sitar music ran on some sort of continuous loop in the background. She gave Sullivan and me a warm smile as we approached. "Erin. I had a feeling you'd be here. And you've brought our designer extraordinaire with you, I see."

"Hello, Mrs. Stanley," Steve said, exuding charm from every pore.

"Please. It's Cassandra. We already discussed this

matter, now, didn't we?"

"We did indeed. My apologies, Cassandra."

I barely resisted the urge to roll my eyes. This was a harmless flirtation, but it made me feel like a third wheel. If I were to treat my male clients this way, I'd feel like a complete slut. "Can I speak to Willow for a moment?" I asked.

Cassandra blinked, as though I'd asked my question in Hungarian. "Willow isn't here."

"I must have misunderstood her work schedule—"

"Rather drastically, Erin. Willow doesn't work for me anymore."

"She quit?"

"Actually . . . I fired her. For stealing from me."

"Oh my God," I said.

"When did this happen?" Steve asked.

"Last week." She frowned. "Willow begged me not to mention the unfortunate incident to anyone in the neighborhood, especially not to Francine, who hired her to babysit all this summer, you know. She even got Diana to plead for my silence, as well."

Maybe in exchange for agreeing to pose as Abby Chambers.

"I haven't told Francine about it yet, but as I already warned Willow, I *will* if she makes even the slightest misstep. The thing is, Lisa totally adores her, and she truly *is* exceptional with kids. So I'm trying to oblige, but, well, you're here at the store, and I'm certainly not going to *lie* for her."

"Willow told me that she was working here tonight."

She narrowed her eyes at me. "Of course she did. I should have picked up on the vibrations. I'm certainly feeling the barbs in your aura now."

Annoyed, I clenched my jaw and deliberately put some extra-sharp "barbs" in my aura, but said nothing.

"You caught Willow red-handed?" Sullivan asked. "Stealing?"

She nodded. "She claimed she had no choice . . . that she was desperate, and that she fully intended to pay me back at the earliest opportunity. Turns out she'd stolen from me the previous two times she worked as well. But Diana wound up reimbursing me."

"I wonder why. Diana is just her landlady, right? They didn't know each other prior to Willow's renting the room, did they?"

Cassandra had begun to busy herself with adjusting the patchouli bottles on the top shelf of the display case. "No, but Diana's taken Willow under her wing of late."

"Did you find out what she needed the money for?" Steve asked, and I looked at him, surprised he was asking a question that was none of our business.

"Not for certain. I have my suspicions that she was involved with an older man and was trying to dress up for him. A married man," she added firmly. "But heaven only knows what story she gave Diana to explain everything away. Whatever it was, Diana no doubt swallowed it hook, line, and sinker. She always does."

"Thanks for your time, Cassandra," I said. "We'd better get going—"

"She's a strange girl," Cassandra interrupted sadly. "I'm getting the worst vibrations from her lately. Her aura and chakras are in hideous shape. No good is going to come from whatever it is that she's up to," she said grimly.

We walked back to my office at a good clip; it was getting near our official date time. As we reached my van, Sullivan asked, "What the heck is a 'chakra'?"

"I have no earthly idea. But then, I have a barbed aura, so what do I know?"

He chuckled, but his amusement quickly faded. "Willow said she had something important to talk to me about tonight. Guess I should call her after all." He forced a smile. "Anyway. I'll come pick you up in half an hour or so."

"I'm looking forward to it," I said as I slid behind the wheel of my van. In truth, though, Cassandra's vague warnings of impending doom were contagious. Now I, too, had the feeling that something dreadful was going to happen.

Two hours later, I was beginning to wonder if the "dreadful" thing in my immediate future was our dinner date itself. The maître d' had written down Sullivan's reservation for tomorrow night by mistake. I worried that Sullivan was really the one who made the error, unconsciously sabotaging our dinner. Getting into a fancy restaurant with no reservations on a Friday night in Crestview was impossible, so we waited, and they finally crammed us around a small table near the kitchen door.

We immediately agreed that we weren't going to talk about work, but that left us with nothing to talk about except our disappointment in our cruddy table, which shook every time a waiter rushed past and the kitchen door banged open. Mysteriously, despite our proximity to the kitchen, our entrées were as cold as our conversation.

Finally, our check arrived. Sullivan insisted on leaving the tip as well, despite my offer, and we left. Minutes later, he pulled into a space in front of Audrey's walkway and shut off the engine.

He chuckled. "You know, Erin, there's a saying in theater: bad dress rehearsal, great show."

"So I've heard. But what's the connection?"

"It's all looking up from here. This was about as bad as a first date can get."

"Not really. You could have lost your wallet. We could have wound up having to wash dishes to pay for our meal. We could have gotten mugged. The car could have gotten towed, or we could have gotten into a car wreck."

"Or we could have gotten food poisoning," Sullivan added.

"True. Although, I've *had* food poisoning before, and that can take a few hours to show up."

"Ah. So there's still time. Nice thought, Gilbert. Thanks." He was staring through the windshield at Bob and Cassandra's house as he spoke. "I know we said we weren't talking about work, but I gotta tell you, there's something strange about the Stanleys. I get the strongest feeling sometimes that Bob's afraid to leave me alone in his house. It's like he's scared I'll find a damning secret under a loose floorboard."

"You're actually complaining to me that *your* clients are strange? After having spent last night at a séance at *my* client's house?"

"Which was officiated by *my* client. Get this: I'm supposed to be using circa late-eighteen-hundred color schemes, right? So I get their approval on some New England–blue milk paint that's precisely right for the room. I come in the next day, and the paint can's missing. I figure, maybe Bob or Cassandra moved it into the room, so I go look. There's Cassandra, in a yoga position in the center of the floor, humming in a monotone, like she's in this deep trance. I wait a minute or two, but finally I can't stand it, so I start to leave the room to ask Bob what's up with the paint. Just as I turn away, she says, 'Chartreuse.' 'Pardon?' I say. She opens her eyes and says to me, 'I'm talking to the walls, and they want to be dressed in chartreuse.' "

I laughed. "You'll have to teach your client's walls how to enunciate better, Sullivan. No self-respecting historic wall that *I've* ever met wants to be yellow-green."

"Even if it did, authentic paints of that era didn't come in that hue. Try telling Cassandra that, though." He got out of his van, circled to my side, and opened my door for me. Bugle, Diana Durst's beagle, was barking relentlessly. That meant we were going to have to say good night over the dog's racket. On the other hand, a glance over my shoulder reassured me that Audrey's Irish crystal chandelier was glittering through the transom above the door like sparkling diamonds, so the view, at least, was grand.

As he helped me step down, I couldn't resist grinning at him, and he asked, "What's with the Cheshire-cat grin, Gilbert?"

"Poor you. Must be killing you and your competitive spirit to know I'm getting all of *my* problems with my design worked out, whereas *you've* gone from New England–blue to chartreuse."

He took my hand and gave it a gentle squeeze. "Ah. But, you see, that's where *you* come in. You're now my boss. You can nix the eye-popping green for me, and I can tell Cassandra that my hands are tied."

"Aha! So *that's* what this is about. You're sucking up to me so that I'll help you with your client."

"Alas," he said, heaving an exaggerated sigh, "you see right through me, Gilbert."

We stopped by the front door. My heart was now hammering in my chest as the realization hit me with the force of a lightning bolt that I wanted him. Simultaneously, as though this were a near-death experience, my life started to flash before my eyes. So many memories were painful: learning that I'd been adopted as a toddler, my adoptive mother dying, my adoptive father walking out of the house for the last time, my biological father finding me only to die before we could acknowledge the connection . . .

Yet there were good things, too. I loved my home

here with Audrey. I loved my work. I needed a chance to enjoy the life I'd designed for myself, just as it was now, before I made any more major changes.

"What's the matter?" Sullivan asked.

I didn't answer.

"All of a sudden you look like you just realized you were standing on a razor blade."

"Do I? Have you *seen* someone's expression who was standing on a razor?"

"I hope not. Is your foot bleeding?"

I laughed. "No, it isn't. Thanks, Sullivan. I had a nice time tonight."

"You lie like a flea-market rug, Gilbert."

My anxieties suddenly lifted. "Well, okay. Technically, this wasn't exactly an enchanted evening. I'm having a nice time *now,* though."

"And, lucky for me, there's still one way we can salvage this date."

He was staring into my eyes and started to draw me close. *This is it—he's going to kiss me!*

At that instant, a woman's scream pierced the air.

chapter 7

Steve drew away, and I grabbed his arm. "Which direction did that come from?" I asked.

The woman screamed a second time. It was coming from behind Audrey's house. Steve and I took off at a dead run.

Where's Audrey? I thought, fighting off panic. She'd become my family, my support structure. If something had happened to her, I didn't know how I'd cope.

We rounded the house and saw Audrey and Diana. They were next door, in Francine's backyard. Diana was in hysterics, wailing, "No!" and blubbering; Audrey was kneeling beside a dark shape on the ground.

I jumped over the short fence, unable to process what I was seeing.

Audrey was shaking her head at Steve, who'd beaten me there.

The dark shape by Audrey was a person—wearing a black hooded sweatshirt. I gasped. Willow McAndrews. Her limbs were at awkward, unnatural angles. She must have fallen from Francine's third-story roof.

Sobbing, Diana flung herself into Steve's arms. "I came out to see why Bugle kept barking," she cried. "I found her—"

"Erin," Steve said crisply. "Call nine-one-one."

I fumbled for the cell phone in my purse. From the angle of her neck, it was clear that it was broken, and from the vacant eyes, I knew, too, that the ambulance would arrive too late. Willow was just twenty-three, far too young to die.

A door banged and the Stanleys came rushing toward us—Bob fully dressed, Cassandra in a bathrobe and slippers. They must have heard the screams, too. I came to realize that there was a distant keening as well, rising from some vantage point over our heads. I looked up at Francine's house and saw the tormented features of Lisa, staring down at us from the roof.

With a horrid vision of Lisa, too, taking a dive off the roof, I ran. I heard Sullivan call my name, but paid no attention. Francine's back door was locked.

I tore around the house, leapt onto the porch, and tried the front door. Unlocked. I threw it open and dashed toward the staircase. Lisa was already heading down the stairs. She wailed "No, no!" with every step, and tears streamed down her cheeks. I tossed my purse and my cell phone in a corner and waited for her.

"It's Willow, isn't it?" she cried. "I've got to go be with her. This is my fault!"

She tried to rush past me, but I grabbed her and held tight. "Don't go out there, Lisa. There's nothing you can do for her."

"She's dead? Oh my God!" Weeping as though her heart had broken, she collapsed in my arms. All I could do was cry along with her.

Sullivan charged through the door. "Is everyone okay in here?"

Not knowing the answer myself, I ignored the question and instead asked Lisa, "Are you here alone?"

She nodded against my shoulder. I scanned our surroundings. Suddenly this long center hallway seemed bleak and cavernous, the arched entranceways gaping at us.

"Lisa," Steve said, "what happened? How did Willow fall?"

She was sobbing so hard it was a struggle for her to

answer. “I don’t know,” she sputtered. “I wasn’t there when it happened. I was looking for her. She let herself in the house. I heard her crying and . . . I couldn’t find her.” Struggling to catch her breath between sobs, she added harshly, “I told Mom how half my friends are babysitters themselves. That I didn’t need a babysitter. Willow’d still be alive if Mom had just listened to me!”

“Why was Willow on your roof?” I asked.

“I don’t know,” Lisa wailed. “She wasn’t even supposed to *be* here tonight.”

My thoughts were racing. Why would Willow enter the house when she’d been so adamant she couldn’t babysit Lisa tonight? Surely she hadn’t broken into the house next door to her own just to commit suicide. But could she have fallen by accident? “Where were you when you heard Willow crying?” I asked Lisa. “Upstairs?”

Again she nodded, gasping for air. “In my room. I was reading on my bed, when I heard noises . . . like . . . footsteps and things . . . and then a girl crying. I thought maybe . . . that maybe there really *was* a ghost, after all. Like, maybe *Abby* was crying. All this junk has been happening here . . . stuff getting torn off the walls and everything. . . . I was kind of scared, but I went into the tower room, and somebody shoved me. From behind. Then he locked me in the closet.”

“It was a man?” Sullivan asked.

“The closet in the tower room?” I asked simultaneously. There was only one closet in the room, next to the door.

Tugging on a fistful of messy, unbraided red hair, Lisa ignored both questions and said, "Somebody pushed Willow off the roof. Whoever locked me in the closet."

"There's a lock on the door to the closet?" Sullivan whispered to me.

I shook my head, bewildered.

Lisa said emphatically, "Something was blocking it, or something. I couldn't get out. I kept banging against it and rattling the doorknob, and it finally opened."

I studied her tear-streaked face. "And you didn't even know Willow was planning to come over here tonight?"

"No. She *canceled*. Remember? While you were here. She had to work!"

Sullivan and I exchanged glances. I wondered if Diana was still in hysterics, or if Sullivan had helped her to—"Oh, shoot!" I cried. "I started to call the police, but—"

"I called them," Sullivan said quietly. "Audrey's outside, on my cell phone with the dispatcher now."

Lisa staggered toward the nearest room—the parlor—dropped onto the floor, and hugged her knees, rocking. I asked, "Do you have your mom's cell phone number?"

She nodded. "Dial memory one on the phone in the kitchen. But if the concert's still going, it won't actually ring. Mom won't answer till she's done playing."

I strode into the kitchen and dialed on the cordless phone. Francine answered on the first ring, her

"Hello?" already tense.

"Francine, it's Erin. Lisa's fine, but something terrible has happened to Willow." Too agitated to stay put, I paced in a tight circle in the kitchen. In my current mental state, the black-and-white alternating floor tiles were making me dizzy.

"To *Willow?* Erin, what are you talking about?"

"Willow fell off your roof."

"My God! She wasn't even supposed to be there! She canceled!"

"I know." The scream of police sirens in the distance registered with me; they'd be here momentarily.

"Ralph said it was all fixed and safe up there! I specifically asked him about the railing, and he said everything was rock-solid. How could this have happened?"

"I have no idea, Francine. The police are on their way and—"

"The *police* are coming? You mean, along with the paramedics, right? How bad is she hurt?"

The doorbell rang. The police were clearly here. I covered my free ear, assuming that Steve would get the door. I swallowed the lump in my throat and said quietly to Francine, "Willow's dead. Her neck was broken."

"Oh, dear God . . ." There was a pause, then her voice raised an octave as she demanded, "Where was Lisa when this happened?"

"She said she was trapped in the tower-room closet."

Another pause. "Tell her I'll be right there."

I could see by the flashing red lights through the sidelight as I made my way down the hall that at least two emergency vehicles were now parked in front of the house. I ducked into the den. Lisa had crawled underneath the grand piano, her head bent, her body curled tight. I told her that her mother was coming and promised that I'd be right back, then headed to the foyer, where Sullivan stood speaking with two uniformed officers. To my relief, they were my friend Linda Delgardio and her partner.

With long black hair and eyes so dark they were almost black as well, Linda was a smart and vivacious woman, and we'd become quite close over the past several months. Now she gave my arm a quick squeeze and asked, "You all right?" I nodded, and she asked Sullivan to have a seat while she spoke to Lisa, and instructed her partner, whom I knew only as Officer Mansfield, to take my "statement."

Steve gave me a long, sad look and said, "If I don't happen to see you again tonight, take care, Erin."

"You too, Steve," I replied as Officer Mansfield tried to usher me down the hall.

I insisted on checking in with Lisa, just to assure her that I'd be speaking to an officer but would be "nearby," then Mansfield led me into the kitchen. I gave him what little information I had: I'd seen Lisa on the roof and had immediately run inside to check on her. Through the glass, I could see two more uniformed officers talking to Audrey and Diana. Mansfield listened carefully, thanked me, then said he was going "out back," where Willow's crumpled body lay. He left through the front door. I gathered my purse, which I'd flung with so much force that the snap had opened. I spotted the babysitting check for Willow that I hadn't had the chance to give her. I set that facedown by the kitchen phone.

Left to my own devices, I headed straight back to the parlor and noiselessly slid the pocket French doors open. In the center of the room, Lisa and Linda faced each other, seated in matching side chairs. As I entered, Linda immediately caught my eye and shook her head a little as Lisa said to her, "I just came into the room, and then someone shoved me from behind and trapped me in the closet."

A floorboard creaked under my foot as I stepped hastily back into the hallway. Lisa gasped and turned. At the sight of a friendly face, she started to cry again. "Who would kill Willow? She was really cool. She liked everybody!"

"I don't know, Lisa," I replied.

Lisa returned her attention to Linda and exclaimed, "When I got the closet door open, I could hear something was happening outside . . . but I couldn't see much through the window. I went up the stairs to ask Willow what everyone was screaming about." She took a shaky breath. "She wasn't there. I looked over the railing, and that's when I saw her . . . and—"

She broke off at a noise that sounded as if the front door had been flung open. A deep voice outside was yelling, "You can't go in there, ma'am!" With all of the determination of a mother lioness charging toward her threatened cub, Francine stormed into the room, trailed by an officer I didn't recognize. She was wearing a long black gown, and her hair was pinned up.

"Where's Lisa?" she demanded of me.

"She's right in—"

She swept past me and promptly drew Lisa into her arms, who once again began to weep, but managed to say, "Mom! How'd you get here so fast? I thought you were performing in a concert in Denver."

"It ended early. There was an electrical problem at the theater." She took her child's face in her hands and studied her. "Oh, my poor baby. Are you all right? You're not hurt?"

"I'm fine, Mom. But Willow . . . somebody threw her off the roof and she . . . she . . ."

"I know, sweetie. Erin told me."

"This is your house, ma'am?" Linda asked gently, rising to face her.

Francine rose to her full height as well; she had a couple of inches on Linda. "That's right. And this is my daughter. I have *not* consented to her being interrogated by the police!"

"I was just trying to tell them what happened, Mom! Somebody killed Willow!"

"She's traumatized," Francine continued, undeterred. "I need all of you out of here this minute."

"We can't do that, ma'am. There's been a possible homicide here tonight."

"On our *roof,* not inside the house."

"We need to close off the entire house while we investigate. We can take you and your daughter to a nice hotel room for the night, and we—"

"I'll take care of finding accommodations myself, Officer. Come on, Lisa. Let's get you out of here right now."

"But . . . I don't have anything packed, and—"

"Don't worry about that now."

"Ma'am, your daughter was a witness to a suspicious death. It's immensely helpful to our investigation to be able to—"

"My ex-husband is a lawyer. I know my rights. Lisa is a minor, and I absolutely forbid you to talk to her. Furthermore, this is my home, and I have an expectation of privacy here. Whatever additional information you need to extract from my daughter will have to be obtained on my terms, when *I* decide it's okay for her to speak with you."

"Mom! I didn't do it! I wasn't even on the roof yet!"

I interjected, "This is Linda Delgardio, Francine. She's a friend of mine, and I can assure you—"

"Erin, I would think you'd have more common sense, and just . . . just basic human decency than to allow a police interrogation of my daughter to occur right in front of you!"

"Francine, they're just—" I took a deep breath and realized she was too frightened to be rational at the moment. "I apologize, Francine. Everything has been happening very quickly."

"Mom!" Lisa cried, tugging on her mother's arm.

"You don't have to worry! I didn't *do* it!"

Francine merely shushed her, and Lisa started to weep softly again.

"We're simply gathering information, ma'am," Linda said in deferential tones.

"Fine. Look all you want, as long as you keep your distance from my child. I'll call the police station in the morning." Francine, with Lisa in tight tow, stormed out the front door.

The air still seemed to crackle with Francine's anger seconds after the door had slammed behind her. The young officer who'd followed her inside said, "I'm standing guard at the front door from now on."

Linda nodded, and he left. I sank onto the Hepplewhite chair in the hallway, not knowing what to do, not sure where Sullivan had gone; probably one of the officers had taken him to a squad car for his interview. I didn't want to go out to the backyard again and see Willow's twisted body. I wanted desperately to put this evening on rewind and somehow alter Willow's course, spare her this hideous ending.

Linda said, "I'm going to take a quick look upstairs. Would you mind waiting for me here?"

"I'll go up with you."

"It's better if you wait right here, Erin. Have you stayed on the main floor since you arrived?"

"Well, yes, but if you're thinking in terms of fingerprints, mine will be all over the house. I was upstairs just this afternoon."

"Still, though. There could be footprints on the stairs.

I'll only be a minute."

I sank back into the chair. She was gone for at least ten minutes, and when she came back, she ushered me into the parlor and had me take the same seat that Lisa had recently vacated. Then she sat across from me and asked, "Do you know Lisa very well, Erin?"

"Not really. She likes Hildi a lot, and vice versa. That's how we started talking one day, about ten months ago, when I first moved into the neighborhood. She was complimenting me over my cat . . . said her mother was allergic, but that cats were her favorite animal. Later she got really interested in hearing about interior design. She told me she thought it was 'cool to be able to poke around in people's houses.' She reminds me of my sister, I guess. They're almost the exact same age."

"Your sister? That's your adoptive father's daughter, right?"

"Yes. She lives in California with him and his wife."

"What type of kid is Lisa Findley?"

"Pardon?"

"Do you think she's telling the truth about what happened here tonight?"

"Yes. Don't you?"

She frowned. "The logistics are a little off, is all. Worries me."

I nodded, well accustomed to remembering details about interiors. I too had picked up on a minor contradiction in Lisa's story.

"The closet is right next to the doorway to the room.

So if someone shoved Lisa from behind as she entered, she would have been pushed *away* from the closet, not toward it. She could have turned back, though, to switch on the light, for instance."

I frowned. That explanation didn't work. During his first day on the job, Ralph had removed the ceiling fixture in preparation for my changes to the ceiling and for moving the chandelier from its second-floor quarters. A pair of old table lamps had been placed on the floor temporarily, but they were nowhere near the closet.

Lisa's statement about the door being jammed shut worried me as well. There was no furniture in the room whatsoever; it would have been hard for anyone to locate something quickly to use as a brace to keep the door shut.

Apparently reading my mind, Linda chastised, "Erin. Don't play amateur sleuth. It's a bad idea. I know you were actually a big help to us last spring, but don't forget how high a price you nearly paid in the process. Besides, you'll muck up the evidence."

"It's just that I'm scared for Lisa's sake. What if she saw the killer's face and is too scared to say so?" A stray thought flitted through my brain: if the killer was somebody connected to Francine, Lisa could be keeping the identity quiet in a misguided attempt to protect her mother. "Do you think Lisa's safe?"

Measuring each word, Linda replied, "Erin, I can't speculate with you about anything. For one thing, it's my job *not* to discuss the case. For another, it's important that you keep in mind that Lisa Findley is not your sister."

"What do you mean?" I asked, already bristling. In a recent girls' night out, I'd told Linda how much it upset me that my adoptive father wouldn't allow me and my half-sister, Jessie, to spend time with each other.

"You need to stay uninvolved, Erin. I know how you are, how deeply you care about your clients. Let us do our jobs. Don't get in the middle of this, like the last time."

"That was different."

"Good. Because you really have no way to know how accurate anything Lisa says is."

Something about her careful diction and emphasis of her words made me read between the lines. "Jeez, Linda. It sounds as if maybe Francine was *right* to rush her out of here. I don't know Lisa real well, but I did see how distraught she was as she came down the stairs. She did *not* push Willow off the roof!"

Linda crossed her arms and regarded me. "Okay. That's the difference right there between you and me. You look at Lisa Findley, and you see a girl who likes your cat and reminds you of your sister and is traumatized by a terrible death. Whereas I see a witness whose story doesn't quite add up and who was seen on the roof just after the victim fell."

"She's a twelve-year-old child, Linda. She did not push her babysitter off the roof!"

She held my gaze. "Want me to walk back to your house with you?" she asked gently.

"No, thanks. I can manage." I couldn't even meet Linda's eyes as I rose and left the house.

Audrey was sitting in her dining room, head in her hands, when I entered. She barely nodded to acknowledge my hello. Like most of the house, this room was what rosy-painting real estate agents such as Diana Durst would call "eclectic," but was really a hodgepodge. It featured a truly stunning mahogany eight-seat table set, with an antique pine hutch straight out of an old farmhouse. An ultramodern serving table sat beside a Victorian settee. One and a half walls boasted wallpaper. The others were merely primed. Audrey had cut up most of the wallpaper to use as wrapping paper last Christmas; she had used the fabric intended for the now-barren windows as ribbon. I gave her a quick hug, then slipped into the chair beside her. Because Audrey was normally so exuberant and indefatigable, her behavior was akin to a blatant display of immeasurable sorrow.

"Oh my God, Erin. It takes a lot to scare me, but this has done it."

"Me too."

Her eyes looked like dark holes. "What makes matters all the worse, I think I saw Hugh Black skulking away from Francine's house."

"When?" I asked, alarmed.

"Just as I heard Diana scream when she saw Willow's body. I looked out the kitchen door and saw what looked like Hugh's silhouette in Francine's side yard. Whoever it was ducked into the shadows and darted away while I ran to Diana to see if I could help."

"My God. Did you tell the police?"

"Of course. But Diana didn't see the man at all. And all I could see was his silhouette."

"Does Hugh have an alibi?"

"I don't know. I haven't talked to him, and I don't know if the police have, either. It's just . . ." She sighed. "My instincts are telling me that it was Hugh, Erin."

"Even if it was, he might have simply slipped away because he didn't want to get involved in the police investigation. People do stuff like that all the time, you know. It's not admirable, but it certainly doesn't make them guilty."

She sighed again heavily. "No, Erin. I meant that my instincts are telling me not just that Hugh was the man in the shadows, but that he's the killer."

"My God. He's really so horrible that he can be violent?"

She rose. "I can't talk about this anymore right now. It's making me depressed. I have to go do something magnificent now, while the day is still young."

"But . . . it's after midnight."

"Which, technically, makes this a brand-new day."

"What magnificent achievement do you have in mind?" I asked as she headed toward the kitchen.

"I don't know yet. But I'll let you know once it's accomplished."

"On that note, I'm going to bed." We said our good

nights, and I clung to the hope that the morning would bring something "magnificent" for us all—the proof that Willow's death had merely been a tragic accident.

Saturday was normally a busy workday for me, by virtue of my clients having the day off from work. Today I was having a hard time concentrating. When a client canceled our midafternoon appointment, I rescheduled my remaining appointment until next week to allow me to spend the remainder of the weekend at home with Audrey. I snatched up my calla lily, not wanting to waste it on an empty office till Monday, and raced home, only to discover an empty house; Audrey was apparently off running errands or socializing.

Deciding that work would help me calm my nerves, I placed my lily on the top of Audrey's curio cabinet in the parlor where Hildi couldn't possibly get to it, spread out my designs and materials on the kitchen island, and soon absorbed myself in rethinking Francine's design with the wallpaper we'd selected. Keeping the octagonal room dimensions in mind, I decided to go with three accent walls on the northern side of the house boasting the wallpaper and to paint the remaining walls in a cornsilk yellow with glossy white trim. I'd chosen a rich crown molding to draw the eye upward and relished the notion of showcasing the sexy planes of the new coved ceiling, which would resemble an inverted, round-cut diamond.

Someone tapped on the back door, and I looked up to

see Lisa Findley peering at me through a pane of the door. Even from this brief and distant glimpse, the girl was obviously a jumble of angst. I immediately invited her in, gave her a hug, and asked, "Are you and your mom back inside your house again?"

"As of an hour ago." She jammed her hands into the pockets of her jeans and said shyly, "Erin? There's some stuff I . . . kind of remembered last night, after that policewoman left?"

"Officer Delgardio?"

She nodded and freed her hands to tug at a fistful of her hair, more wavy than ever now that the braids had been removed.

"Let's have a seat." I pulled out one of the slat-backed country-style chairs and took a seat across from hers.

She propped her elbows on the pine surface of the kitchen table and laced her fingers tightly. For a moment, she rested her chin on her hands as though in prayer, then she began to fidget with her hair again. "See, Erin, I don't know why Willow said she wouldn't come over last night. We were going to sneak up to the roof together and try to hold our own private séance. We'd already made a secret pact."

"And you don't—"

"It's going to pass on to me now."

"*What* is?"

"The curse. Whatever this . . . ghost is doing. Abby. Throwing people off the roof."

She started crying. I snatched the box of tissues from

the corner and offered her one. She accepted it and struggled to compose herself. "It really is all my fault, Erin. I . . . I lied. I gave Willow a key to our house. She made me promise not to tell my mom. She said she just needed it for emergencies, but that Mom would get all paranoid if she knew."

"Did you believe that was the real reason she wanted a key? For emergencies?"

She shook her head and swiped at her tears. "She was . . . kind of in on everything with me. We were just . . . Look, I don't know why this sounded like so much fun at the time, but Willow knew all about Abby. I guess she'd read some history stuff. Everyone knows she's this ghost. I dunno . . . It just seemed like so much fun to make everyone think she was back. But then, at the séance, I didn't even mean to say the things I said, and . . ." She let her voice fade.

"The two of you were trying to spook your mom. How? By making noises at night and things like that?"

"It was just supposed to be for a couple of times."

"So did Willow tear down the wallpaper?"

"I think so. She *swore* to me she didn't, though. And she started to get real nervous about stuff, for the last day or two. She canceled babysitting last night. Only, then I heard her sneak inside the house."

"Through the front door?"

She nodded. "Unless it was someone else. Whoever pushed her, I mean."

"You never actually saw the intruder?"

"No. But there's this one real noisy step. It's pretty close to my bedroom. I can hear it creak, even when my door's closed. So, I heard someone I figured was Willow walk past my room, and I tiptoed after her, up to the tower room. By then I could hear footsteps on the roof, and I hid in the closet. I was just, like, going to make some noises and pop out at her when she came back down. As a joke. You know? I didn't mean anything bad to happen. But then, when I'd been in there for a minute or two, I heard a *second* person go past and up the stairs to the roof. I got all freaked out, so I stayed hidden. Then I heard the screams from below when . . . when they found Willow, so I ran upstairs to the roof. And that's when you saw me."

"Did you hear footsteps a second time? *Leaving* the roof, while you were still hiding in the closet?"

"Yeah, but by then I was really scared, because I couldn't figure out what was happening . . . why someone would be following Willow onto the roof."

"Why did you make up the story about getting shoved in the closet?"

"I don't know."

I waited. Often "I don't know" really means "I don't want to say because it'll make one of us feel bad."

"I should have been braver," Lisa said quietly. "At least nicer to her. To Willow, I mean. I should have let her know right away that I'd heard her. I was mad at her for treating me like a little kid when she told my mom she couldn't come. And I could tell she was lying about why. Then, when I heard someone else come up the stairs, I got too scared."

"Lisa, Willow's death wasn't your fault. You could have gotten badly hurt if you'd confronted whoever followed her up the stairs."

"*Or* maybe he'd have run away, and Willow would still be alive."

"That's really unlikely, Lisa," I said. Holding her gaze, I asked, "What you're telling me now is the complete truth? You're not leaving anything out?"

She said sharply, "It's the truth, the whole truth, and blah, blah, blah."

"Did you tell your mother the full story?"

"Not yet."

"We'd better call her right now."

"No, see, the thing is, I—"

"Lisa, this is the best way to handle things. The three of us will go to the police station together, and you'll tell Officer Delgardio exactly what you just told me. It's going to be all right."

She shook her head vehemently. "You don't understand, Erin. It *isn't* going to be all right!" She reached over the table to grab my wrist. "You've got to help me, Erin! The police are going to think I did this! They'll think I'm lying about someone else being on the roof with her." She released my arm and grabbed her hair with both hands.

"But your mother is your biggest ally, Lisa. She can—"

"My mom is never going to understand! She's afraid that I just had a—" She broke off. "She's never going to trust me again, now that I've been lying to her about the ghost."

"Lisa, parents were once children themselves, you know. Your mother won't like hearing about all this, but she'll cope."

"You don't understand! She thinks I did it! She thinks I pushed Willow off our roof! That's why she was acting like that last night!"

"But why would she—"

"I don't want to talk about it, okay?" she shrieked. She took a couple of shallow breaths. "I know I'm just twelve, but I have the right to keep some things to myself, you know? It's not about Willow. It's just . . . something that happened before we moved here." In a small voice, she added, "Sometimes things just happen. And they mess up your life forever."

My heart ached for her. Maybe the events of my life lately had made me unduly suspicious, but I couldn't help but worry that perhaps she'd had some violent episode in her past that Francine was afraid she'd repeated. "Lisa, are you sure you don't want to talk about it? Maybe if you did, you wouldn't feel—"

"I *do* talk about it. Just not to you. So let's call my mom and go to the police station. It's no big deal. I know the drill. So does my mom." She threw the door open and said viciously, "Mom's home now. Let's just get this over with."

chapter 8

Creative inspiration can't be rushed. All you can do when you're in dire need of its presence is to leave the lights on, keep all the doors and windows wide open, and keep on working.

—Audrey Munroe

DOMESTIC BLISS

Driving home from the police station Saturday evening, I had not a doubt in my mind that Francine and Lisa were hiding some incident in Lisa's past that made the girl a suspect in Willow's death. Maybe Lisa had a sealed juvenile record. Even so, she'd been utterly convincing in this more thorough version of what she'd witnessed last night. What now kept playing over and over in my head was how Lisa had grabbed my wrist and pleaded, "You've got to help me, Erin!" It broke my heart.

As I pulled into a parking space on my street, a sense of doom got a stranglehold on me. Maybe I'd made the biggest mistake of my life when I accepted Francine as a client. Suddenly my neighborhood, which I so dearly loved with all its stately manors and timeless elegance, was no longer so genteel. Someone had died a stone's throw away from my home. My next-door neighbors, the Stanleys, weren't as kindhearted as they'd always seemed. Even Audrey didn't seem up to her usual zaniness of late. She was instead dealing with a possibly violent ex-husband.

My home was no longer my haven. My dream job had turned into a nightmare. Maybe my life was spinning out of control. Weighed down with these heavy thoughts, I made my way up the slate walkway, aware of—but unable to appreciate—the astonishing approach to the home. The glimmering chandelier in the foyer shone through the transom and sidelights like a dazzling beacon: now it felt like an illuminated target.

I unlocked the front door and let myself inside. I tossed my purse in the closet, entered the parlor through the French doors, and was dismayed at the sight that greeted me. Audrey was sitting cross-legged on the floor, surrounded by armfuls of . . . feathers. Nearby, Hildi was batting at fluffy white down with her front paw.

"Audrey? What are you doing?"

She twisted to look at me over her shoulder. "I need your help, Erin. I'm in so much trouble!"

"What's happened?" I asked, picking my way quickly through the mess to join her. I pushed off a stack of papers and sat down on the ottoman in front of her. When she didn't immediately answer, I asked, "Did somebody kill a flock of birds in here?"

"I am still one segment short for my show on Monday. And yet I just can*not* get my brain to work.

I guess it was the shock of finding Willow last night. But in any case, I have no ideas for the show. None. Zip. Nada."

"So . . . you want me to help you come up with an idea for *Domestic Bliss* . . . that uses feathers?"

Hildi pounced on a feather and murdered it.

"No, this is just indicative of how desperate I am. I found a bag of feathers in the basement and thought I'd do eight minutes on 'Fun with Feathers.' But to be honest, I'm not having that much fun. Unlike your cat. It would never do to have me tape Hildi and show her chasing a handful of goose down around a room for several minutes, although, admittedly, I've actually considered the notion. But my producer would fire me on the spot."

"How can I help?"

"Brainstorm with me. Just . . . blurt out some ideas."

I looked around the chaotic room. "How about tips from house cleaners, or professional organizers? Someone who can talk about the ill effects of clutter."

She shook her head, closed her eyes, and decreed, "Too long."

"You could ask them to keep it short, to just discuss—"

"No, I mean your suggestions are too long. You're using too many words. We have to do this rapid-fire . . . one-word suggestions. Just whatever pops into your brain."

I scanned the room. "Cats. Pet ownership. Messy

floors. Missing phones. Storage space. Sofas. Fabrics. Light fixtures. Ceiling art. Tuna fish."

"Tuna fish. Interesting."

"You could come up with some delicious tuna casseroles."

She grimaced. "Not possible. That's an oxymoron. Maybe pan-seared ahi." She pondered for a moment. "No, this segment really shouldn't involve cooking. I'm already doing a kitchen segment. It'll throw the show out of balance." She hugged her knees and looked at me, gesturing for me to continue. "Back to it," she commanded. "You're doing fine."

"Um . . . roommates. Paint. Spills. Birds. Kleenex tissues."

"That's it!" she cried, hopping to her feet.

"So . . . you're going to do a segment on Kleenex?"

"No, but you just gave me a great idea. Wait right there. I'll show you."

She went upstairs, and I coaxed Hildi onto my lap. She'd finally tired of the feline version of "Slaughter on Feather Avenue." "Hi, sweetface," I said to her. "Those darned things just won't turn into a bird for you, will they?" She lovingly touched noses with me and rubbed her cheek against mine.

Audrey returned, carrying a T-shirt. "Ta-da!" she cried, holding it aloft. "Here's Monday's segment . . . hobo art!"

"Hobo art?"

"Yes, indeed. A professor noticed the graffiti in and around train stations and figured out that they were symbols from the homeless people to communicate with one another. I can start my TV segment by saying, 'We often talk about ways to spruce up your home on this show, but for a few minutes today, let's talk about those who *don't* have homes.'" She made a Vanna White gesture. "You can see the symbols on this shirt, along with the translations for each one. Things like 'free phone,' 'hobos arrested on sight,' 'work available,' and so on. I'll get someone who sells these shirts to talk about the symbols and what they mean, and explain how buying the T-shirt helps the homeless . . . that they make a donation for each shirt you buy."

I studied the shirt, which truly was fascinating. "You got that idea from 'tuna fish' and 'Kleenex tissues'?"

"Oh, who knows how the creative mind works?"

I read one of the symbol translations aloud, amused. "'Kind woman, tell a pathetic story.' Huh. I guess that means the hobos should tell her a sad story to gain her sympathy, but the way it's written, it's as if it's the woman's pathetic story."

Audrey's cheeks turned a rosy-pink shade.

"Hey!" I cried. "Is that what made you think of hobo art? Were you sitting here, listening to me talk, thinking 'How pathetic'?"

She gave me a benign smile, patted my shoulder, and said, "What matters is the idea itself, not how it hit me." She sighed happily and headed for the kitchen. "I'll fix us some dinner."

Still perturbed, I said to Hildi, "Crazy landlady, drives roommate wild."

"I heard that," Audrey called, laughing.

chapter 9

By ten o'clock Sunday morning, I'd finally deserted all self-delusions of being able to sleep in to make up for yet another restless night. I was deeply concerned about Lisa, as well as disappointed in Sullivan for not calling me yesterday. I was even more disappointed in myself for hoping, against logic, that he *would* call.

When I emerged only partially refreshed from my shower, Audrey knocked on the bathroom door to tell me that Sullivan had phoned fifteen minutes earlier and wanted me to call him back. Thinking he was a day late, I thanked her and quickly dressed in casual clothes appropriate for the hot summer day—a pale pink polo shirt, black shorts, and flip-flops.

Deciding that Lisa took precedence over Sullivan, I went to her house. I took the circuitous front-door route. I had lost all desire to cut through our backyards and walk across the very spot where poor Willow had landed. Though the sky was clear and a bright azure blue, my spirits were so low that the Findley manor with its dark gray exterior looked dreary and forbidding as I made my way up the slate walkway. I battled the sensation that I was trespassing and turned the key on the antique doorbell, feeling as though I were violating a "Do Not Touch" sign in a museum.

Francine's stone-cold expression and frigid greeting did little to alter my gloomy mood. "This is a surprise," she said in a chilly voice, holding the door for me. "I thought you didn't work on Sundays."

"Erin's not here to work," a voice I recognized as Cassandra's called from the living room. "She's here because she's worried about Lisa."

"That's true, actually," I muttered, mildly impressed at Cassandra's perceptiveness, if not her prescience.

Frowning, Francine turned on a heel and I followed. Seated on the gold camelback sofa beside Cassandra, who, as usual, was wearing khakis and a peasant blouse, was Diana, clad in a short denim skirt and red T-shirt and sandals. Before I could ask how Lisa was doing, Diana chirped, "I'm sure Erin's here for the same reason we are, Francine." I slipped into the Hepplewhite chair next to the walnut drum table topped with pewter-framed photographs of Lisa beaming at the camera. "Willow's death has just been so upsetting for us all. We need to stick together."

"Absolutely," Cassandra chimed in.

"I suppose so," Francine said with little enthusiasm from her perch in my favorite chair in the room, a stunning mahogany Sheraton upholstered in ivory damask with light vertical stripes. Judging by her voice and her tight expression, she wasn't really into this spirit of

Musketeerism, and neither was I. Lisa had me convinced with yesterday afternoon's amended version of the horrid events she'd witnessed. Two nights ago Willow had been murdered, and most likely by someone with a connection to her and to this house. I wasn't about to "stick together" with three out of just a handful of viable suspects.

Lisa descended the stairs and peeked around the corner, spotted me, and ventured into the room. I said, "Hi," but my voice was drowned out by Diana's hardy cry, "There she is!" She added, "Hello, dear. We're all so sorry about what happened Friday night. I know you and Willow had really bonded, and I'm so terribly sorry for your loss."

As if needing to keep her hands busy, Lisa opened the glass doors of the étagère, removed one of the figurines, and, studying it, eased herself into a cross-legged perch on the floor halfway between her mother's chair and mine. "Did she used to talk about me?" Lisa asked Diana shyly, her focus squarely on the porcelain piece in her hand—a cat or dog. I felt a pang: she was begging for a compliment from Willow, even now.

"That's precisely what I was just going to tell you about, Lisa. She told me just two days ago how much she enjoyed sitting for you. She said you were great fun."

Lisa cocked an eyebrow and muttered, "That doesn't sound like something Willow would say." She set the tiny figurine on the floor in front of her. It was a black cat.

Diana chuckled. "Oh, those weren't her exact words. It was more along the lines of your being 'a blast to hang with.' "

Lisa pursed her lips and said nothing.

Cassandra and I exchanged glances, and she blurted out, "Willow still *does* think you're terrific, Lisa. I had a dream about her just last night, and she was walking down the sidewalk with you, arm in arm. When we're asleep is when the spirits of our loved ones have the least distance to travel to contact us. I'm sure it was a message, directly from Willow."

Lisa rolled her eyes. "Yeah. Great. Either that or it was, like, a *dream*."

Francine gripped the arms of her chair with white-knuckle force, but said gently, "Lisa, honey? Would you mind bringing out the tray I was preparing in the kitchen? I forgot all about it when Erin arrived."

"Sure, Mom." She returned the cat to its showcase and left by way of the den.

Francine rose and briskly slid the pocket doors shut. Then she whirled and, in a vitriolic hiss to Cassandra and Diana, said, "Don't you dare patronize my daughter! She's twelve, not two! She can see through put-ons faster than any of us!"

Diana made a conciliatory gesture. "Everything I said was true, in spirit. Willow wasn't especially communicative. But I know she enjoyed Lisa immensely."

"And I *did* have the dream last night!" Cassandra protested, twisting a lock of her long, sandy-blond hair around a beringed finger. She sighed and continued in a dispirited voice, "Though I suspect it had more to do with Willow's trying to apologize to *me* than with anything regarding Lisa."

Diana's cheeks immediately colored. I remembered that Cassandra had told me Friday evening that it was Diana who had picked up the tab for Willow's thievery.

Francine reclaimed her seat and asked skeptically, "Why did Willow owe you an apology?"

Cassandra squirmed, and Diana's face remained beet red. "Oh, well, I guess there's no harm in telling you now," Cassandra said. "The thing is, I caught Willow stealing from my cash register the week before last, so I had no choice but to fire her."

"Willow was always scrupulous about her babysitting charges, and I never hesitated to leave my purse out in the open when she was in the house," Francine told her coldly. "You're certain?"

"I'm positive," Cassandra replied with a grim nod. "I caught her red-handed, holding a fistful of twenties, which she'd—"

Lisa marched into the room through the open archway to the foyer. She dropped the tray of crackers, cheese, and strawberries onto the coffee table, a half-dozen strawberries toppling over the side. "That's a *lie!*" she shrieked.

Cassandra sputtered, "Oh, Lisa, I didn't realize—"

"Willow told me three weeks ago you were itching to fire her! She said she knew too much about how you'd been lying about your profits and cheating the IRS!"

"What? That's outrageous!"

"I'll bet anything you set her up! You made it *look* like she was stealing from you! Willow told me you'd pull something like that!"

Cassandra's jaw dropped. Like all of us, she seemed too shocked by the outburst to know what to say. "Lisa, I assure you . . ."

But the girl had bolted from the room. A moment later, a door upstairs slammed.

"Oh, dear," Cassandra said, shifting her gaze to Francine, who was massaging her temples with her hand. "Obviously Willow was *already* stealing from me and knew she'd get caught soon, so she fed a story to your daughter making me out to be the bad guy."

Seething, Francine lowered her hand. Through clenched teeth, she retorted, "More important, you've upset my daughter unnecessarily at an extremely trying time."

Diana chimed in, "Plus, it's *not* like Willow to steal. She lived in my house for nearly four months, and I should know better than anyone. I'm totally with Francine on this one."

Cassandra retorted, "That's not what you said when I first told you about the theft. And when you *volunteered* to cover my losses."

Diana sniffed. "I was merely trying to keep the peace, Cassandra. I believed then and I believe now that you misinterpreted what you saw."

"The sight of one's employee stuffing cash into her pocket is pretty difficult to misinterpret! Especially when your cash register is suddenly short two hundred dollars!"

"All right, all right," Diana said. "Maybe she *was* stealing. She must have felt trapped. Her credit cards were maxed to the limit, and she told me she had to upgrade her wardrobe to look more sophisticated, because she'd become smitten with an older man." Steve Sullivan's name popped into my head immediately, but Diana added under her breath, "I just hope she wasn't talking about Hugh Black."

Francine's jaw dropped. "Why on earth would you think she meant Hugh Black?"

"I've just been picking up on some . . . innuendos between them over the past couple of weeks." She leaned closer to Francine and said gently, "And you should know, my dear . . . Hugh was in the neighborhood Friday night. Both Audrey and I saw him."

My stomach knotted. Diana was exaggerating at best and lying at worst. She'd told Audrey she *hadn't* seen the man lurking in Francine's yard.

Francine was looking at me. "Did you see him, too, Erin?"

"No. I arrived after Diana and Audrey."

"Well, Diana," Francine said evenly, "it appears that having your eyes turn green has affected your vision. You *want* to have seen Hugh, to stir up trouble among your more affluent neighbors. It's common knowledge that you're jealous of all our estates, compared to your little house. Willow told me all about how you constantly used to whine about our extravagant homes, compared to yours."

"What?" Diana shrieked. "I'm merely reporting what I saw the other night!"

"I think everyone's tensions are running high right now," I said firmly.

Ignoring me, Francine sniped to Diana, "And I certainly don't appreciate how you drove up the price of the house when I purchased it three years ago!"

"I did nothing of the sort! I quoted you the asking price, and you lowballed it, but the owners demanded their full price."

"After not getting any offers for six months. They were desperate to sell. It was on *your* advice that they refused our offer and countered with full price only."

"That is just not true!" Diana leapt to her feet. "Who told you that?"

"Ralph Appleby. And he should be here any moment, so you can verify this with him." Francine glanced at me and explained, "He's taking the glass panes out of some windows in the tower room. He collects old glass, apparently."

I didn't know how to reply to such a triviality, under the circumstances. One thing was certain: these women were *not* the Three Musketeers.

Diana dropped back into her seat. "Fine. I'd be only too happy to hear what Ralph has to say for himself about the price of this house."

On cue, the doorbell rang. Francine snapped, "Nobody move!" and went to answer. Diana and Cassandra both became fascinated with the tops of their own shoes. I hadn't even been living in Colorado three years ago, but I knew all too well that these homes were worth millions of dollars and rarely came on the market. My hunch was that Ralph had been talking through his hat. He probably had no more knowledge of what price the market would bear three years ago than I did. "Aha, Ralph. Just the man I wanted to see. Come with me." Francine all but dragged him into the living room. "Tell everyone what you said to me the other day about the price I paid for this house."

"Er, I said it was high," he mumbled. "I'm going to go get to—"

"And why did you think it was too much money?"

"Because it needs tons of work."

"No, I mean, what did you say was Diana Durst's role in regards to the asking price of my house?"

"That's quite enough, Francine." Diana rose imperiously, flicking her dark hair back from her shoulders repeatedly, as though she'd suddenly acquired some sort of compulsive tic. "It's obvious that Ralph Appleby and I have a difference of opinion." She gave Francine a scathing look. "For what it's worth, Francine, as the listing agent, I *reduced* my own commission in an effort to lower their asking price to market value. I most certainly did *not* drive up the price of your house."

Ralph muttered, "I gotta go upstairs and—"

"Ralph," Francine interrupted, "did you or did you not tell me Friday afternoon that you had done an inspection upon Diana's request when she first listed this house, and you made a report of all the things that needed repair?"

"Er, yeah, uh—"

Francine whirled to face Diana, adding triumphantly, "And that *you,* Diana, told Ralph *not* to file the thing once you'd seen how extensive the list was!"

Diana tossed her dark hair off her shoulders. "Have it your way, Francine. But in Colorado real estate, it's strictly buyer beware, and we all know that. It was your responsibility to hire a house inspector, not the sellers', and certainly not mine." Her nose in the air, she brushed past Ralph and Francine, but then whirled on a heel to face them again. "By the way, I *also* saw Hugh sneaking out of your house late *Wednesday* night. Not to mention his staggering around your yard in the middle of the night last month, so drunk he could scarcely stand up, trying to plant rosebushes. Which, no matter what you say, is *not* romantic, but just plain weird. I wonder if Audrey Munroe knows that you two are up to the same old tricks." She marched out the door.

Ralph instantly slunk away and up the stairs. "I should get going, too," I said, wondering to myself if there had ever been a less effective consolatory visit among neighbors. "I'll call you tomorrow about our schedule," I murmured to Francine as I started for the door.

"Me too. I should have left five minutes ago," Cassandra said. "See you soon, Francine. I'm sure things will look better then."

Cassandra and I left together. She said, "What a disaster! We might as well have set fire to the place and stomped on Lisa's toes in the process. Honestly, I don't know what I was thinking, bringing up the whole business of the theft at a time like this."

"I should have done something to stem the tide."

"You tried, at least. None of us was willing to let go."

Her phrasing chilled me, reminding me of how Lisa had begged to be "let go" at the séance. Just for a moment, I wondered if that truly was Abby Chambers, asking the killer to confess and thereby set her spirit free.

Cassandra and I said our good-byes at Audrey's walkway. The phone was ringing as I opened the door, and there was still no sign of Audrey, who was probably at church, so I rushed to follow the sound, found the handset on the coffee table in the den, and answered.

"Is this Erin Gilbert?" a deep, unfamiliar voice asked. "The interior designer?"

"Yes."

"A friend recommended that I seek your services. If you're willing to take on a small job, that is. I have a one-bedroom apartment and far too much furniture to fit right. I'd just like some advice getting the place set up."

"I'd be happy to do that. When would you—"

"How does right now work for you? I'm knee-deep in furniture. I'm obviously going to need to haul some things to a storage unit before I have to return the moving van first thing Monday morning, or I'll get charged for an extra day."

Glancing at my watch, I said, "Sundays are my day off. I'm afraid I'm—"

"I'll pay you double your normal rates."

That was difficult to resist. "I suppose I could get there in thirty or forty minutes, after I have time for some lunch. I could set my fee on an hourly—"

"Whatever you want to charge is fine. Let me give you my address."

He rattled off the address, on a major east-west corridor in Crestview, and just as I pointed out that he hadn't yet given me his name, he said, "Someone's here to install my computer cable. See you around noon." The line went dead.

I hesitated, confused and suspicious. A cable man had come to his door on a Sunday? No way was I so reckless as to go alone to some man's apartment I'd never met, without even knowing his name. I was just about to use the reverse-calling function when the phone rang again.

So much for being able to call him back, I thought as I answered. Maybe it would be the man calling me back, having realized his gaffe.

"Hey, Gilbert. Waiting by the phone for my call?"

"Hi, Sullivan." Happily, my pulse didn't quicken, though that was probably the result of his less-than-timely crack about my waiting breathlessly for him to call me. Sullivan and I were just not meant to be together. A body had been discovered, right as the man tried to kiss me; if ever the Fates were sending me negative vibes, that was it. "Actually, I was just about to dial star sixty-nine to find out who just now hired me."

He chuckled. "You're getting to be such a hot designer you get hired without even learning the client's name? Doesn't that make it difficult to bill them?"

I gave him a capsule version of my previous phone call, and he said, "For all we know, this guy might have found access to an empty apartment for the day. He's probably a pervert."

"I know. If I go at all, which I'm already ruling against doing, I'll have my pepper spray at the ready."

"*And* I'm coming with you."

"Excuse me?"

"Hey. It's the least I can do. If I hadn't called just now, you'd have been able to ring him back. And I *have* heard of perverts pulling crap like this on real estate agents. Just in case this is some kind of a predator, luring women to his lair, I want to wring the guy's neck." He paused. "How 'bout I come pick you up in half an hour or so?"

Although there was undoubtedly more than one good reason I should simply write this off as a crank caller, none occurred to me, and I was now too curious to resist. Hildi, meanwhile, had pranced into the room demanding attention. I stroked her fur. "Okay, Sullivan. Thanks. See you then."

An hour later, Sullivan, as promised, accompanied me

to the apartment. He'd reverted to his indifferent behavior toward me—no now-we're-an-item vibrations, no awkwardness over our less-than-super date—and I guess that was good. If he wasn't going to bring up the fact that we'd almost shared a moment as we were saying good night, I certainly wouldn't. In any case, it all seemed so irrelevant in comparison to Willow's death.

"There's the moving van," I said as we parked behind the building. "Looks like maybe he is on the up-and-up."

"Hope so, but I'm still prepared to be your muscle."

"Sounds good to me." I reached into my purse and showed him the tiny metal spray can. Unwilling to take things too seriously, I said, "Okay. How about this: you ring the doorbell, and if I don't like the looks of him when he answers, I spritz him in the eye, then you beat the living daylights out him?"

Sullivan merely asked, "Is that pepper spray a recent acquisition?"

"Yes. Audrey bought it for me. She worries."

"Smart lady," he muttered.

I opened my mouth to protest, but realized he had a point and held my tongue. We navigated our way to the mystery client's door. This was one of the seedier apartment complexes I'd seen in Crestview, and I muttered to Sullivan that I might indeed need him to be my "muscle" if the client refused to pay. I knocked on the unadorned pecan door, Sullivan standing at the ready just behind me.

The door was swept open.

"Hugh!" I cried in surprise.

He gave me a cocksure grin. "You recognized me. We met so briefly, I wasn't sure you would."

I gazed up at the man, who was indeed huge—at least six-two, two hundred and fifty pounds. Audrey was so petite, the two of them must certainly have made a mismatched couple in more ways than one. "Why did you lure me out here?"

"Because I need your expertise, just like I said." He gestured at the stockpile of furniture in the center of the room, then looked at Steve. "Ah. You brought an assistant. Good. You can help me move the furniture."

"This is Steve Sullivan. Hugh Black." As the two men shook hands, I explained, "Hugh is Audrey's ex-husband. And Steve is—"

"Ready and willing to assist in any way I can," he interrupted, giving me a look that implied I was to follow his lead.

I told Hugh, "You said you had a friend who recommended me."

"And so I do. Francine Findley." He rubbed his hands together. "Since I'm paying by the hour here, mind if we jump right in?"

Sullivan and I exchanged glances, and, reasoning that I might as well make some money off whatever ulterior plan Mr. Black was trying to pull, I said, "Yes, let's."

To my surprise, the assignment turned out to be great

fun. As Hugh had told me over the phone, he had twice the amount of furniture that he could possibly use, and it was all really nice stuff. I was envious of his Euro-country dining table set. It was glossy black-painted hardwood, flawlessly constructed, the ladder-back chairs augmented with delicate gold lines—the perfect touch. The rectangular table was simple, yet the functional details were excellent—no sharp edges, its legs perfectly placed for the six chairs. Hugh also had some vintage World War II posters that were beautifully framed, but he told me right away that he'd already decided to put those back into storage.

As we finished up, leaving it up to him to move the excess furniture in the hallway back to his van, I told him honestly, "You've got excellent taste, Mr. Black."

"Call me Hugh, Erin," he said with a wink. "Actually, all of my furniture was selected for me. I've just got great taste in designers." He grinned at me. "A streak that I'm obviously maintaining now."

"I can't work for you a second time, Mr. Black. Audrey and I are close, and she is obviously not comfortable with your being back in town." I could only imagine how she'd take it if I were to knowingly accept work from her ex-husband who'd had an affair with Francine.

"Ah. I see. Surely you're willing to at least put in a good word with her for me, aren't you? Considering what a super client I've been?"

"Should I do that before or after I tell her that your friend Francine recommended me to you?"

His cocksure grin finally faltered. "Francine and I called things off for good nearly three years ago. We've merely resumed our friendship. That's all we are. Friends."

"Always nice to have." I gestured at the finished room. "Looks like we're all finished here."

He paid me in cash nearly twice what I'd asked, which was already double my usual hourly fee, saying with another wink, "Your assistant deserves a bonus." He hesitated, then added, "By the way, I heard about the babysitter's accident. If you see Frannie before I do, please tell her I'm sorry. I'm sure such a thing happening on her property has left her quite unsettled."

"I'll tell her."

"I thought I saw you in the area last night," Steve said to Hugh. "You drive a silver BMW, right?"

"Yeah, but that wasn't me. I was home last night."

"Huh," Steve said noncommittally. "Enjoy your new place."

"I don't expect to be here long, but thanks."

When we were in Sullivan's van, I handed him half the money, and he shoved two twenties back at me, which I accepted without debate. I then asked, "What was that about? Did you really see his car?"

"I noticed a BMW, yes, but I have no idea what type of wheels he drives. Just wanted to shake him up a bit . . . see what falls out."

"You're talking like a P.I. now."

"Am I?"

"The police want us to keep out of it. Linda Delgardio already told me that flat out."

"I'm not talking about our taking part in car chases and gunplay. We're designers, the touchy-feely warm sorts. We'll simply keep low profiles and keep an eye on everybody."

"Right, Sullivan. Thanks for your help."

"My pleasure, Gilbert."

As he dropped me off at my house and drove away, I realized that we hadn't argued even once during the three hours we'd been together. It was a personal record. But then, as Audrey would say, the day was still young.

Monday afternoon, I had a selection of banisters for Francine to choose from and needed to show her the product brochures. Once again, I decided not to take the friendly shortcut through our backyards and instead rounded the block. Fortunately, despite our prickly parting yesterday when I'd bolted from her house with Cassandra, she greeted me with a smile. "Oh, hi, Erin. I thought you might be Bob Stanley."

"No, just me. Why? Is Bob coming over here?"

"Momentarily. He's been hinting around that he'd like to exercise his power as the architectural review chair."

"But the homeowners' committee decided Steve Sullivan would be the one who needed to approve our plans. And he already did so, verbally, last Friday."

"I know. But Mr. Sullivan won't have to live in this neighborhood after the remodel is complete, whereas *I* do. It's best to get Bob on board now, so we won't have problems later on."

"Good point." I handed her the brochures, explaining that I'd narrowed down our choice of banisters to two. Partway into the conversation, Bob arrived, and Francine greeted him as if he were royalty. She asked me to join them as they went upstairs to look at the work in progress. Ralph was already there, hard at work. The plasterers had come and gone this morning, and the new ceiling was in place and taped, looking like a white-bandaged expanse of gray cardboard. I could instantly see how it would look when finished, though, and my mind's-eye image made me beam with pride. Some of the windows were now sporting brown corrugated cardboard in the place of the panes. The floor-restoration workmen had also been doing their part. Most of the hideous black-speckled paint had been sanded off the floor, although there were still a few loose floorboards where the wall had once stood.

Ralph turned toward us, and his typical look of mild annoyance turned instantly to utter disdain at the sight of Bob Stanley, who looked especially dapper today in his nicely pressed blue slacks and white polo shirt. "What are you doing here?" Ralph grumbled.

"Francine invited me," Bob replied. "I'm just getting a look at how everything's shaping up, that's all."

"Checking up on me, in other words. I don't need your interference, Bob. Neither does Francine."

"Ralph, I'm very capable of speaking for myself!" she objected.

Bob's complexion was now ruddy with his embarrassment. "I feel sorry for you, Ralph. You know that? You must have one hell of a miserable life to be so nasty to everyone."

"I'm not nasty to everyone. Just to killers like you."

"*This* again?" Bob's cheeks were nearly magenta. "How many times do I have to tell you! I had nothing whatsoever to do with Abby's suicide! I wasn't even in the neighborhood at the time! What's the matter with you? Why can't you get that through your thick head? If anyone actually *killed* her, it was probably you! You could have been drunk out of your skull in another one of your drinking binges, or something!"

"I was never a binge drinker!"

"You were a drunk clear back in high school!" Bob fired back.

Ralph took a step toward us. He was holding a claw hammer. Suddenly my vision was riveted to it. "I was completely sober that day . . . and have been ever since! I'd joined AA! It was my birthday present to Abby, you bastard! She said it was all she wanted from me! *You* were the one she was afraid of. She told me she was scared to death of you!"

"That's a lie! She and I were neighbors and friends! *You* were the one supplying her with the booze, and God knows whatever drugs she got hooked on! Face it. You feel so guilty that you've fooled yourself into believing your own lies, Ralph. No way am I going to keep having this ridiculous conversation with you every time we run into each other for the rest of our lives!"

"It's your fault if we do." Ralph lifted the hammer and shook it at Bob. "I am not going to sit back and let you get away with having killed a second innocent young girl. You're going to have to take on someone with the strength and wherewithal to fight back, this time."

So angry now he could scarcely speak, Bob stabbed a finger at Ralph. "I've put up with your crap long enough. I'm suing you for slander." He turned to face us. "Ladies, this obviously is not a good time, but thank you for your hospitality."

He slammed down the stairs. Nobody spoke. Ralph chucked his hammer into his toolbox. I sighed with relief. The moment we heard the front door shut, Francine chided, "Oh, Ralph. Do you honestly think I'd let that man into my house if there were any possibility he was responsible for Willow's death?"

"He *is,* though."

"The two of you have obviously held a grudge for a long time now. I think it affects your opinion of Bob," she said.

"Yeah. Knowing someone's a murderer kind of has a tendency to make me want to hold a grudge. But then, maybe that's just me."

chapter 10

With half an hour free before my next appointment, I decided to pay a visit to Diana Durst.

I was hoping to decipher her behavior yesterday at Francine's house, when she'd asserted that she'd seen Hugh Friday night. Claiming that I had questions about the historic-homes tour, I called her and arranged to come right over.

From the moment she invited me inside and I stepped onto the square of Tuscany-brown travertine tiles, I loved her house. I gushed about how beautifully she'd brought texture into the living room with the Berber area rug and the rough finish on the ceramic vase that sported a spray of magenta-and-white tulips, and she offered to take me on a quick tour. Although I was somewhat pressed for time, my van would have to be on fire for me to decline the opportunity to see a home's interior.

Diana's kitchen was as efficient as a ship's galley and featured my personal favorite cabinetry wood—cherry. She had a country-style pine dinette set in matching reddish hues and an adorable hutch. Upstairs, the bedroom, with its muted blues and greens, was a cozy retreat that bore a striking resemblance to my own bedroom at Audrey's. She declined to show me the second bedroom, which she explained was Willow's and "too depressing," and instead gave me a quick peek at her attic office, with its slanted ceilings and cedar paneling.

Though I liked the décor in every room, her living room remained my favorite. I sank into the embrace of the spring-green overstuffed brushed-corduroy chair while she sat on the nearest cushion of her sofa—a solid taupe with floral-patterned pillows that really popped against their neutral backdrop. She had a well-placed mirror on the opposite wall, adjusted to give the illusion of space without forcing guests to stare at their own reflections.

"Your home reminds me of a guesthouse in the foothills that I decorated when I first arrived in Crestview. I wound up being so pleased with the results that I actually would have preferred living there to the main house."

Her smile became strained. I realized that I'd inadvertently hit a nerve and drawn attention to her home's lack of square footage. "I'm familiar with that house. On Wagonwheel Drive."

"Yes, that's right. Are you friends with the owners?"

"We're just acquaintances," Diana replied. "An associate in my office sold that house. The new owners promptly hired you to decorate it, then they held an open house that we were all invited to. They were so tickled with your work that they went on and on about what you'd said about the key to decorating small houses—use a light palette, lots of mirrors, avoid clutter like the plague, and so on."

I chuckled. No wonder Diana's taste in décor was so similar to mine; it *was* my taste. "It's lucky for me that everyone can't adopt decorating tips as easily as you do, or I'd be out of work in no time."

"Oh, unfortunately, I still couldn't do this all on my own. Actually, I hired Steve Sullivan . . . before you moved into the neighborhood, of course. This is his design . . . after I showed him my photographs of the house on Wagonwheel and told him that's what I wanted for my place."

I tightened my grip on the armrests and tried to prevent myself from digging my nails into the wonderful fabric. "He never mentioned that he'd worked for you."

She giggled. "It was the darnedest thing, actually. I'd meant to hire *you* . . . but all I could remember was that your last name was one of the famous musical collaborations, and I got Gilbert and Sullivan confused."

"That happens," I said casually, though she'd just jabbed me in a raw nerve. One of Sullivan's and my ugliest arguments had been caused by a similar confusion of my getting mistakenly hired by would-be clients of his.

The sight of a Polaroid of Willow that Diana had left on the oval-shaped pine coffee table helped me to regain my focus. I asked, "Have you met Willow's family? Are they coming here to claim her things?"

"They live in Colorado Springs, and they're coming to get everything tomorrow. Everything that the police haven't already taken as evidence, that is."

"What all did they collect?"

"Mostly the contents of her desk . . . photo albums, notebooks, that sort of thing."

I sighed and looked into Diana's dark eyes. "Diana, I have a confession to make. I didn't really come here to discuss the tour. I really wanted to ask you again about the . . . girl on Francine's roof."

"Oh?"

"I've been thinking about this, and I am certain that the girl I saw on Francine's widow's walk was Willow, wearing a red wig."

A look of anxiousness crept onto her features. "Did you tell the police that?"

"Yes. So if you know anything about why Willow was on Francine's roof, you really need to tell the police."

"Why? That was three nights before Willow fell. The two incidents are unrelated." She hesitated, then added hastily, "Even if it *was* Willow, I mean."

"Her decision to go up there the first time could be related to why she sneaked up there the *second* time . . . when she fell."

Diana pursed her bow-like, ruby-painted lips, then replied, "I just don't see how that could be the case, Erin."

"And maybe you're right. But you should let the police decide whether it's useful information or not. They need to know everything they can about Willow, so that they can discover who had a motive to kill her."

"That's only important *if* she was killed, Erin. Maybe this story about there being some trespasser in the house is all a fabrication on Lisa Findley's part. Maybe the girls were horsing around, and Willow fell, and Lisa feels so guilty she's lying."

"*Did* you enlist Willow to impersonate a ghost?"

Her jaw dropped and she sputtered for air in a less-than-convincing display of offense. "Now, why would

I do something crazy like that?"

"To garner new clients for your business."

She began to make an annoying clicking noise with her nails that resembled the ticking clock on *60 Minutes*. "Well, Erin, if there's one thing I've learned after years and years as a Realtor, it's this . . . if you take the 'i' out of 'reality,' what have you got?"

" 'Realty,' " I answered quickly, not bothering to mask my rising exasperation.

She pursed her lips and nodded slowly as though she'd made a profound point, ticking away all the while.

"I'm not following."

"That's as much of an answer as I can give you."

"Do you mean that . . . you separate yourself from reality in order to survive in the realty business?"

"Again, Erin, I've said as much as I'm going to say on the matter."

"Fine. We'll change subjects. Audrey said you told her that you didn't see a man in the shadows on Francine's property, yet yesterday you said you saw Hugh Black there."

She sighed heavily and nodded, eyes averted. Now she began to fidget with her dark hair, silencing her nails. "I was trying to keep the peace. I knew Audrey would be hurt to hear that her ex was at Francine's house. I never should have blurted that out to Francine, but she'd been so horrid, accusing me of price-fixing and being jealous of her house. It just slipped out."

"So you did see Hugh Black there that night? And on

a couple of previous nights? And you told the police that?"

"Of course I told the police. As well as my suspicions that Willow and Hugh might have been dating on the sly. Honestly, Erin! Do you think I'm trying to hide something?"

I almost answered "Of course not" automatically, but stopped myself. "I hope not. But I still believe you should rethink your decision not to tell them about Willow's being on Francine's roof."

She met my gaze, forced a smile, and said, "I hate to kick you out, Erin, but I have a house to show."

"I'll get going, then."

"Have a great day, Erin," she said frostily as she ushered me to the door. "Oh, and I should tell you that if you're ever tired of living in someone else's home, you should let me know. I've seen some charming little bungalows for sale. I'm sure we could work out the financing."

That evening, an unusual number of cars were parked in front of our house, and I had to park two blocks away. A couple I knew vaguely from down the street waved hello as they headed toward the Stanleys' door. Bob and Cassandra must have been hosting a neighborhood party that I hadn't been invited to, which made me feel bad once again about our deteriorating relationship.

Audrey was waiting for me in the foyer. "Don't get comfortable," she warned by way of a greeting.

"You're going to want to join me at the emergency homeowners' association meeting next door."

"At Bob and Cassandra's? Has something else happened?"

She shook her head. "It was just a last-minute thing. Bob is insisting upon hosting a neighborhood meeting to discuss the tragic events at Francine's home."

"Does he want to head up a neighborhood-watch group or something? If so, how can he be sure Willow's killer isn't someone in the neighborhood?"

"Not everyone's as convinced as you and I are that Willow was pushed. But Bob's not pleased with the ad hoc committee decision for you and Mr. Sullivan to serve as each other's watchdog." She held the door for me. "Coming?"

Hildi was meowing as she trotted into the room to join us. I longed to curl up with her and a good book and forget all about the neighborhood turmoil for a couple of hours. "I guess I can't miss this when I'm half of the meeting's agenda."

"No, you can't, and we're already late. Bob specifically told me you were welcome to come, but he's definitely employing some rather unpleasant gamesmanship. I suspect ours was the very last household he notified."

"I hope he notified his *own* designer. Sullivan has a lot invested in this issue, too."

"According to Bob, Mr. Sullivan will be there, but has vowed to merely listen and abide by the majority."

Silence and compliance weren't typical behavior for

Sullivan, but that was something of the pot calling the kettle black. "I thought that the 'majority' had already decided to let the anonymous committee members decide."

Audrey didn't comment, and we went next door. The house was crowded—standing room only—which was annoying to me because now I couldn't get any sense whatsoever of Sullivan's design influences; on my previous visit I'd also gotten no farther than the living room, where Bob had now assembled rows of folding chairs. He was sitting on the stairs that overlooked us all. Two men got up and offered us their seats, which I refused but Audrey accepted.

Diana had the floor and was saying, "Cassandra and I fully believe the ghost is back but means no harm, and we should just proceed with Francine's plans for restoring the house."

Bob countered, "I still disapprove of the remodel plans on Francine's place. After what happened to Willow, it obviously isn't safe up there. It's the tallest structure in the immediate area, and I'm tellin' you right now, folks, it'll prove to be as enticing to kids as a swimming pool without a fence."

"That is *not* a fair comparison!" Francine cried, her cheeks flushed. "I lock my front and back doors! For all intents and purposes, that *is* a fence!"

"Except you're always forgetting to lock your doors," Bob shot back. "According to Erin Gilbert, Willow McAndrews got up there without being let inside, not just once, but *twice!*"

"I don't know for certain that she wasn't let inside either time, and neither do you," Francine retorted, "but that's neither here nor there. Why don't we vote on whether or not I should be forced by everyone to install a cedar privacy fence? My guess is that nobody wants that any more than I do."

"That won't solve Stanley's problem," someone's rumbling voice declared. "He doesn't care about fences, or keeping anyone safe!" I turned toward the voice near the front door and saw that it was Ralph. "He just wants all construction and renovation to come to a complete stop as soon as possible."

Bob hopped to his feet from his perch on the stairs and pointed at the door. "Hey! You are not a homeowner! Get out of our meeting!"

Ralph ignored him. "You just want to stop all remodeling work at the Findleys' house, 'cuz you're afraid someone's going to turn up evidence that points the finger at you."

"That is a bald-faced lie, Ralph! Get out of my house! Now!"

Ralph opened the door, but then pivoted and said with confidence, "Bob Stanley murdered Abby Chambers and doesn't want any old clues dug up. He prob'ly killed Willow McAndrews, too, to protect his dirty secret."

Bob shouted, "It was Ralph Appleby who supplied Abby with the drugs that led to her suicide!"

"That's a filthy lie!" Ralph slammed the door behind him.

The crowded room fell silent. I watched through the window as Ralph stormed off. Audrey rose. "Not to belittle Bob Stanley's concerns," she announced, "but I am a big believer in letting people do their jobs. I suggest that we allow the designers to do theirs, and that we allow the police to investigate the tragic death of Willow McAndrews."

"Hear! hear!" someone with a deep voice called from the back. The voice was familiar, and I turned and spotted Steve Sullivan, who must have remembered his promise to stay silent only after he'd spoken up, because he was now studiously staring at his feet.

"What a thoroughly unpleasant meeting," Audrey remarked as we reclimbed our front porch steps. The proceedings had ended shortly after Sullivan's "Hear! hear!"; the association president put the matter to a vote, and Audrey's suggested position of letting people do their jobs was overwhelmingly supported.

"It's already unlocked," I said with dismay as I fumbled with the key.

"Oh, that's right. My fault. I'd started to lock it after us, but then remembered the back door was unlocked, so there seemed little point in locking the front." She closed the door behind us and threw the deadbolt. "Let's scrape together some leftovers for dinner. On today's show, Chef Michael taught me a trick about frying leftover spaghetti in olive oil, and it truly is delicious."

We chatted as we worked together in the kitchen, until a floorboard above us creaked and we both froze.

"Someone's upstairs," Audrey whispered.

"I'll go look," I said quietly, my pulse thumping.

"I'm coming, too. Just a second." She dashed into the den and returned with the heavy fireplace poker.

"I haven't seen Hildi yet," I whispered. "Maybe she just ran across a squeaky board upstairs."

"That was a footstep," Audrey whispered back tersely. "From a person, not a cat."

We began to climb the stairs, with me in the lead. "Who's up here?" I cried, halfway up the flight.

"You'll give them time to hide!" she chided, again in a harsh whisper.

"From an unarmed interior designer and a hundred-pound woman carrying a poker? They'll be terrified."

Our hunt was ludicrous, I thought as we crept down the hallway. Audrey was just a step behind me, and if there was a prowler and she swung at him, she'd be more than likely to miss her target and strike me. My bedroom was directly over the kitchen, where we'd heard the noise. "Is somebody in here?" I called from just outside my bedroom door, then I threw it open.

The breeze from the window hit me. "Hildi's on the windowsill," I said to Audrey, about to ask if she'd been the one to close up my cat in my room. I heard a little gasp from the direction of my bed.

"Lisa? Is that you?" I asked, playing a hunch as I stared at my lumpy bed.

She peeked out from underneath my silk-filled comforter. "I didn't mean to let the cat climb on the window ledge."

"It's all right. There's a screen. But what are you doing here?"

"I got scared being home alone. My mom went to the meeting. Then I saw Hildi in your window, and I rang your doorbell to warn you, and nobody answered, so I figured I'd just come inside and shut your window so Hildi was safe, but then I heard you come in . . ."

"It's not a problem. As you can see, Hildi is perfectly safe." I gave a quick glance behind me at Audrey, who was uncharacteristically silent. "How about I walk you home, honey?"

She clutched my white and powder-blue comforter to her chin. "Could I stay here tonight?" she pleaded. "I'm sure my mom won't mind. I won't be any trouble. I'll sleep on the couch in your . . . storage room downstairs."

"That's not a 'storage room,'" Audrey protested. "It's the parlor. We just haven't decided which furniture we're keeping after I bought a full lot at an auction."

"Is it all right if I stay?" Lisa asked her.

Audrey asked her in turn, "Do you really want to stay here tonight?"

The girl nodded emphatically. "My mom thinks I'm behind all that ghost stuff . . . and it did kind of start out that way, but I'm not doing any of it now, but she won't believe me and is always furious at me. She won't even let me be with any of my friends. At least this way I can visit with the kitty."

Audrey raised her eyebrows and gave a small shrug,

which meant the decision was up to me. I began, "Let's first check with—"

The phone rang, and I hesitated before picking up the handset from my nightstand, hoping that the caller wasn't Francine, desperately searching for her daughter. The caller blurted out, "Erin, it's Francine. Have you seen Lisa? I told her to stay in the house, but she's nowhere to be found."

"It's okay. She's right here. Just a second, and I'll put—"

"You're getting between me and my daughter, Erin."

"No, I'm not. She simply—"

"Ever since Willow died, you're the only thing she talks about. Erin this. Erin that."

"Let me put your daughter on the phone and—"

"Fine. You do that."

I gritted my teeth, but dutifully passed the phone along to Lisa, saying gently, "Your mom wants to talk to you."

Audrey and I ducked out of my room to give Lisa some privacy. Audrey whispered, "This won't sit well with Francine, Erin. She's so territorial, she probably thinks you're coming between her and her daughter."

I sighed and said nothing. A few seconds later, Lisa happily emerged from my room. "She says it's fine if I sleep over."

"Good," I replied, not knowing what else to say, but thinking that things were now far from "good" with my relationship with my client.

"Come, Lisa," Audrey said. "Let's get you set up in the guest room."

Though I wasn't proud of myself for doing so, I told Lisa that I had a lot of work to do, and let Audrey take over as far as feeding her a late dinner and putting her to bed. It was after ten p.m. when I checked on her. The lights in the room were out, and I could see Lisa's slender form sprawled on top of the sheet with the chenille blanket wadded up by her feet. As I tried to tuck her in, Lisa murmured, "War camps. Prisoner. Abby."

"Lisa?" I whispered.

She didn't reply, but was breathing deeply. I realized she must be talking in her sleep. As I turned away, my sleeve caught on the top of the copper table lamp beside her, and it nearly toppled. I managed to catch it and right it, but the noise woke her.

"Mom?" she called, bolting upright.

"No, it's Erin. I knocked something over. I'm sorry."

She stared at me. In the shadows, her face looked pale and her eyes like dark holes. "Erin? Can you do me a big favor? Please? Can you get my stuffed cat from my mom?"

"I don't want to disturb your mother. She's probably already asleep."

"No, she isn't. All the lights are on next door. *Please?* I always sleep with my kitty, and . . . I really want it."

"I'll try."

I called Francine, who answered on the first ring. Judging by her voice, she'd calmed down. She explained immediately that Lisa never went anywhere overnight without her stuffed toy and offered to meet me at her back door with "Kitty" in hand. Though that meant breaking my vow not to cut through her back-yard again, I agreed. A minute later, I'd apparently been too quick to arrive, because Francine was not in the kitchen. I knocked, then opened the door and called, "Francine?"

"Come upstairs, Erin. I'm having trouble finding the darn thing."

I went up to Lisa's doorway, where Francine was rummaging through Lisa's messy and cluttered room. "It's got to be here someplace," Francine grumbled. "She never sleeps without it."

"Her pillow is missing, too," I pointed out.

"Is it?" Francine said, then looked at the bed to see for herself. "That's strange."

"Does she ever move to a different room to sleep?"

She frowned. "Every now and then. When she finds that she can't fall back to sleep. We'd better search behind the couches downstairs."

I paused for a moment, thinking. Lisa had told me that she'd spotted Hildi in my bedroom window, which she'd have had a clear view of from the tower room. Although I'd been in the room earlier in the afternoon, she might have moved her belongings there when her mother left for the meeting. "I'll go check upstairs."

Francine started to deride my suggestion, but then stopped, pursed her lips, and said, "Let's both take a look."

We climbed the stairs, Francine leading the way, and she opened the door and flicked on the nearest light fixture—a table lamp on the floor. Right beside the lamp was the stuffed cat, along with other items—a sleeping bag, a flashlight, and a pillow—but it was the painting, leaning against the wall by the foot of the sleeping bag, that captured my full attention. Someone, probably Lisa, had done a haphazard job of wiping what looked to be years' worth of dust off the canvas and its simple, inexpensive frame.

The subject was a girl in her early teens with red hair, bright brown eyes, and a breathtaking smile. Even though the painting technique was a bit unrefined, it had an undeniable tenderness. The way that the background blues became lighter surrounding the subject gave the girl an almost ethereal glow. She could have been a much younger, redheaded version of Willow McAndrews. The similarity was downright eerie.

"Where on earth did this come from?" Francine asked, picking up the painting. "Unsigned," she murmured. "I wonder if it's Abby Chambers." She narrowed her eyes and accused. "Did you find this someplace in my house and move it here, Erin?"

"No, this is the first time I've seen it, too. The only logical explanation is that Lisa found it."

A look of heartfelt sorrow passed across Francine's features. "You're right. Maybe she planned to sleep up here beside the portrait because the girl looks so much like Willow, and Lisa misses her. Or else she was trying to perform another séance to exorcise Abby's spirit." She sighed and set the painting back down. "Either way, Lisa's too young to have to endure all of this. If only my ex weren't such a horse's ass! He should let her visit for a few weeks, till this all settles down."

"Can't you insist?"

She let out an angry bark of sarcastic laughter. "You've obviously never been through a nasty divorce. Like I told you before, he's in Europe right now, and he always does the exact opposite of what I ask him to do. If only it made any sense for me to call his hotel room in Paris out of the blue and plead with him *not* to fly Lisa overseas to join him . . . so that he'd turn around and do just that."

I picked up the cat. "I'll take Lisa's stuffed toy back over to her."

"Thanks." She grabbed my arm and searched my eyes, her own immeasurably sad. "Erin, don't ask her about the portrait tonight. Let her get a good night's sleep for a change."

chapter 11

Ceilings are the most neglected, under-decorated surfaces of our homes. Positive experiences lift us in an upward direction, so why not give everyone in your house good reason to keep their chins up as they admire your beautiful ceilings?

—Audrey Munroe

DOMESTIC BLISS

After getting Lisa to sleep once more, Audrey and I were both too keyed up ourselves to sleep, and we sat amid the disarray in the den, my mood worsening by the minute as I filled her in on the discovery of the portrait. Afterward, we lapsed into silence and watched Hildi pick her way across the detritus on the floor till she reached, to my disappointment, Audrey's seat on the Sheraton chair and leaped into her lap, rather than mine. Audrey cooed praises into my fickle feline's ear. Hildi lapped them up like so much cream.

"Audrey, explain something to me. Why won't you ever let me get the front rooms of the house looking nice and put together? Why do you persist in keeping them in chaos?"

With a fingertip, she absently stroked the face of

the porcelain harlequin figurine on the base of a delightful table lamp that was all but buried in clutter. "I like it this way. This home is my life. I don't want it to be finished."

My jaw dropped a little in surprise. Audrey was so vivacious that it had never occurred to me that she could possibly be making an almost maudlin connection between her house and her golden years. "None of us ever has to think of a room as being 'finished.' We can always update and improve our spaces, or just switch things around for the sake of embracing change. And we can alter your rooms seasonally from now until the end of time, if you'd like." I hesitated. "And, while we're on the subject, I don't want you to think that you have to keep me busy or else I'll start to feel like a freeloader and move out. I'm always willing and able to pay you actual rent money, you know."

"Oh, it isn't that." She caressed Hildi's fur. "I just truly like the freedom of not having a room look so meticulously designed that I can't turn it upside down without feeling as though I've just spilled India ink on a finished painting."

Speaking of painting, I looked with despair at the north wall. The sunny yellow Venetian plaster I'd applied to these walls a few months ago had been so wonderful; Audrey too had raved about the cheery, warm effect. Even so, she had chosen to experiment with some stencils on that wall and had applied a collection of flora and fauna designs—

mostly birds, leaves, flowers, and fruits—at irregular intervals. So that they would "show up on the yellow background" and allow her to choose the best among the many designs, she'd used blue oil-based paint.

"We were getting so close to agreeing on an old-world Italian design for this room," I said. "All that was left to do was purchase the furniture."

"I did rather make a mess of that one wall," she admitted sheepishly. "It was just such a nice, large surface to work with, I couldn't resist. At least I didn't ruin the ceiling. I do so love the medallion."

"So do I. That's something, anyway." I stared up at the delicate lines of the ceiling decoration. It was a highly unusual piece that wouldn't have worked on just any ceiling. The medallion was shaped like a bouquet of roses, with leaves ringing its edges, and the buds clustered around the circular support for the chandelier.

"I love the way you came up with the paint for the medallion by mixing some of the yellow paint of the walls with the bone-white ceiling paint. That was the perfect touch. And I love how perfect the size is for the chandelier and the ceiling height and dimensions."

Glumly, I interjected, "And *I* love how the ceiling is the one part of the room that isn't suffering from clutter."

She clicked her tongue. "*You* suffer from a one-track mind at times, my dear. I require project rooms in order to come up with all the creative segments on my show."

I sat up. "Okay. Here's a thought. We take out the wall between the two guest rooms upstairs. We turn that into a nice big project room. Then, if you'd like, I can turn this den into a combination guest room/den."

She stroked Hildi in silence for a moment. "To be honest, dear, I've already considered that idea, but ultimately rejected it."

"Why?"

"I need to be on the main level to be creative. The upstairs needs to be my retreat from my day job. I can be tranquil upstairs, but I just cannot be creative."

"And yet you once tried to turn the bathtub upstairs into a terrarium. That was very creative." *Albeit extremely wrongheaded.*

Audrey spread her arms. "And look what a disaster that turned out to be. We had to replace the entire tub."

"So you're saying you'd have used better judgment if only the bathtub had been located on the main floor?"

"Possibly. For whatever reason . . . force of habit or the extra altitude upstairs making me light-headed, I can think better downstairs than I do upstairs." She arched her eyebrow. "And since you brought it up, no offense, my dear, but you really should have tried harder to dissuade me from that fiasco."

"I'd only just moved in! The tub was in your private bathroom!"

"Which I'd told you on day one that *you* could use whenever you wanted."

"And then, two weeks after 'day one,' you filled the tub with dirt and planted ferns."

"You hadn't used the bathtub *once.* Naturally, I assumed you were strictly a showerer, to coin a word. In any case, that whole tub-to-terrarium incident clearly demonstrates that I think best when my 'project spaces' are located downstairs, so my point has been made." I clenched my teeth, but she lifted her index finger and continued brightly, "However, I'm willing to compromise."

"You are?"

"Yes. I've given this a lot of thought and have been meaning to tell you this for weeks now: there's no need for me to extend my projects into the dining room. Let's get that room into shape."

"Wonderful!" Last winter we'd been well on our way to transforming the dining room into a glorious space, until she had sliced and diced the wallpaper and curtain fabrics for use as wrapping paper and ribbons. "Should I reorder the draperies and wallpaper that you . . . wound up reallocating? Or should we start over from scratch?"

"Let's start from scratch. But I'd prefer not to rush into wall treatments or curtains."

"We can begin to look at the furniture, but—"

"Oh, no, no. Heavens! We'll be moving way too

fast for me if you want to discuss the room's contents already."

"That only leaves the floor and the ceiling," I said evenly, my voice deflated.

As though annoyed at our too-noisy conversation, Hildi hopped down from Audrey's lap and pranced out of the room. Audrey said cheerfully, "Well, the floor is also going to take me some time to consider. But you can go ahead and order whatever ceiling medallions and trim you'd like, Erin. You do such marvelous work, I'm sure it's going to be glorious."

chapter 12

The next morning, with unfaithful Hildi curled in Lisa's lap as we sat at the kitchen counter, Lisa and I chatted over our bowls of Wheaties. I pretended not to notice that she was periodically allowing Hildi to lick milk from her spoon.

By eight-thirty, clutching her stuffed cat to her chest, Lisa dashed across the back lawns to her home. An hour later, however, she was dawdling by my car when I left my house. She sat on the curb, peeling the bark from tiny twigs and stacking them in a square, Lincoln Logs style. I was wearing reasonably casual olive-green slacks and plunked down beside her. It was clear at a glance that she was merely biding her time, waiting for me.

She lowered the headphones of her iPod and said, "Hey."

"Hey. How's it going?"

She shrugged. "The usual. My mom hates me. My house is haunted. How's it going for you?"

"Your mom does *not* hate you, Lisa."

Another shrug. "She's mad at me all the time."

"She's under a tremendous amount of stress."

"So am I!"

"True. And I'm sure your mom realizes that. But I suspect that, because she's your mom and she *loves* you, knowing that you've got all this pressure on you too makes things doubly hard on her."

Lisa rolled her eyes. She snatched up the ant-sized corral she was building and began to flick the twigs, one by one, onto the street.

Regardless of how it would sit with her mother, I couldn't just drive off and leave her sitting here. "Is your mom home right now?"

"I think so."

"I've got almost two hours where I'm going to be making some fabric selections for draperies and upholstery. If your mother says it's okay, do you want to come with me?"

"Sure." She was playing it cool, but she had a bounce to her step as I unlocked the van and she hopped into the passenger seat. We made the short drive around the block to her house.

Lisa waited in my van while I spoke to her mother on their porch. Francine said, "Fine, fine," to my suggestion. She never cracked a smile and seemed to be distracted, but she also said she was "fine," with no further elaborations, when I asked if everything was all right. Lisa, on the other hand, said, "Yippee!" when I returned and told her that her mother had no objections to our plans.

"How old is Hildi?" Lisa asked as I got back behind the wheel and pulled away from the curb.

"She's about four. I got her from the animal shelter two years ago, when I first moved to Crestview." We stopped at a red light, and I asked, "Why were you so worried about her when you saw her on my window ledge last night?"

"I'm not supposed to talk about that."

"About . . . your entering Audrey's house, you mean?"

"No, about what happened. To Taffy."

"Taffy?"

Silence. Finally, Lisa said, "It was almost four years ago. Just before we moved here. Taffy was my orange-colored cat. There was this tree near my window, and Taffy loved to try to swat at the birds from the ledge. Mom kept telling me not to let her do that, because the screens were down, but this friend of mine thought it was really funny to watch her." She cleared her throat, fidgeting with my dented glove-box door. "So, this one time, we kind of got the idea of tossing Taffy onto the tree branch so she really could catch the bird? It was just a second-floor window, and we knew how cats always land on their feet . . . and my friend was telling me that she heard of cats falling, like, ten stories and not getting hurt. Only . . . Taffy kind of squirmed, and then my mom saw me from the yard and yelled 'No!' at me, and I kind of tried to stop, but it was too late. Taffy wound up landing on the cement back porch and got hurt really bad, and my dad and mom thought I did it on purpose. I didn't! It was just . . . a stupid thing that I did while I was goofing around. You know?"

The light had turned green, and in a way it was nice not to have to make eye contact. "That must have been so terrible, for all of you," I murmured, meaning it, but well aware that the poor cat had suffered the most for Lisa's actions.

"My parents gave Taffy away and took me to see a shrink. Like I'd ever hurt my cat on purpose! But they were all really freaked out by it. Like *I* wasn't? I'll never forgive myself for being so dumb. But it really was just an awful accident. And . . . now I guess my mom thinks I've moved on to shoving my babysitter off the roof!"

"She can't possibly really believe that, Lisa." As soon as the words were out of my mouth, though, I knew I'd spoken too soon. If Francine did secretly suspect her own daughter, it certainly explained the woman's reactions the night Willow died. Worry niggled at me. Shouldn't Francine have automatically believed that her daughter was *incapable* of evil acts? Was there more to the story than Lisa was telling me?

I sneaked a glance at Lisa. "I found your stuffed cat in the tower room last night. By a portrait of Abby Chambers."

"Yeah," she muttered, her voice forlorn. "I forgot I'd left it up there last night. My mom wasn't home and . . . the painting looks a bit like Willow, so . . . it was silly, but I felt safer that way. Like she was watching over me."

"Where did you find it?"

"In the closet."

"Of the tower room?"

She nodded.

"How come no one else noticed it all these years? It obviously belonged to the Chambers family."

"It was lying flat on the top shelf. I guess nobody looked up there."

I said evenly, "That's really hard to believe, Lisa, since your mom and I are a couple of inches taller than you, but didn't see it there."

"I found it back when we first moved into the house. I knew someone else would see it there and take it away, so I've been hiding it in my room ever since."

She must have read the skepticism in my silence, because she cried, "I found it in the closet, Erin, I swear to God."

We arrived at the fabric store and pulled into a parking space.

Lisa pivoted in her seat and said, "So we're going to pick out cloth for curtains now?"

"And for some upholstery, as well. For two different homes in south Crestview. Then you can help me put my presentation boards together."

"This is so cool! I can't wait to tell my friend about

this. She wants to redo her room when they get back from vacation in two weeks. Now I'll be able to really help her!"

Lisa proved to be one of the most eager and quickest studies I've ever met, and the morning flew by. Having her with me also allowed me to get a strong feel for her likes and dislikes, which would be useful when designing her bedroom. We headed back to our neighborhood for lunch. I decided to continue our conversation from the drive to the fabric store and asked, "Why didn't you show your mom that portrait of Abby when you first found it?"

"I thought she might make me get rid of it . . . that she'd say it belonged to Abby's cousins or a museum or something."

"Did you ever show it to Willow?"

"Yeah. It was kind of our secret. Willow thought it was freaky how much it looked like her."

"Did she comment on that? Say that they were related . . . distant cousins, or anything?"

"No way. It was just a coincidence that they looked similar. And it's not like they're twins or anything. Abby had red hair like mine, not dark blond like Willow's."

At another red light, I turned to look at her. "Lisa, I need you to be honest with me. Are you still playing tricks on your mother? Pretending to be Abby?"

She winced. "No. Like I kind of told you before. Willow thought it'd be fun. But it's no fun at all when you're doing it all by yourself."

I held my tongue, and at length, she continued. "When everyone was at the meeting over at Mr. and Mrs. Stanley's house . . . I tried to, like, talk to them on the other side? To talk to Abby and Willow, I mean. And find out who pushed Willow. But it didn't work, and I saw Hildi on your window ledge, and forgot to hide the portrait."

"Did your mom ask you about the portrait this morning?"

She frowned, then nodded. "She was really mad at me for keeping secrets from her. Like *she's* one to—" She broke off and her cheeks colored. "That's why I'm really glad you invited me to come to work with you today."

"So were you faking it at the séance when you—"

"No, I *swear* I didn't. I . . . had started to, though. Willow's the one who told me about the chemistry class that Mr. Stanley and Abby were in ages and ages ago. I guess Willow kind of read his yearbook signatures when she was watching Steve Sullivan work. But then, Abby really did take over my body. And sometimes *I've* heard noises at night, too. The ghost is *real,* Erin! I think Abby's the one who shoved me in the closet to protect me."

My thoughts were in a jumble. I wanted to believe Lisa. Linda Delgardio had already lectured me on what I saw when I looked at Lisa versus what she, as a police officer, saw. All I knew was if I couldn't even trust that a child I'd come to care about was innocent of murder, the very foundations of this world and my place within it had crumbled. Though we were just a few blocks from her house, I signaled and pulled over to the curb. "Lisa, I'm going to ask you this just one more time, and you've got to promise to tell me the truth."

"I promise."

"Are you absolutely positive there was someone else on your roof with Willow the night she died?"

"Yes! I swear to God!"

I searched her earnest face and I believed her. "You've got to never again hide a single item or play a single ghost trick on anyone. Willow was *murdered*. The police are trying to investigate and figure out who did it. You've got to be absolutely up-front about everything, or the police are going to conclude you and Willow were horsing around on the roof, and she fell, and you're covering for what happened."

"Okay. Got it."

"You have to do this for me, Lisa, or I won't be able to help you. You can't lie to me first, then tell me another story. There is just too much at stake here for playing games."

"I know. I'm sorry. I'll never do it again. I promise. Cross my heart and hope to die."

The vow brought me little comfort. I was scared to the bone at the possibility that she'd witnessed more that night than she was willing to admit. And if the killer believed that Lisa was a witness, her life could be in jeopardy.

• • •

By the time we returned, Francine was in much better spirits. I grabbed my digital camera and asked if I could take some in-progress photographs, and she said, "Absolutely. This is a good time. You'll have the room all to yourself."

"Really? Ralph's truck is parked out front."

"He's brown-bagging it, at the park across Tenth Street."

Lisa started to follow me upstairs, but Francine said, "Let's let Erin take her pictures in peace, shall we? I want to hear about your day while I'm making your sandwich."

Lisa grimaced, but pivoted and joined her mom, and I went up the stairs alone. On the second floor, I heard strange noises above me.

Someone was scraping metal against the wood floor in the tower room. I had a creepy vision of Dickensian chains being dragged across the floorboards. Totally spooked, I climbed the flight to the tower room. The scraping noise continued, and I hesitated outside the door, afraid that I'd discover an empty room and would have to report to Linda Delgardio and to everyone else that I too was now convinced that the house was indeed haunted.

Vowing to get this over with quickly, I turned the knob and flung the door open in one motion. I sighed with relief as I saw that the "ghost" was merely Ralph Appleby. He was using a handheld planer, smoothing a floorboard the old-fashioned way.

He turned to see who'd entered, and I smiled at him. "Hi, Ralph. Francine thought you were at lunch."

He went back to work. The new planks were already indistinguishable from the original ones, at least to my eye. "Changed my mind."

Determined to goad him into conversation, I asked, "How are you doing today, Ralph?"

"Still never able to get an even break. My life sucks."

I sat down on the floor behind him. "You're upset about the meeting at Bob Stanley's house, I assume?" He didn't reply, so I went on, "Do you still think he's guilty of Abby's murder?"

"Yeah, but nobody ever listens to me."

"*I'm* listening to you." For one thing, I was intensely curious about what was behind Bob Stanley's accusing Ralph of supplying the drugs that killed Abby. There wasn't an easy way for me to work that into a conversation, however.

Finally, he grumbled, "Hell. Why should I go caring about some young girl's life? It's not like anyone ever gave a rat's ass about mine."

I replied quietly, "I'm sorry you've had it so rough, Ralph."

"Rough," he spat. "You pretty girls got no idea how rough things can be."

Annoyed, I snapped, "If nothing else, somebody cared enough to keep you alive as a baby till you were capable of feeding and dressing yourself. And so maybe pretty girls like Willow had easier childhoods than you did, but someone shoved her off a rooftop when she was just twenty-three. Personally, I'd call that worse than 'rough.' "

He turned and peered at me from beneath his heavy brow, which jutted over his eyes like a roof eave. I half expected him to say something nasty, but instead he replied, "You got a point there. I probably made more 'n enough folks want to drop me off a bridge over the years. I ain't no beauty queen. Ain't no Miss Congeniality, either."

"We all have our surly moods," I muttered, as noncommittal a response as I could muster.

He sat up and dragged his palm across his pate and managed to accidentally plant a curled woodchip on his fringe of dark hair. "Just not all that crazy about people, when you come straight down to it. I do better on my own. Only time I ever felt like shooting the breeze with anyone was clear back when I got plastered as a teen. But, like I said, Abby made me promise to quit drinking, and I never break a promise."

This being the first time Ralph was actually willing to talk with me, I seized the opportunity and asked, "You weren't in the neighborhood when Willow died, were you?"

"I was home in Lafayette." He glared at me. "Why?"

I need to keep in mind that I'm not a police officer, I scolded myself. "Audrey said she thought she saw a man in the backyard that night, who ran off. She thought it was someone she knew, and I was hoping maybe you were here late and possibly saw him, too."

"Wasn't me." He got to his feet. "Talked to the spiral

staircase rep this morning. Said they'd ship it next week. You still haven't given me your final plans for this room." Then he mumbled, "'Scuse me. Lunch break," and trudged down the stairs.

I started to take my pictures. The room was beginning to shape up nicely. Having the dreadful wall gone was a big improvement, and the ceiling would soon be wonderful but was currently an eyesore, as were the too-small windows with the boarded-up panes. The place was now reminiscent of a Rapunzel-like tower. Soon a chill seeped into me, as distinct as if I'd stepped into Audrey's wine cellar. *Abby?* I thought, at least managing to resist talking out loud. *If that's you, please go away.* I took my final flash pictures and pocketed my camera.

Although the chill in the air subsided, a powerful presence remained. A whistling noise behind me made me jump. It sounded disturbingly like a girl's voice, asking *"Who?"*

I crossed the room to the nearest window and pressed down on the window sash. It was the breeze, playing a trick on my all-too-easily-spooked state of mind.

Just as I turned away from the noisy window, however, I thought I saw something move. That got my heart going, till I realized that it was just a beam of sunlight, dappled by the leaves on the trees.

"Get a grip on yourself, Erin," I scolded, needing to hear my own voice.

Although I was convinced the apparition had merely been the play of sunlight, I crossed the room to investigate. I knelt and ran my hand over that surface of the wall and felt distinct depressions in the old plaster. As though I were searching for a smear on a countertop that can only be seen at certain vantage points, I peered at the surface from another angle and now clearly saw two childlike handprints, as though a child had played patty-cake with the wall while the plaster was still wet.

My eyes misted. It was heartbreaking to see the reminders of a playful moment in the life of the little girl who was going to die on her fifteenth birthday.

chapter 13

Later that afternoon, I worked on a kitchen remodel in Lafayette, a small town outside of Crestview. Because Ralph Appleby also lived in this town, I decided that I could drop off a copy of my final designs now and eliminate one item from my mental TTD (things to do) list. I looked up his address and found that he lived on West Emma Street, not far from my client's house, so I drove there without calling, planning to put my sketches in his mailbox. Just to tease him, maybe I'd attach a sticky-pad note with a happy face on it and dot my *i*'s with little hearts.

My drop-off / drive-off plans were instantly foiled. Ralph had a slot by his front door instead of a mailbox, and as I pulled into his driveway, his garage door rose. Clad in work boots, denim overalls, and a yellowed T-shirt, Ralph stood blocking the entrance with his arms crossed, watching to see who'd deigned to pull into his driveway. A cloud of cigarette smoke arose from his single-car garage, which had me on the verge of lecturing about fire safety as I emerged from my van, until I noticed that his pickup was parked on the street. He'd converted his garage into a woodworking shop.

"Oh. It's you," he said, then turned his back on me and walked toward a workbench.

I followed him, saying, "Hi, Ralph. Beautiful afternoon, isn't it?" I scanned my surroundings in awe. Scattered throughout the workshop were various mallets and chisels as well as the resulting relief carvings; he'd done a small but eye-catching rendition of an iris in a vase. That piece would look spectacular in a shadow-box frame with a linen mat and a touch of gold trim. "Wow! Ralph, you're such a talented artist!"

"Window installers arrived at Francine's, so I had to clear out," he muttered. "You brought the final plans for Francine's room, I guess."

"Yes. I thought I'd drop them off now so you'd have plenty of time to study them." My vision fell on a photograph on his workbench. It was a wallet-sized picture of Willow McAndrews. He'd sketched out a life-sized drawing of her and had transferred the sketch onto a creamy-white basswood board, which he was about halfway through carving—a portrait of Willow in relief. I realized at once that Ralph Appleby was the artist who'd painted the unsigned portrait of Abby Chambers that Lisa had found. "Your drawings are excellent, too."

"Makes it easier to do the actual carving when I got drawings to scale."

"You're carving a portrait of Willow McAndrews from just that one small picture? That must be a major challenge."

He shrugged. "Use whatever photo I got." He pointed with his chin at the wallet-sized shot. "Diana found me that one in her desk and let me have it. I'm gonna see if someone in her family wants a portrait of her. Need to finish it by the funeral, so I gotta get back to work now."

"When *is* that? I haven't seen anything about it in the paper."

"Tomorrow afternoon. Down in Colorado Springs. That's her hometown, turns out."

Colorado Springs was a two-hour drive from Crestview. "I didn't realize you were a friend of her family."

"I'm not. I do 'em as a tribute to young people I know who've died before their time. When they come out good enough, I give 'em to the parents."

What a sad—and slightly eerie—ritual, I thought. Hoping he'd finally acknowledge the compliment, I said, "I had no idea you were such a talented artist, Ralph."

He shrugged. "It's just a hobby. Beats carving duck decoys."

Still awestruck, I wandered over to the workbench along the back wall. He had at least a dozen relief portraits in two stacks. "Mind if I look through these?" I picked up the top one and saw that the next was of the same girl—Abby Chambers. So was the top carving on the second stack. He'd carved the likeness of Abby over and over.

"Yeah, I do." He jerked the portrait from my hands and set it back down. "These were just my practice pieces. Back when I was learning how to carve, in high school." He draped a tattered, ratty-looking, pea-green towel over his carvings.

I forced a smile. "This girl looks a lot like Willow."

"Not in person, they didn't. Weren't nothing alike." I could tell by the set of his jaw that this was the last he would say on the subject.

"Here are the plans for the room. Let me know if you have any questions or concerns with them." I set my drawings on his bench.

"I'll do that," he said, and stood at the ready beside the button for his opener. He gestured that I should leave and muttered, "I gotta lock the door behind you."

Feeling increasingly uneasy, I drove to my office. There was already a message on my machine from Ralph, saying he had some questions about my design. The way he said "questions," it was clear that he meant he had *problems* with it. I called him back, and we agreed to meet at five o'clock, if that was convenient for Francine. I phoned her to ask, and she said, "Absolutely," and added that the windows were "just marvelous," doubling my resolve to get there on time so I could see for myself.

• • •

Ralph's pickup wasn't there when I arrived, but my glimpse of a pair of the new windows on the west side of the house captured my focus. The enhanced appearance even when viewed from outside made me a little giddy. A large piece of plywood was in place of the window that faced the street, temporarily covering up the opening for the piano movers' use; because of the impossible approach through the narrow staircase and low attic, we needed to have Francine's Steinway crane-lifted upstairs. Francine was so nervous about this procedure that she insisted it take place at the earliest possible opportunity, even though this meant we would be completing the room around her gorgeous piano. Heaven help us all if something were to go wrong and her piano was damaged.

I rang the bell. Francine greeted me warmly, saying, "The windows are utterly fantastic, Erin!"

"I saw the two on the west side. Have you already contacted the piano movers?"

"Yes, and they'll arrive tomorrow morning, so hopefully the installers will be back to finish up tomorrow afternoon. I'm hoping they can get the other four windows done then."

Four windows would be installed in one afternoon, *after* the completion of a challenging feat in the morning? Not very likely. She had gotten spoiled by Ralph Appleby's feverish workaholic ways.

She grinned and gave my arm a squeeze, and I decided to let her stay happy for a few minutes before pointing out that if we were betting on which would show up for a visit tomorrow afternoon, Santa Claus or the window installers, the smart money was on Kris Kringle.

"Feel free to go upstairs and see for yourself, Erin. I'll send Ralph up when he arrives." She started to turn away, then hesitated and reached into her slacks pocket, saying, "Oh. Before I forget, here." She tossed a key to me. "I might have a last-minute gig tomorrow. That key is to my back door. I gave the construction foreman your work and home numbers. If they have any scheduling problems while I'm not here, I wanted to make sure that they can still get in."

"That's fine, but please don't be too disappointed if the installers can't finish up that quickly. They're contracted by—"

She held up a hand, cutting me off, and said, "You can just give my key back whenever the house is done."

I forced a smile. "Will do." I climbed the stairs, my excitement rising with each step, as usual. I held my breath as I threw open the door and wound up hugging myself with delight at the vision that greeted me. Although there was a world of work yet to be done, I could see by the room's bones that this space was eventually going to be sublime. The lines were sexy, the planes and angles divine.

I strolled to the center of the room, only to have a strange, unpleasant sensation suddenly overcome me. It felt for all the world as though I were being watched.

I chastised myself for being so paranoid, but couldn't shake the feeling, even so.

I felt drawn to the small section of wall where I'd found the child-sized handprint and knelt to examine it once more. The baseboard directly below the indentations was slightly loose, something I hadn't noticed before. The vibrations from the power tools as they installed the large windows must have shaken it loose.

I pushed the baseboard back into place with the heel of my hand, but then began to wonder why this small section of trim slid in and out of place so easily. Its two finishing nails were there for show only. Maybe the baseboard was hiding a small cubbyhole. I pried the two-foot-long section free. There was an inch-wide gap where the floorboards met with the wall. I curled my fingers into it to investigate and touched a small object. It felt like a hard, plastic toy. I managed to pinch it between my fingertips and to work it free.

The object was an inch-tall plastic soldier, dressed in a German World War II uniform. To my disgust, the soldier had been stabbed, a miniature nooselike string had been tied around his neck, and he was dappled with blood-red paint spots.

Just then I heard Ralph's heavy footfalls on the steps and quickly pocketed the toy. I got the board back into place and managed to stand up just as Ralph appeared. My hello sounded breathy and unnatural.

"Got here a bit late," he said. "Traffic."

"You said you had some questions."

He nodded. " 'Bout the room dimensions." He was

paying the new windows no mind and instead stared at the baseboard where I'd just found the toy soldier. In spite of myself, I glanced down to make sure the baseboard was still in place. He peered at me. "You all right?"

"Of course. Absolutely. There's just . . . something bothersome about this room."

He frowned and crossed his arms. "I'm trying to fix it."

"Fix what?"

"The room. How it makes you cranky."

"It makes *me* cranky?" He was nobody to talk about others being cranky.

"When you're in it for any amount of time, you start to feel a little out of sorts. *That's* what we gotta fix with your design. You notice how all the dimensions are off by an inch or so?"

"Yes, but that's often par for the course with old houses."

"Only in this room. Rest of the house is built better." He sneered as he scanned our surroundings. "Everything's slightly off-center. Floor. Walls. Ceiling. Place is a bit like one of them fun houses. It's all just off-kilter enough to give you optical illusions. Make you feel like you're falling when you look out the window."

I didn't agree with his assessment in the least, but asked, "You can *fix* that?"

He shook his head. "Not without tearing the whole tower down and rebuilding it from scratch, or at least gutting the room. Suggested as much to Francine, but she said no . . . it wasn't worth the added expense."

"Not to mention how peeved that'd make Bob Stanley, our historian watchdog."

Ralph smirked and said under his breath, "Major reason I wanted to go ahead with it."

"Is that what you wanted to talk with me about? The room's being . . . off-kilter?"

"Kinda." He wandered back toward the door. "Ever measure the attic outside this room, where the closet cuts into it?"

"Yes. I had to do that to complete my floor plans. Why?"

"Closet's short by almost eighteen inches."

"It is?" My thoughts raced. There was hidden space behind the closet! That explained Lisa's story; she'd lied about the logistics of *where* in the closet she'd found Abby's portrait.

"You want I should do anything about it?" he asked, meeting my gaze, for once. "I could take down the plasterboard right now, get you that wasted closet space back."

"Did you tell Francine about this?"

He shook his head. "Figured I'd tell *you* first."

"It's really Francine, not me, who'll be regaining the wasted closet space."

Ralph said nothing, but held my gaze.

He was creeping me out; I had visions of skeletons *behind* closets now. "Are you implying there's something hidden back there I might want to know about?"

He shrugged. “I got no idea what’s back there.”

This was now reminding me of Geraldo Rivera and Al Capone’s vault. I’d rather not have Ralph be present if and when I looked back there. “Let me think about it for a while.”

He nodded.

“The new windows look great, don’t they, Ralph?”

He shrugged again. “Hope Abby likes ’em.”

“Abby?”

“Lisa, I mean.”

Though he hastily turned away, he’d obviously been horrified at his gaffe.

I went home. Audrey wasn’t there, and I was surprised and a little hurt to see that she’d apparently tossed out my calla lily. The petals were getting slightly wilted, but the flower was still lovely. I checked in every room in the house, but the crystal bud vase and the lily itself were no longer on the curio cabinet and weren’t on display anywhere else.

For safekeeping, I removed the mutilated toy soldier from my pocket and stashed it in the drawer in the charming artisan-style coffee table in the den. (Fortunately, Audrey had grown tired of the previous table, which resembled a stack of three enormous books and was never to my taste.) I’d have to contact Linda Delgardio to give the toy soldier to her, although it probably had nothing to do with either Willow’s or Abby’s death. Maybe something significant was hidden behind the closet, however.

In need of a sounding board, I glanced out the dining room window to see if Sullivan's van was in the Stanleys' driveway. It was. I kept an eye out for him, and my vigilance was soon rewarded when I saw him emerge and head to his van.

I dashed out the front door and called, "Got a minute, Sullivan?"

"Sure thing. Come on over."

I rounded the shrubbery that formed the border between Audrey's and the Stanleys' properties. "Are you done for the day?"

He glanced over his shoulder. In a lowered voice he said, "Whether I want to be or not."

I could hear what sounded like angry voices through the closed window. "They're arguing? What about?"

"I try not to spy on my clients. But it's something about a painting." Sullivan smirked at me.

"I wonder if it's got something to do with the portrait of Abby that Lisa found."

"Lisa found a portrait of the ghost girl?"

"In the third-floor closet." Sullivan was technically my boss—or rather my overseer—at Francine's. I should ask his opinion about the space behind the closet. "Can you come to the Findleys' house with me . . . right now? We'll explain to Francine that I'm consulting with you about what to do about the asymmetrical walls."

He said, "Sure. Hop in," and I caught him up on Ralph's information about the unorthodox closet space during the short drive to Francine's house.

He gathered up a few hand tools and a flashlight to bring with us. I said, "Eighteen inches would be wide enough room for a skinny person to pass through."

"Such as a thin child." He rang the doorbell and charmed our way into the house. Francine was sitting down to an early and solo dinner—Lisa was at a friend's house—and she gladly gave us private access to the tower room. We headed up the stairs. Sullivan scanned the attic with its new octagonal window and said nothing, but stared at the glorious, ethereal ceiling when we entered the tower room. He stood with arms akimbo, admiring the space, and finally said, "I approve, Gilbert. Nice to see my underling does such good work."

"Your 'underling'?" He was once again studying the ceiling, and I said, "Are there any pigs flying up there?"

"Funny." He joined me in front of the closet, where we stood staring for a moment at the back wall.

"It's bizarre that anyone would build such a small hiding spot," I said, more for my own benefit than for Sullivan's. "I mean, this closet wall is just eight feet long, twelve feet high. A hundred fifty or so cubic feet of dead space is nothing."

Sullivan ran his palm along the surface of the wall. "The bottom third or so of the Sheetrock isn't fastened to the studs. They trimmed out the closet with corner bead and a chair rail to cover up the seams. All we have to do is remove the trim to access the crawl space back there."

"I commented on the trim myself when Francine first showed me the room. Our theory was that Abby liked to sit in this closet . . . maybe have tea parties when she was little. Which would explain why the chair rail is so low, to protect the wall."

He got hold of one piece of corner trim with his fingertips and tugged on it. "It's loose." He pried it away from the wall in a matter of seconds. Like the baseboard, the finishing nails were mostly for show. As he'd surmised, it was covering a seam in the drywall. He grinned at me. "Maybe the previous owners didn't believe in keeping their money in a bank. They could have stashed their cash back there."

"My theory is that Lisa's been back there already and found the portrait hidden there. If she found bags of money too, I doubt she'd just leave them there."

"Let's have a look."

"Without the homeowner's permission? We've got no right to do this. It's unethical." Which was not to say that I wasn't dying to do it.

"Yeah, but it also could give us valuable information to help solve a murder."

"True," I said quickly. "I'm game."

"I'll have to remember to twist your arm a little harder next time we're in a predicament like this."

"By 'predicament,' you mean investigating a murder? I hope *that* won't ever happen again."

We got to work and removed the second piece of corner bead and the chair rail, which was attached with screws. This was surely the least responsible thing I'd ever done as a designer, and I moaned, "How can I justify this to Francine? It's her house, after all, and she's paying me to design her room, not to tear up the back of her closet to see what's behind it."

"If we have to, we can always tell Francine the truth."

"That we were dying of curiosity?"

"That we wanted to uncover a possible source for the strange noises she's been hearing." Sullivan focused the beam of the flashlight through the gap. "Too small for me."

"But not for me." Though just barely, I managed to squeeze below the permanent portion of drywall and stand up behind the closet. At that, I had to keep my head facing sideways, or I'd bash my nose against the studs.

"You all right?" Sullivan handed me the flashlight.

"So far. Good thing I don't have claustrophobia. Though I might develop it before I get out of here."

"Anything interesting?"

"No, just a couple of huge bags of money," I joked.

"Is there a crawl space above the ceiling? Or under the floor?"

"I doubt it," I answered. I shone the beam above me and hopped a bit to see if the floorboards jiggled. "Nope. It's so stuffy and stifling hot in here. It's just dead air, with no circulation."

I squeezed my way from one side of the closet to the other, checking for telltale cracks of light or temperature shifts. "Nothing in here," I called out to Steve.

With effort, I turned to negotiate my way out the low opening. As I shone my beam to the opposite wall, I found a message. It was written on an unfinished two-by-four, placed directly above and opposite the opening in the closet. It read: *Leave me alone! Or DIE!*

chapter 14

"I'm getting out of here," I announced, my voice shaky. Easier said than done; there wasn't enough room to crouch and duck through the opening. I sat down, eased my legs through, then tried to crab-walk out. Halfway there, my shoulders got wedged between studs. I tried to shimmy my way free, to no avail.

"Are you stuck, Gilbert?" Sullivan asked, already cracking up.

"No, I'm working on my latest limbo moves," I snapped. "Give me a hand!"

Laughing merrily, he pulled me by my ankles till I managed to fully emerge. Thank goodness I was wearing pants! Standing by my feet as I lay on my back, he wisecracked, "That must be how doctors do a breech delivery."

I thrust my foot at him, kicking him in the leg. "This isn't funny, Sullivan! There's a second death threat written in there!"

"A death threat?" he repeated, rubbing his shin.

"Someone wrote, 'Leave me alone, or die' on a two-by-four."

"Where is it, exactly?" Sullivan snatched the flashlight from my grasp. He knelt in the closet to peer behind the Sheetrock.

"On the far wall, just above and opposite the opening. It's written on a horizontal board . . . one that serves no structural purpose." I scooted over to him and yanked the flashlight away from him. "I'll show you."

I lay on my stomach, supporting my upper body on my elbows, and swept the beam along the far wall. "There," I said, pointing with my chin. Sullivan squeezed beside me, having trouble angling his broad shoulders such that we could both see. He had to stretch alongside me, and it flitted through my brain that this could easily become a deeply embarrassing moment if Francine should enter the room and find us lying side by side with our heads in a cubbyhole behind her closet. Not to mention that I was starting to get jittery from being pressed so close to him.

"Huh." He reached up and ran his fingertips along the writing. "That's ink from a ballpoint pen."

"It was written onto the board with so much force it's practically embossed. Must have been rough on the pen to have been stabbed into the wood like that. So now all we have to do is locate an abused Bic, and we've got our killer." I sat up.

"Doesn't give us much in the way of clues. I'm pretty sure ballpoints have been around for more than fifty years, back before this room was built. And I can reach the board from where I am, so even someone too large to squeeze into that tight space still could have written it there."

I turned off the flashlight and got to my feet. Sullivan sat up and met my gaze. "My guess is that was written very recently . . . and the message writer assumed you'd be tearing out the closet."

"I *was* going to, until Francine changed her mind about the picture windows and keeping the wall intact. The closet was shown as being removed in the before-and-after plans that were circulated throughout the neighborhood."

He nodded. "Someone's trying to scare you off this job."

Resenting Sullivan's junior-detective tone of voice, I said snidely, "You think?"

He studied my features with a solemn expression on his own face. "Let's team up on the two houses, Gilbert. Watch each other's backs."

"Why?"

"Because it's safer. Ever stop to think what might have happened to you last spring if I hadn't gotten there in time?"

He was referring to a terrifying encounter with a killer that had almost cost me my life. "Thanks for reminding me. That still gives me nightmares, you know, and I really don't appreciate being dragged down memory lane."

He held up a hand in a silent apology.

I sighed, feeling guilty. Against my will, I'd reverted to sniping at him over every little thing. Why was it that I was capable of getting along with anyone on the planet *except* Steve Sullivan? Even so, having a partner *was* safer for me. "Okay," I said, softening my voice. "I suppose that's what the homeowners' committee indirectly suggested that we do anyway, since we're supposed to be acting as each other's supervisors. How's the Stanleys' house coming along?"

"Great, actually. No problems. I did an end-around regarding the chartreuse paint." He grinned. "I lobbied Bob to choose New England blue, and he convinced Cassandra to go with my instructions, as opposed to the room's."

"And you've convinced them to put the bay window in the den now, right, instead of in the front of the house?"

"Yep. Already installed. Looks great. Everything's all set."

In spite of myself, his breezy replies were starting to get under my skin. "What do you mean by it's 'all set'? That your work's already complete?"

"No, but it's damned close. We've just got the kitchen left to do. The Stanleys' place is going like clockwork." He shoved the drywall back into place and began to fasten the screws on the chair rail.

"So, in other words, you don't want my help on *your* house, you just want to help me on *my* house."

In patronizing tones, he replied, "You can help me, Gilbert. Just . . . not for a while. You're great with the finishing touches, so when—"

"In other words, *you* want to be in charge at both houses, yet you'll let me fluff up the pillows and align the tassels on the throw rugs. Dream on, Sullivan! I'm lead designer on this project. You're lead on the Stanleys', and we're both equally open to input from the other. That's the deal. Otherwise, we watch each other's backs from a distance, just like always."

Turning from the closet to glower at me, he said, "Which means you play Lone Ranger while you're stumbling across death threats and young women are getting tossed off the roof."

"Yes. I'd rather take some calculated risks than desert my vision for this house." Even as I said this, part of me was telling the rest of me that I was being grossly unfair; Sullivan had volunteered to do this to protect me, not to horn in on my design job.

Sullivan, meanwhile, threw up his hands and snarled, "Fine. We're equal partners."

"Fine."

"Here." He thrust the screwdriver at me and stood up. "I've got the screws halfway in. You can screw 'em in the rest of the way, pardner."

Although my cheeks grew warm, I resisted making an off-color joke, sure that he was trying to goad me into doing so and unwilling to give him the satisfaction. I went to work on tightening the screws.

"Hurry up," he demanded. "I've got an appointment clear across town."

The doorbell rang, and I could hear the sounds of Francine letting someone inside. I resealed the back of the closet and took just a moment to collect myself, admiring the simple but effective hiding space.

Without measuring the room dimensions and contemplating how odd it was to put corner trim and chair railing inside a closet, the space was undetectable.

I led the way downstairs, chastising myself with every step for being so mean to Sullivan. But this was my dream job, damn it, the one house in all of Crestview that I'd told myself I most wanted to experience—to enhance and to learn from! Sullivan was going to criticize my every decision!

I felt a pang as I turned the corner at the bottom of the staircase and faced the stunning arched entranceway of the foyer, its every line and plane such perfection. Bathed in afternoon sunlight from the open doorway, the space was a vision. Hallways are normally an ideal place to hang artwork and photographs, but Francine had correctly sensed that, with their ornate carved trim, these creamy-butter plaster walls were best left bare. The craftsmanship and glorious sheen of the walnut flooring alone was magical. And yet this majestic building had twice been mutated into the scene of terrible deaths.

Diana and Francine must have cleared up their differences, because they were chatting in the foyer as if they were the best of friends. Diana spotted us and said brightly, "Speak of the devil. Here they are now."

Francine furrowed her brow and asked me, "Are the room dimensions hopelessly lopsided? Ralph told me weeks ago about the room's basic construction not being up to his exacting standards, but it's fine even so, don't you think?"

"Absolutely. Everything's coming along magnificently." Not counting the nasty warning hidden behind the closet. Was Ralph right to accuse the imprecise dimensions in the tower room of making its inhabitants "cranky"? Could that disharmony have fueled the murders? No, that was nuts. No way could I pass the blame for my own snarky behavior onto a room. Unfortunately. I forced a smile as I met Diana's gaze. Francine had a right to know about her own closet, but I wasn't going to tell her about it in front of Diana.

"Are you two working together now?" Diana asked Sullivan and me.

"Yes," we answered, just as Francine was saying "No."

"Actually," I explained, "we're each other's supervisors on the two houses, so now that things are moving along so nicely, we're going to join forces more often."

"Oh." She hesitated, glancing at me and then at him. "That's fine with me, of course, but Ralph Appleby is so . . . temperamental. Does this mean you'll be *Ralph's* supervisor, as well?"

"It's best if we don't suggest anything of the sort to him," Sullivan said with a smile. "Erin and I will make our partnership work," he added. "You'll see."

"I can vouch for that," Diana interjected. "Steve designed my living room, and Erin loves it."

Determined not to choke on the words, I said, "That's true. I do love that particular design."

"Unfortunately, I've got to go, but I'll look forward to seeing you lovely ladies tomorrow." Sullivan's parting line made both Diana and Francine light up like Tiffany lamps, but seemed as fake as a two-cent plastic rosebud to me. He let himself out. I felt a stab of regret as I watched him close the door. In the past few minutes, the two of us had demolished the last remaining glint of warmth and intimacy we'd shared when we'd almost kissed.

"Erin? Francine and I were just discussing the notion that you should join us and Cassandra tomorrow when we discuss the home tour. It'll just take a half hour or so. Ten o'clock tomorrow morning, at my house. Can you make it?"

Francine said to me, "As long as my Steinway is safely upstairs by ten a.m., there shouldn't be any major catastrophes here for you to deal with. For once."

Despite her naive timetable, I gave her a smile and checked my Day-Timer. "Yes, I just have to shift a couple of things around." I hesitated. "Oh, wait. Ralph told me just today that Willow's funeral is tomorrow afternoon. Do you know what time?"

"Four p.m." Diana's mood instantly darkened. "The details are in today's paper. I'm arranging a car pool. We're leaving here at one forty-five." She touched Francine's arm. "You and Lisa can ride down with me."

Francine shook her head. "I can't make it. As I told Erin earlier, there's a good possibility that I'll be filling in for the organist of a touring concert group in Denver tomorrow. And Lisa's too young for funerals."

I glanced at Francine, surprised at her borderline heartlessness. Willow had been their babysitter and had died in a fall off their roof! I shifted my gaze to Diana. "I'm not sure if Audrey is able to go to the funeral, or if she'll want to drive. Can I give you a call tonight if I need a ride, Diana?"

"You betcha." An instant later, her eyes lit up. "Oh, oh!" She hopped a little in a sudden burst of excitement. "I just got a wonderful idea! For our morning meeting, that is. We're going to be discussing some of the basic logistics—hours of operation of the tour, procedures, the hosts for each place . . . and so forth. And you know who is absolutely fantastic at planning details like that?"

She paused, but neither of us ventured to guess.

"Audrey! She's so great at details. And she's a local celebrity to boot! If we announce that she's the hostess for your or Cassandra's home, she'll bring in lots more people to the tour!"

Francine's face fell. Diana's eyes widened at her reaction. "Oh, dear. You and she aren't still feuding, are you? You seemed to get along just fine at the séance."

"It's not a problem," Francine said. "But you know what, Diana? As I've been saying all along, I'm planning on taking Lisa out of town for the entire length of the tour anyway. So you really don't need me at your meeting tomorrow. Plus, I really should be here while they're moving my piano."

Diana arched her eyebrow. "Are you sure? You're

willing to sign off on whatever Cassandra and I think is best?"

Something in Diana's tone, as well as in her words, made me suddenly suspect that she had set up this turn in the conversation. After all, Francine had been the major stumbling block in Diana's plans to use "Abby" as the chief attraction for the tour, and Diana was much likelier to get her way without having to take Francine's wishes into consideration.

"As long as Erin is included in the decision-making process, it'll all be fine with me." Francine gave my shoulder a rather aggressive squeeze. "I'm sure Erin will guard my interests just beautifully."

"I'll do my best."

"Wonderful," Diana cried as though sincerely delighted. "I'll give Audrey a call to discuss the meeting and the car-pool arrangements, and we'll gather at my house at ten. This will be the very thing to shore up our spirits so we can face the ordeal of poor Willow's funeral."

To Francine's severe annoyance, but hardly to my surprise, the following morning the piano movers called to say that the crane had "mechanical difficulties," and all progress in the tower room was forced to a screeching stop. I reminded her that we'd been prepared for this scenario when we originally devised the schedule, and we could begin working on Lisa's bedroom in the interim.

Shortly after ten, Audrey and I joined Cassandra and

Diana in Diana's cozy living room. Once again, I immensely enjoyed the muted earth tones and off-whites in this room, all the pieces so harmonized and inviting. Audrey and I took seats on the plush taupe sofa, with Cassandra and Diana settling into the over-stuffed armchairs to either side.

The four of us barely exchanged a word before Diana gushed to Audrey, "I'm so excited that you're willing to lend us a hand. Having your name power behind us this year will be every bit as big a bonanza for the historic tour as Abby is."

"Abby?" Audrey repeated.

"Oh, you betcha." Diana beamed. "A real live ghost on a historic-homes tour is right up there with a real live celebrity for a tour guide."

A "live ghost" seemed quite an oxymoron, but I ignored that and stated firmly, "Francine has said she doesn't want Abby's presence to be publicized. Remember?"

Diana replied, "Oh, Francine will be fine. She's not even going to be here for the tour."

"She appointed me as her spokesperson, Diana, and as such, the answer is no."

Through a forced smile, Diana retorted, "I don't recall having asked a question, but fine, point taken. No publicity about Abby Chambers."

"Good," I replied, "because if Francine catches wind of your publicizing any ghost rumors, she can consider that a breach of contract. She'll withdraw her house from the tour."

Cassandra kept her eyes averted, but Diana's flew

wide. She fluffed up her hair, took a sip of Darjeeling tea, then asked Audrey which house she'd prefer to show—Bob and Cassandra's or Francine's.

"I have to choose?" Audrey asked.

"Yes."

"I'll go with Francine's, then."

"Wonderful," Diana said.

"Are you sure you wouldn't rather be *our* guide?" Cassandra asked hopefully.

"I'm sure. You know how much Bob will relish being his own tour guide. He's so marvelous at embellishing his historical descriptions."

"You can say that again," Cassandra muttered, and crossed her arms over her ample chest.

"Willow would have been a terrific host as well," Diana said sadly. "That's who I'd originally tapped as the tour guide for Francine's home."

Cassandra chuckled and fidgeted with a few errant strands of her sandy-brown hair. "Oh, come now, Diana. The men would have enjoyed ogling her, but she'd have been terrible! Willow had no interest in people's homes whatsoever!"

"That's not true," Diana protested. "She had the perfect qualities for a career in real estate. I'd been grooming Willow to become my partner once she graduated from C.U. in December."

"You were?" I asked in surprise.

"Absolutely. Willow was going to get her license. We were going to open our own office in another year or two."

"That . . . really surprises me, Diana," Cassandra said. "Considering."

"Considering *what?*" Diana ticked off on her fingers. "Willow was intelligent, attractive, personable, and responsible. She'd have made an excellent junior partner."

"*Considering* that Willow never once mentioned your joint plans to me," Cassandra replied tartly. "She told me she was going to California as soon as she finally managed to get her degree. She used to ramble on and on about how great California was."

"Well," Diana said, her voice sharp, "we'd only just decided on the partnership when she fell, and anyway, you were the last person Willow would feel comfortable talking to about anything personal, once she found out who your daughter was."

"Diana!" Cassandra sprang to her feet. "Don't you dare insinuate that my daughter's death had anything whatsoever to do with my relationship with Willow!"

"I simply meant that—"

"Not. Another. Word. Diana!" Cassandra punctuated each word by stabbing her finger at Diana's face.

Audrey had paled and stiffened. Clearly we were equally shocked by this sudden unpleasant twist to our conversation.

Diana looked at us and covered her mouth in horror. "Oh, Cassandra! Oh, my goodness. I'm so sorry! I didn't realize you still haven't told Audrey and Erin about . . . your past."

With hands fisted and voice simmering, Cassandra

retorted, "As you well know, Diana, I prefer to keep some things *private.*"

"Please forgive me!"

Cassandra's eyes remained smoldering. With no attempt to make the action look anything other than staged, she gaped in feigned surprise at her retro Mickey Mouse watch. "Oh, dear. Look at the time. I've got to return to my shop. I'll be down in Colorado Springs all afternoon for the funeral, and I'm not sure my trainee is ready for this much responsibility."

"Cassandra, please wait." Diana rose. "I'm truly terribly sorry for me and my big mouth. Please don't storm off like this. We haven't worked out any details of the tour."

"We'll touch base again soon. It's still two months away, after all. There's plenty of time."

"We can all try to meet again tomorrow," Diana pleaded. "Okay?"

Cassandra shook her head. "Just fill me in later on what you decide." She gave Audrey and me a wan smile. "Sorry I have to rush out."

"Quite all right, my dear," Audrey replied kindly. "We'll see you this afternoon at the service." Audrey and I had already decided to drive down together in her Mercedes.

The silence was thick after the door latch clicked shut behind Cassandra. Diana sank back down into her seat and said, "Oh, dear. I'm afraid I let a lion-sized cat out of the bag. I should have assumed that Erin didn't know. But, Audrey, I never dreamed you hadn't heard about Cassandra's deceased daughter. After all, you've been living next door to Cassandra for six years now, ever since she married Bob."

"No, she never said a word," Audrey said sadly.

"Well, the thing is," Diana began with a disconcerting relish, "although Cassandra never talks about it, seven years ago, before she met Bob and moved to Crestview, Cassandra's only child . . . a teenaged daughter . . . was killed in a one-car accident."

"That's so awful!" I exclaimed, but instantly began to worry that there was some vendetta-type connection to Willow's death; maybe Willow had been in the car as well and had been clowning around with the driver, or something.

"Some seventeen-year-old boy was driving. He was drunk. He was a close friend of Willow's. Her boyfriend, actually. In fact, it was quite a coincidence that she wound up answering my room-for-rent ad on the bulletin board at C.U. and moving so close to Cassandra. Small world, as they say."

Was Diana lying about how Willow came to rent a room from her? In any case, Cassandra Stanley had hired the girlfriend of the boy whose drunk driving had killed her daughter. Had Cassandra unconsciously turned Willow into a surrogate daughter? In which case, Willow's petty thievery would have felt like an enormous betrayal to Cassandra.

In a much more appropriate reaction, Audrey cried, "Oh, poor Cassandra! I can't imagine having to endure the heartbreak of burying one's only child!"

"Cassandra gets too upset to talk about the tragedy," Diana said. "After the accident, she left Colorado Springs, moved to Crestview, then met and married our local confirmed bachelor, Bob Stanley." The bitterness in her voice made me wonder if Diana's sights had been set on Bob at the time.

She continued, "You know, the only reason I'm even including the Stanleys' home on the tour is because Bob and Cassandra insisted on it, once they learned about Francine's participation. The Stanleys are ridiculously competitive. And no matter what Francine or Ralph says, Francine's house is an extraordinary property . . . worth every penny her ex-husband paid for it."

Diana's snide tone, coming on the heels of revealing Cassandra's devastating loss, infuriated me. "Why are you bringing that up now?" I snapped. "Neither Bob nor Cassandra is here to defend themselves."

Audrey added furiously, "And you've already upset Cassandra so badly that she's left in a huff."

Diana's jaw dropped, and she sat there blinking. "I didn't mean to upset Cassandra. I shouldn't have brought up Willow's ties to her daughter. That was thoughtless of me."

"It certainly was," Audrey retorted. "If Cassandra wanted me and Erin to know about her personal tragedy of losing a child, she would have told us herself. You obviously betrayed her trust." Audrey rose, and I was more than happy to follow suit. "Find someone else to act as your shill for the historic-homes tour, Diana. I think it's best if I remove myself from the entire venture."

"Audrey!" Diana cried. "You're completely overreacting!"

"Maybe so, but that's my prerogative."

We left.

The funeral was a lengthy, dreary affair, but Cassandra and Diana appeared to have set aside their differences. If Ralph Appleby had managed to complete his portrait of Willow in time to give it to the McAndrewses, there was no sign of his artwork or him at the service. Afterward I spoke privately with Linda Delgardio, who'd made the drive there, and gave her the plastic soldier, though I was increasingly certain it had nothing whatsoever to do with Willow's murder. When I told her about the argument at Francine's house that morning, Linda curled her lip a little, but said nothing.

The next morning, Francine agreed to let me come make some final measurements and take some "before" pictures of Lisa's second-floor room with its soaring ceilings. Lisa was, once again, at a friend's house. I decided to aim at creating a bedroom for a young adult—using a bold, broad color palette and featuring plenty of storage space plus work space for studying. I envisioned a sleigh bed with accent pillows in blues and purples, a borderline-traditional desk and dresser but with a more modern, sexy flair to the legs, and a fun overstuffed chair in the corner with a playful pattern.

Francine was practicing with the earphones plugged

in, silencing her instrument as I worked, but ten minutes after I'd arrived, I began to hear what sounded like an old orchestra piece being played on a scratchy album. I couldn't tell what direction the sound was coming from, and I stepped out to see if it was emerging from the current music room across the hall or, as I feared, from the empty room above us. The instant I stepped through the doorway, the music stopped.

I finished my preliminary planning and went to tell Francine good-bye. She removed her earphones, and we chatted a bit about my ideas for Lisa's room. Afterward, I asked, "Were you playing with your headphones disconnected a few minutes ago?"

"No, why?"

"I could hear some sort of tune in the background. It must have come from outside. It was probably just someone's blaring car radio." Although why some radio station would be playing such an eerie, old-fashioned song was beyond me.

Francine had paled. "Did it go something like this?" She unplugged the headphones and played the simple tune I'd just now been hearing.

"Yes, that's the song." Though it definitely hadn't been an organ playing it.

Francine's cheeks remained flushed. "Lisa used to hum that to me. When we first moved here. I didn't think anything of it, until she started humming it again a couple of months ago. I know so many melodies, but not that one, and I asked her about it. She said it was a song that Abby liked to play on her parents' record player."

"How strange." Conflicting explanations occurred simultaneously to me. One was that this tale of Abby and her favorite song had been yet another devious trick that Willow and Lisa had played on Francine. Another explanation was that Francine was lying to me. I didn't want to think about the third possibility. "Did Lisa ride her bike to her friend's house this morning?"

"No, I had to drive her clear to the other side of town. It's not Lisa playing tricks this time, Erin."

So who'd been playing the music just now? Maybe Francine was indeed lying to me. Maybe it had been her electric organ after all, and her electronic controls had been on a different setting. "Why do you use the earphones? Don't you want to hear how your instrument will sound to an audience?"

"It's become such an ingrained habit, I can't break it. My ex-husband always used to get all upset about the 'noise' I was making, so I took to wearing the earphones whenever I'm home."

"Can you play a song for me?"

"I'd be happy to. Have a seat. I'll get us both some iced tea, all right? I have a pitcher of sun tea that's just now finished brewing."

"That sounds great. Thanks."

She smiled, rose, and headed toward the kitchen.

This was the perfect opportunity for me to examine her organ. If her musical instrument, like electronic keyboards, was capable of producing the sounds I'd heard, Francine would certainly never be so foolish as to let me hear those tones in whatever piece she was going to play for me. I crept over to the keyboard to see if there were any telltale switches or dials.

No sooner did I reach the instrument than there was a creaking noise over my head. I looked up just in time to see the chandelier falling straight toward me.

chapter 15

The chandelier's fall magically jerked to a stop, and I dived out from under it. An instant later, the enormous light fixture crashed to the floor behind me.

"Erin?" Francine shrieked as she charged back into the room. "Oh my God! The chandelier! Oh my God! How did that happen?"

I sat up and struggled to regain my wits, annoyed in spite of myself at the question. Did she think I'd decided to swing on her chandelier the moment she left the room?

The electrical wiring in the light fixture, I realized as I looked at the debris behind me, had delayed the fall of the heavy fixture for one miraculous second, just long enough for me to get out of the way.

The piano bench had been flattened. The keyboard was now off-kilter and badly damaged. The arms of the chandelier were hopelessly mangled. I got to my feet, brushing off my slacks. "I barely had the—"

"My organ! Oh my God! My instrument!"

Francine fell to her knees and was cradling a key that had broken off the keyboard. "This is going to take months to repair!" Dropping the key, she pressed the heels of her hands against her temples, moaning, "There's only one manufacturer of electric organs like this one in the area. Who knows if he'll even be able to fix it! My career's ruined! Not that I *have* a career. They chose another stand-in at yesterday's concert. I haven't had a gig in months."

"I thought you had a concert just last week. The night Willow died."

"Oh, that . . . fell through." She rose. "Help me move the chandelier."

"No. Don't touch it. Let's let the police examine it."

She froze. "The police? This was an accident. You and I are the only people in the house."

"Light fixtures don't fall on their own accord. Someone had to have loosened the bolts." I glanced at the ceiling, the hairs at the back of my neck rising. "Are . . . you sure nobody's upstairs?"

"Positive."

Despite her confident reply, I remained skeptical. She had just gotten through telling me she'd driven Lisa to a friend's house, so someone could have sneaked inside the house in the interim; Willow had scaled the stone siding to reach the third floor, and now the windows were missing several panes. Even so, the idea of going upstairs myself to investigate did not appeal to me. "At least nobody got hurt. Or killed."

"True. My God. I could have been killed if this had happened just two minutes earlier." She pointed at the flattened bench. "I'd have been sitting right there."

I rubbed at my sore elbow and grabbed my cell phone, hoping she didn't expect my sympathy. "I'll see if my friend Officer Linda Delgardio can be the one to come out."

Linda arrived twenty minutes later. We escorted her to the damaged second-floor room. Francine insisted that she hadn't seen or heard anything to indicate that the supports for the heavy fixture had been loosened. "Did either of you touch the chandelier?" Linda asked.

"No," I said.

Francine added, "Erin wouldn't even let me move it to get it off my electric organ."

"Good. Maybe we can get some prints."

"Lisa sometimes makes a game of jumping up and touching it," Francine quickly interjected.

"Okay," Linda said while jotting a note in her pad. "If we find her prints on the chandelier, we'll know to eliminate them."

Francine pursed her lips and gave a grim nod.

"Do you use a cleaning service?"

Francine shook her head. "I fired them two months ago. 'Maid for You' was their name. For what it's worth, I don't recommend them. I doubt they ever touched my chandelier, let alone cleaned it."

"How long has the light been hanging there?" Linda

asked as she looked up from her notes. "Did it predate your buying the house?"

"No, I hired Ralph Appleby to hang it for me there nearly two years ago."

"His prints should be on it, too, then," Linda muttered.

I studied the supports for the heavy light fixture. "Look at this, Linda." I pointed at the metal rod visible in the hole in the ceiling. "Ralph installed the chandelier from underneath it by using that support rod. It lengthens as you twist it, till the spikes on either end bite into the joists. It's still securely fastened. The bolts fastening the fixture to the rod were removed."

"So could the bolts have been accessed from above, or below?" she asked, standing beside me to shine the beam of her flashlight into the hole.

"Either way, but it'd have been safer and easier for whoever sabotaged it to reach them from above."

"Through the *floorboards?*" Francine asked.

"Remember that Ralph was replacing a couple of the boards upstairs."

"Let's go take a look," Linda suggested.

We all tromped up the stairs. The floor was sanded and ready to be sealed, and only by tracing back from where we knew the wall had once stood were we able to identify the new planks Ralph had installed.

"Nobody could have gotten at the bolts through the new floorboards," Francine declared triumphantly. "They're too far away from the center of the room, where the chandelier's hanging. See? It was just an accident."

"Not from those boards, but maybe by removing another board directly above the light," Linda said thoughtfully.

"There are dents in this one," I said. "Right around the nail holes. And the nail heads are nicked."

Linda joined me to examine the board.

"That damage could have been done by the sander," Francine said.

"No, from these dents you can see precisely where a crowbar was used." I pressed down on the plank. It wobbled. "And look. The board's loose. That's how the bolts were accessed. Someone pulled up this plank, then stuck smaller nails in the holes to keep it in place."

"Have either of you been up here this morning?" Linda asked.

"No," we answered in unison.

"But nobody could have snuck up here today." Francine added, "I've been home all morning, and I—" She broke off. "Oh, that's right. The house was empty when I was driving Lisa to her friend's house. But even so, there are no intruders here now. At least, I don't . . . *think* there are."

Francine's bravura faded along with her voice as she eyed the closed door to the closet.

"I'll check the premises," Linda said firmly, "just to be certain."

Nobody was lurking in any of the rooms or the closets. Even Francine admitted it was possible that someone had scaled a wall in broad daylight and gotten in and out through a window in the tower room. However, with all the carpenters and movers going in and out of the house the past several days, it was more likely that someone had donned a workman's coveralls to sneak into the house and loosened the chandelier's bolts, leaving one or two barely attached so that the hundred-pound fixture would eventually fall. Maybe the motive was to scare Francine into selling her house or stopping the remodel. In any case, I was certain that the target had been Francine, not me.

That afternoon Sullivan and I had an appointment to work at Bob and Cassandra's. I headed over there a few minutes early. The front door was open. I rang the doorbell and heard Bob call, "Cassandra? Can you get that?" There was a pause. "Cassandra?" After a second pause, he strode into the foyer himself and smiled broadly at me. He was wearing shorts and sandals and looked remarkably fit.

"Why, if it isn't little Erin!"

"Hi, Bob." I had to admit that his familiar greeting had, once again, managed to cheer some of the glum out of me.

"Come on in!"

He held the door for me, and I brushed past him. I should have suggested this compromise—of Sullivan and my working together on both jobs—myself weeks ago; I had missed Bob's company, ever since the neighborhood brouhaha had begun. "Looks like I've beaten Sullivan here, but I thought I could use the head start familiarizing myself with what you all have in mind."

Bob ushered me upstairs, where Sullivan's plans were spread out on a built-in desk in the spare bedroom the Stanleys had converted into a library. "Make yourself comfortable, little lady, and I'll send Steve right up when he arrives."

"Thanks." Okay, I inwardly grumbled, not so crazy about the "little lady" designation. I took a seat in the pine slat-back desk chair and dutifully started to study Sullivan's plans, but couldn't get past the first drawing, which showed the den and the infamous bay window. The one *I'd* envisioned—back when we'd been planning on replacing the front windows—had been nearly twice this size.

It was unwise of me to start picturing my own designs for the Stanleys' house after being so adamant that Sullivan was to play second fiddle at Francine's. I pushed my chair back and scanned my surroundings. This room featured lovely built-ins that ran the length of two adjacent walls. The carpenter had done a nice job of varying the placement of the vertical supports so that such a large expanse of shelving wasn't monotonous. Some of the shelves had been crammed too full, tarnishing the room's ambience, which was something I would mention to them when it came time for the final brush-up preparations for the tour.

Just above the desk, a book caught my eye. Its jacket was bowed out from the spine, a bit too large for the book itself. Curious, I grabbed the book and peeked under its jacket. Underneath was a Colorado history book, which had the look and feel of a self-published work, although the jacket was for a Hemingway novel.

I riffled through its pages. The book naturally opened to a page, and the top paragraph on the right-hand side might as well have been highlighted, my eyes so quickly fell on its text:

> The house was built for Dr. Stuart in the late eighteen hundreds and is one of the grandest homes in all of Crestview. A considerable controversy erupted, however, when Bernard Chambers and his wife—a couple with a questionable background—bought the home from the Stuarts in the fifties and promptly constructed the infamous octagonal tower. At least a dozen neighbors protested that the tower was an eyesore and were even more offended when Bernard Chambers built a deck on its roof. Chambers soon came to deeply regret that decision when, in the 1960s, his only child, fourteen-year-old Abby Chambers, jumped to her death from the third-floor roof.

A board creaked. Someone was standing behind me. Hoping it was Sullivan, I turned and saw Bob, his jaw muscles working and his gaze withering. "Looking through my personal items, Erin? Do you always take such liberties with your clients' possessions?"

"I'm sorry, Bob. I didn't mean to pry. When I saw what it was, I couldn't help but want to read the history of the house that I'm currently designing."

"I should have put this away," he said, snatching the

book from my hands and slamming it shut. He wedged it into a shelf at my eye level and then jammed it into place with the heel of his hand. The paper jacket was badly creased in the process.

Anxious, I got up and pushed the small desk chair back into place, my stomach in knots. Hoping that Bob's anger would pass as quickly as it had emerged, I asked, "What did it mean when it said that Abby's parents had a 'questionable background'?"

"Mr. Chambers was Jewish and was born in Switzerland, so he had a foreign accent." Though Bob's tone was still harsh, he was ever the rabid local historian. He continued, "There were some anti-Semitic idiots in the neighborhood at the time who insisted he'd gotten his money by embezzling it, but that was never proven. He was a nice, quiet man, and—"

A thump on the roof made us both jump and look up at the ceiling. "Huh." He glanced at the wide-open window. "That explains why Cassandra didn't hear me calling for her earlier. She's sitting on the roof again." He glared at me. "Seems like the women in this neighborhood are making her daft." He pivoted and left the room.

I stared after him. Maybe he felt I was invading his turf in boning up on local history as well as reading his book without his permission. The one paragraph was the extent of the information on the Findleys' house. If there were any secrets in that particular book, they had to be well hidden.

The last time I'd been in this room, over a month ago, I'd noticed the spines of two CHS yearbooks. My looking through those truly would have been nosy of me. I glanced at the shelf, but the books were no longer there. Out of idle curiosity, I scanned the four shelves tall enough to hold yearbooks, but they were nowhere in sight.

Hoping Bob's wife was in a better mood than Bob himself was, I leaned out the window and found Cassandra sitting between the dormers, gazing at the Findleys' house. "Hi, Cassandra. I'm here to work on your design with Steve Sullivan."

She glanced at me and, thankfully, smiled. "I *thought* I recognized your voice. Good afternoon, Erin. I was just . . . meditating. I do this a lot. The roof pitch is negligible, and the foliage from our cottonwoods makes it quite private up here. Care to join me?"

"Sure," I said, and easily climbed out the window while she scooted over. "The trees really do make it so nice and cool . . . and almost cozy up here."

"Yes, but I can see the widow's walk very clearly." She forced a chuckle. "Just think how nervous that would make Francine, if she realized how well I can see what she's doing when she's up there."

Francine told me she had acrophobia. "What do you mean?"

Cassandra shrugged. "I spotted her up there a couple of times, searching for something."

"After we'd taken down the wall to the staircase, I assume."

"No, before then, actually. It struck me as so odd, because she once told me she was terrified by heights, yet there she was way up there on her roof. She had to have climbed quite a tall ladder to get there."

"Maybe her phobia comes and goes."

"Indeed. And she must have dropped something between the floorboards during one of her non-phobic spells."

I nodded and said nothing, though I couldn't help but wonder if there was a connection between Francine's search and Willow's having pocketed a small object that she'd said was a quarter.

A silence grew, and I mulled over whether or not to express my sympathies for the loss of her daughter. I asked myself what my mother's advice to me would have been and knew at once she would have told me, "Honesty is always the best policy." (My adoptive mother had been a wise and wonderful woman, but she did have an annoying tendency to spout clichés.)

"Cassandra? I don't want to upset you again and probably shouldn't mention it, but now that Diana told me about your loss, I wanted to say how very sorry I am."

She winced. "That's why I'm up here now, as a matter of fact. I've been trying to talk with Katelyn. My daughter."

Her climbing out on her roof to talk with her dead daughter was so sad that I added, "I know there's no greater loss than that of your child. I can't even begin to fathom it."

Cassandra tucked an errant lock of her wavy hair behind her ear. "Katelyn's death is what got me involved in the occult in the first place. Maybe it's just a superstition, but I'm afraid that . . . she'll go away if I talk about her. That she'll stop appearing in my dreams and stop conversing with me." She sighed and added, "I've been up here half an hour, and nothing."

I didn't know how to respond and held my tongue.

Cassandra gave me a sad smile. "You think I'm crazy."

"No, I don't. I—"

"Bob doesn't believe it, either, but he humors me, most of the time. Meanwhile, my daughter told me that Abby doesn't like Bob. And that neither does Willow."

"Did Katelyn tell you *why* they don't like him?"

"No." She frowned. "He *is* my husband. I'm sure Katelyn didn't want to turn me against him."

Bugle started barking, which drew our attention. "There goes Francine," Cassandra said.

Wearing a tight, hot-pink sleeveless dress, Francine trotted toward the carriage-house-cum-garage, her exaggerated gait making it obvious she was wearing heels. She was certainly dressed to kill, especially for the middle of the day.

Francine tossed some small object into Diana's backyard, and Bugle promptly quit barking to chase after it.

Cassandra clicked her tongue. "She's throwing dog biscuits again. She does that whenever she wants to shut Bugle up so she can sneak out without Diana noticing. I guess Francine doesn't realize she's inadvertently trained the dog to bark for a treat every time she leaves the house."

My thoughts snapped back unwittingly to Bugle's barking the night I'd spied "Abby" on Francine's roof, and to how he'd barked the night of the murder.

There'd been a bounce to Francine's step as she made her way to her garage that made me suspect she was off to meet a man. Perhaps this was a lovers' rendezvous with Hugh Black. I wondered if Lisa was home alone.

"Gilbert?" a deep voice called from below. I looked down. Sullivan, standing in the Stanleys' backyard. "Hello, Cassandra. How are you?"

We both grinned and waved at him. I could get used to looking down on him like this.

"Shouldn't you be looking at the *interior* of the house, not the neighbors' lawns?" he said.

"Be right there," I replied. I scooted toward the open window, then hesitated when I realized Cassandra was staying put. "We're going to discuss Sullivan's plans for the kitchen now. You're joining us, aren't you?"

"Not this time. I told Bob he could handle it." She added glumly, "These past few days, I've kind of lost interest in the whole redecorating thing. If it were up to me, we'd cancel out on the homes tour entirely."

Bob, Sullivan, and I moved to the kitchen for our discussion. We sat around his chrome-edged, white-and-silver-flecked Formica table, which had fallen so out of fashion that it was retro and actually quite appealing. Though I tried to stay mum—I counted all the way to twenty in silence—I did voice my concern that some of their choices regarding the kitchen upgrade would make the room a bit out of step with the rest of the house. I suggested that they might want to reconsider at least the ultramodern cabinets. To my surprise, Sullivan agreed with me and had even come prepared with several pamphlets of product lines that reflected a classic style, more in keeping with a historical home.

Afterward, we left together, and he promptly ushered me into his van, shut the doors, and declared, "So, Gilbert. Any particular reason you were hanging out on the roof with a murder suspect?"

I almost retorted that it was safer than hanging out underneath large chandeliers, but answered instead, "I feel sorry for her and wanted to establish some camaraderie. Yesterday Diana blabbed about Cassandra's daughter from a previous marriage having been killed in a car accident. Apparently her daughter went to high school with Willow in Colorado Springs, and Willow's boyfriend was drunk behind the wheel."

"Huh. I've been through every inch of their house. I've never seen as much as a photograph of a girl who could have been her child."

"She doesn't like the painful reminders, and she thinks talking about her daughter might . . . drive away her spirit, or something." I paused. "In which case, wouldn't you have to wonder why Cassandra would hire, and then fire, someone so closely related to a personal tragedy?"

At a client's house in south Crestview a couple of

hours later, my cell phone rang, its sound muted from its perch inside a compartment of my purse. I answered, "Interiors by Gilbert. Erin speaking."

"Erin. You need to come home. Now."

"Audrey? What's wrong?"

"You'll see when you get here." She hung up.

I apologized profusely to my client and explained that I had an emergency at home and left. I drove home, agonizing over every red light along the way, imagining the house in flames, or Hildi on death's doorway. I was relieved to see that the house looked fine from the outside. I found a parking space right in front of the walkway.

Audrey met me in the foyer. She was holding a standard-sized white envelope. Handing it to me, she said, "Someone stuck this through our mail slot." The envelope was unsealed, and I looked inside.

An orange flower, pressed flat, was inside, along with a note. On a small piece of white paper in shaky block letters were the words:

NEXT TIME, ERIN, I WON'T MISS!!

chapter 16

What does 'next time I won't miss' mean?" Audrey asked.

"The falling chandelier," I promptly replied.

"What 'falling chandelier'?" Audrey asked in alarm.

"This morning I nearly got clocked by the crystal chandelier in Francine's music room. It's similar to the one in our foyer, but larger. I'm moving it up to the third floor. Once it gets repaired, that is."

"Someone nearly killed you today?" Audrey cried, my attempt at distracting her with a few designer details having missed its mark. Not unlike the chandelier.

"No, Audrey. It was just a coincidence that I happened to be in the room when it fell."

"Well, it certainly doesn't *sound* like a mere coincidence to me, now that you've been sent a note like this!"

I returned my attention to the crushed flower in the envelope. "This looks just like the lily that Steve Sullivan gave me before our date last Friday. It vanished a couple of days ago. It was starting to wilt, and I assumed you'd thrown it out."

"That flower you had on the curio cabinet in the parlor?" Audrey asked.

Hildi meowed a greeting to me, but I was too intrigued by our most recent mystery to respond.

"Yes, the one in the crystal bud vase."

"I didn't throw it out. I assumed *you* did. In fact, I was looking for that vase yesterday. It was the perfect size for an iris from the back garden with a broken stem."

Bewildered, I wandered into the parlor, heading straight for the plump sage sofa. Some people have comfort foods; I have comfort furniture. I started to snatch up the damask accent pillow, but Hildi provided even better solace by hopping onto my lap. I hugged her in gratitude and said to Audrey, "We need to think back and figure out who's been at our house since this flower first disappeared."

"That's going to be a challenge. Quite a few neighbors have been stopping by. That tends to happen when anything unsettling happens around here, and a young woman's murder more than qualifies." She paused, then grinned. "So Steve Sullivan brought you that flower?"

"Audrey, that's hardly the issue right now. The flower was here on Tuesday when I left for work. It was gone that evening when I returned."

"So it disappeared the night before last. Now I just have to remember who was here on which day." She rubbed her forehead, muttering under her breath, "It's not as if I have visitors sign and time-stamp a guest book." She paced along the narrow clutter-free path from the foyer to the dining room. Watching her, I made a mental note to rotate the luxurious Oriental rug soon to reduce traffic-pattern wear. "Bob Stanley stopped by looking for you one day. I think it was Tuesday. Diana came over to chat about the home tour. That had to have been Tuesday, because it was right before she asked me to be a hostess. I think Cassandra came by for tea that afternoon. Though it could have been Monday. . . ."

"No visits from Francine? Or Hugh?"

"Please. Not much chance of either of them coming

here. Oh, wait. Hugh *was* here. Asking me out. But he only came in as far as the foyer. And I was with him the whole time." She furrowed her brow. "No, that's wrong. I'd gotten him a glass of water. He'd gone into one of his patented coughing routines as a stall tactic."

I sighed. I nudged Hildi off my lap and reached for the phone. "I'm calling Linda Delgardio. Unfortunately, she probably thinks we consider her our own personal police officer, by now."

Linda arrived in less than fifteen minutes. The three of us took seats at the dining room table—currently the least cluttered room with adequate seating—and Audrey filled her in on all the details regarding the calla lily I'd gotten from Steve and how she'd discovered the envelope and its contents. Linda asked me, "Do you think the note is referring to the chandelier?"

"Yes, but—"

"You knew about that?" Audrey interrupted, glaring first at Linda, then at me. "Apparently I'm the last to know that somebody nearly killed you today!"

"I couldn't have been the intended target, though." I said to Linda, "You searched the house. There was nobody else there."

She replied, "Is it possible somebody sneaked down the stairs and out of the house before I arrived?"

I hesitated and could feel the heat from Audrey's glare as she awaited the answer. "I guess that's possible," I reluctantly admitted.

Audrey slapped the table, making me flinch. I

couldn't help but look to see if she'd dented the mahogany, but the rich, glossy surface appeared to be fine.

"We went downstairs after the crash and waited for you in the kitchen," I said. "Francine was flustered, so she turned on her radio to listen to music and calm herself. I guess it's possible someone could have slipped down the stairs after us, stayed out of sight, and then crept out the back door when we both went to the front door to let you in. It is a big house, and it's built so solidly there're only one or two noisy steps. Even so, I can't imagine anyone taking such a big gamble." Plus, I *really* didn't want to accept the possibility that a killer had turned his or her sights on me.

"You never know what someone will decide they can get away with," Linda countered bluntly, rising. "Especially when they think a possible witness is going to be dead."

Audrey gasped and gave me a piercing look that I knew was a precursor to a mammoth lecture on the subject of my personal safety. She got to her feet and stood over me, her arms crossed. Somewhere at that moment, my mother was no doubt looking down on us, pleased that at least her disciplinarian role had been nicely filled by my landlady.

Linda collected the envelope and its strange contents from the table. "I'm going to take this to the lab." She winked at Audrey, then touched my shoulder. "Not that this warning will do any good, but, please, Erin, consider staying at a friend's house for a while.

Preferably one on the East Coast."

Early the next morning, Francine called me, ecstatic with the news that the movers were finally coming over in half an hour. True to their word this time, they arrived, and Francine, Lisa, and I watched as the crane safely lifted her beloved piano—wrapped up like a mummy—to the top floor. Virtually the entire neighborhood came out to witness the event as well, with Diana eventually having to put Bugle inside the house to mute his barking.

Afterward, Francine checked her piano and pronounced it unharmed. She then promptly had the workers wrap it back up in the company's mummy wrappings, which she arranged to purchase. She vowed the instrument would remain snuggly under wraps until the room had been completed around her grand piano. She also paid the movers to take her electric organ to wherever she'd arranged to have it repaired.

The moment the movers left, she insisted on calling the window installers herself to give them the news that they could now put the remaining windows in place. I'd never seen her—or Lisa—happier: the latter had a burst of very un-preteenager-like sharing of her mother's joy.

After leaving Francine's, I called Steve Sullivan from my office and told him about my near miss with a crashing chandelier and the threatening note that I'd received and had given to the police. Afterward I said, "This is just a product of how warped my mind gets when I'm exhausted, but I had a bout of insomnia last night and envisioned someone hiding behind the closet, having placed a tapered pin in the place of the chandelier bolt and tying the pin to a string, so that he could yank on the string, and the chandelier would drop when he heard my voice below him."

"You're right," Sullivan said promptly. "Your brain's warped. You're talking about someone being able to pull a pin free that's supporting a hundred pounds, just by tugging on a string."

"Physically impossible, I know. Still, I need to go back upstairs and reexamine that hiding space. I'd like to see if I can identify the voices of the occupants in the room below when I'm inside it."

"That reminds me. Did you tell Linda about that crawl space?"

"Oh. Good point. No, I haven't. Maybe the police already know about it, though. They had the room sealed off as a crime scene, and Lisa had claimed to be trapped in the closet by the killer."

"The police had no reason to be looking for cubby-holes behind the closet. If they'd found it, they'd've torn up the whole back of the closet and would've seen the 'Leave me alone or die.' "

"Another good point."

"I'm on a roll."

"Yes, you're a regular pincushion today, full of good points. I'll tell Linda about the crawl space tomorrow. After I've had a chance to check it out again for myself. After all, *I'm* the one who wound up nearly getting flattened. I have a meeting with the Findleys at four o'clock this afternoon to discuss Lisa's bedroom. Can you come, too? I need you to keep Lisa and Francine distracted downstairs while I check out the closet. I've got the room plans already worked up, so you'll just need to go over those with them."

"It'd make more sense for *me* to look at the closet space and for *you* to be showing them your new plans."

"Except you're never going to fit in that tiny space . . . and there won't be a good excuse for you to be rattling around in the tower room while we're discussing Lisa's bedroom. So this time I get to be the snoop."

"Lisa, the time has come," Francine announced in a no-nonsense voice in front of Sullivan and me some three hours later. "We're either remodeling your room, or it stays as is."

"Fine. Let's go for it. I already decided I want to stay in my bedroom. That tower room's too creepy."

I helped Sullivan get started with the presentation, which we gave in Lisa's bedroom. Five minutes into the discussion, I interrupted Sullivan and said, "While he's showing you this, I want to run upstairs and take some more window measurements, now that the piano's finally up there. I'll just be a few minutes."

I dashed upstairs before anyone could object. I'd brought a screwdriver in my purse, and I opened the back of the closet as quickly and quietly as I could. There was no need to test the theory of someone having hidden themselves in the small space, thereby foiling Linda's search. The drywall and chair rail could only have been put into place from the *front* of the closet.

I knelt in the closet, hearing nothing at all. Last night I'd assumed that voices would carry between floors the easiest from the closet—the landing in the attic notwithstanding—but now that I was here, another possibility hit me: there was a heating duct in the floor. By pressing my ear to the duct, I could hear the murmuring of the conversation in Lisa's bedroom. Yesterday Francine's and my voices would surely have carried much better from the room directly below this one. This duct was only two or three strides from the center of the room. Anyone familiar with my and Francine's patterns could indeed have timed the drop of the chandelier; he or she would only have needed to be aware that Francine practiced in that room every day, and that I went in to say good-bye to her every day before I left.

A sunbeam slanted across the lovely unfinished heart-pine floor, illuminating the closet. Somehow it seemed like a message from on high that I was missing something. I crossed the room again, lay down on the closet floor, and stared up at the two-by-four with its leave-me-alone-or-die message. The board bearing the words wasn't level. I pushed against it and realized the board hadn't been fastened into place, it had simply been wedged between the two studs. Out of curiosity, I started to work it free.

As I pulled out the short two-by-four, something

metallic fell from one end. Perplexed, I examined the piece of wood in my hands. A wide, shallow hole had been bored into one end of the board.

I retrieved what I first assumed was a coin. It looked like a dull metal tag, perhaps made of zinc. The tag was oval shaped and bore a pair of four-digit numbers, and the large letter *A* stamped on it. The information embossed in the top and bottom halves of the oval was identical.

Footsteps! Someone was coming up the stairs. Heart racing, I stuck the tag into the pocket of my slacks, jammed the board back between the studs, and tried to wrestle the drywall in place.

"Yeah, Erin's up here now. Measuring for the window treatments," Sullivan was saying in a half shout, obviously trying to give me some warning.

The screws weren't going in fast enough! It felt as though my stupid fingers were only capable of moving at half speed.

"Thought she already did that," a voice rumbled. I instantly recognized the low tones. Ralph Appleby.

The doorknob was turning. There was no time to get the last screws tight. There was *also* no reason for me to be sitting by the closet when measuring windows. I scrambled to my feet. Why had Ralph come into the house without ringing the doorbell? And where the hell was my tape measure?

The door swung open. I tried to hide my screwdriver in my waistband. To my horror, a fingernail caught on the fabric of my slacks, and the metal tag I'd only just now found popped out of my pocket. It skittered across the floor, directly in front of the door. I lunged after it, only to have Ralph Appleby grab it just a half second ahead of my grasp.

"Oops," I said to him. "That's mine. I dropped it." I got to my feet, trying to muster as much dignity as possible, considering I'd all but prostrated myself in front of him.

He ignored me and studied the tag in his hand. Meanwhile, Sullivan, a step behind Ralph, was staring aghast at me. I gave him a grimace in a silent *Well? Too late to do anything about this now!*

Ralph finally handed the metal tag back to me, glowering. "This is *yours?*"

"Yes. I dropped it."

"You were in the military?"

"No, my father was. It's one of his dog tags."

"And he was in World War II?"

"Yes." I was adopted; he could have been almost any age at the time, I reasoned wildly, in silence. Despite my reassuring logic, my cheeks were growing warmer by the moment.

Ralph continued to hold my gaze, his own expression increasingly skeptical. "Fighting as a German soldier?"

"Um . . ." That was a bit too much of a stretch. "Not that I know of. Gee. Maybe that isn't my father's after all."

He held my gaze.

"How did you know it was a German soldier's dog

tag?" Sullivan asked him.

"My dad served in World War II. He died when I was just a baby and Mom gave me his dog tags. It was all I had to remember him by." He shrugged. "Did some research on ID tags."

My thoughts raced. Apparently the owner of this dog tag was trying to hide his affiliation during the war. "Ralph, do you know if Abby's father served in World War II, by any chance?"

"Abby told me he didn't . . . that he was living in Switzerland during the war."

Yikes! If Ralph was the killer, I'd just tipped my hand by letting him know I suspected the tags were a clue to Abby's death. To shift the focus off me and the German dog tags, I blurted out, "Lisa found the portrait you did of Abby."

He dragged his palm across his scalp. "*What* portrait?"

"The one you did years ago, in high school. Lisa found it hidden behind her closet and she's been hiding it in her room ever since. She forgot to hide it one time, though, and her mother and I spotted it."

I gave Sullivan a quick glance and realized he knew very little about the portrait; I'd merely mentioned it in passing once. He was keeping his features inscrutable.

Ralph sighed and asked, "How'd you know I painted it?"

"From the drawings you did of Willow for the bust. I recognized your style."

He grunted. "Haven't taken an art class since I

dropped out of high school after my junior year. Haven't improved much."

"Did you know the portrait was back there, Ralph?" I asked.

"Back where?"

"Behind the closet. In the secret storage space."

He patted his stomach. "Look at me, Erin. Think I can fit into a gap that's just eighteen inches wide?"

I studied his craggy features and put two and two together. "You built it yourself, didn't you? That's how you knew it was there."

He hesitated, blinked a couple of times, but then nodded. "Abby asked me to build it. She knew I was working construction on weekends. Said she needed a hiding space in her room. I cut out the Sheetrock from the back wall of her closet and moved it forward. Put in that phony chair rail and trim to cover up the opening. Her parents never even noticed."

"Why did she feel she needed a hiding place?"

"Wouldn't really tell me. As Stanley likes to broadcast to anyone who'll listen, she was experimenting with drugs a little. So were lots of kids, though."

"Yourself included?" I asked.

"And I got caught at it and had to pay the price," he retorted. "That was a long time ago. I don't use drugs now." He glanced at the closet and said sadly, "Figured she needed a place to hide some personal belongings, case she needed to run away."

"Were her parents abusive?" Sullivan asked.

"No way. But Stanley lived right next door. Figured

maybe she'd been looking for a place to hide from *him*."

"Did you ever have any proof that Bob killed her?" I asked gently.

He nodded. "In art class one time we were passing notes back and forth. Abby wrote me that Stanley was stalking her . . . trying to force her into going out with him. I kept the note. Figured I might need to give it to the police someday. But then his goons took it off me."

"His *goons?*" Sullivan repeated.

"I was just a scrawny kid then. Stanley was a pip-squeak himself, but his dad gave him lots of money, so he bought himself some big friends . . . linebackers on the football team."

"And they knew about the note somehow?" I asked.

"It fell out of the shelf of my locker when they were banging me into it. Broke my collarbone in the process. Stanley snatched up Abby's note . . . started to read it out loud like it was a love note he could taunt me with . . . till he realized who wrote it 'n' what it was about. Then he just wadded it up in his fist. Six weeks later, Abby was dead. Then, when her parents had me build the wall, I snuck a look behind the closet, hoping I'd find some evidence . . . her diary or another note, sayin' how scared she was that he'd hurt her, but . . . just the portrait was back there. Nothing else."

Sullivan asked, "Did you tell the police about your suspicions at the time?"

"Tried to. Hell, I had a juvie record. Got caught with some pot when I was sixteen. The Stanleys were these big-deal upper-crusters. Ran a business supporting a couple hundred families. Whose story were the cops gonna believe?" He snorted with disgust. "Whole thing made me so sick, I never did return to high school for my senior year."

"Yet you've worked off and on in Bob's neighborhood for years now," I said. "You and he have peacefully coexisted until now, right? What changed?"

He smirked. "I guess I like being the fly in Stanley's ointment. Figure it has to drive him nuts . . . having me, here, right under his nose, knowing what he did. And now that he's killed again, I ain't letting him get away a second time." He held my gaze for a long moment. "*That's* what changed."

He crossed the room, eyeing the piano in its wrappings. "Gotta get to work now." He shook his head, muttering, "Francine's too stubborn for her own good. Now the floor refinishers gotta finish the floor in two stages, so we can move the piano into place without scuffing the boards up."

As I descended the stairs with Sullivan, I whispered, "What if Willow knew about the hidden space behind the closet? And that the dog tag is what she really found on the roof? Maybe that's why the killer came into the house that night. Willow planned to reveal the German dog tag in its new hiding spot in the closet. Maybe she even saw that Lisa was hiding there, so she led the killer onto the roof to give Lisa time to escape."

He shook his head. "No way. If Willow had something she was blackmailing somebody over, she'd have held on to it."

"True." I sighed.

Lisa dashed out of her room to greet us in the hallway. "There you are," she said with a big smile. "My mom was about to send a search party up for you."

"Sullivan and I had to talk to Ralph for a few minutes. Shall we get back to our plans for your fantastic new room?"

The following morning, to my considerable annoyance, Bugle, Diana's dog, was barking incessantly. This being a Saturday, he was probably annoying the whole neighborhood as well. I toyed with the notion of hollering out the back door at him, then realized that Bugle's barks were coming from the front of our house. Diana had installed one of those "invisible fences," and I'd never known the dog to escape till now.

About to leave and head to my office, I decided to check on Bugle in the process. I gathered my keys and purse and went out to the front porch. Hugh Black was heading up the walkway.

I locked up. Hugh smiled and continued toward me. "Good morning, Erin," he said, climbing the porch steps. "Is Audrey home?"

"No, she's interviewing an expert on stamp collecting this morning."

"Oh, right." He waited for me and walked back down

the steps by my side. "That silly television show of hers is still on."

"I very much doubt that Audrey would like to hear her job described as 'silly.' "

"*Domestic Bliss with Audrey Munroe* is not exactly . . . *CNN Headline News*, though." He dutifully turned with me as I headed toward my car, parked closer to the Stanleys' house than to mine, but gave a longing glance at Audrey's door. "Has she said anything about me, Erin? About the chances of our getting back together again?"

"Yes, and I've got to say, they don't look good."

He remained glued to my side as I rounded my van and unlocked my door. "Any advice?"

I slid behind the wheel of my car. "Such as 'give up,' you mean?"

He glared at me through the open door. "For an interior designer and a woman, you don't seem to have a whole lot of empathy for other people."

Though it was ridiculous to take offense at anything the man said to me, his remark stung. "You don't know me well enough to judge my level of empathy."

"And *you* don't know me well enough to judge my relationship with my ex-wife."

Sorely tempted to point out that I *did* know his ex-wife well enough to draw some solid conclusions about their former marriage, I chose not to respond. I watched in my rearview mirror as Hugh stormed off toward his own car—a silver BMW. I started my engine. Although Diana's beagle was not in sight, he was still barking relentlessly.

I took a quick detour and drove around the corner, trying to follow the unmistakably shrill bark. I spotted the beagle in the corner lot two houses down from Diana's. I parked and coaxed him toward me. Bugle took a few steps, then sat down and started barking again, but I closed the gap, scooped him up, and carried him the short distance to Diana's front door. The screen door was shut, but the main door was wide open. I rang the doorbell and called, "Diana?" Just then, Bugle scrambled from my arms, so I opened the screen door rather than have him run away again. Bugle barged inside, and I stepped inside after him, calling, "It's Erin. I found—"

I gasped as I peered into the living room. Diana was sprawled on the floor. Her skin tones were the ice-blue color of death. Beside her, Cassandra Stanley knelt, her eyes wide, clutching a pink heart-shaped satin pillow in both hands.

chapter 17

Bugle trotted over to Diana's motionless body and sat down, panting. I was too shocked to move. This was my hometown, my quaint, picturesque neighborhood, almost my very own backyard. What in God's name was happening? Was Diana, too, now dead?

My world was being turned upside down and shaken like a snow-dome souvenir.

"Erin," Cassandra said as she rose and dropped the pillow. "Thank God you're here. We've got to call the police! Somebody killed Diana!"

I studied her tense features, unable to decide whether Cassandra was merely shocked at her grim discovery or upset that I had stumbled onto the scene before she could slip away. Diana was wearing a pink terry-cloth bathrobe over purple pajamas, a shiny synthetic blend. "Maybe she's still alive. Maybe we can save her."

I started to bend over Diana, but Cassandra put a hand on my shoulder. "She's passed to the Other Side, Erin. I can tell."

"But have you tried to revive her? Maybe she's just—"

"I'm Red Cross certified. There's no pulse. She's not breathing. The pillow was on her face when I got here. Somebody suffocated her."

I had to battle back tears. "When?"

"I don't know. Last night, maybe."

"I meant, when did you get here? What were you doing here?"

"I was out taking a walk and saw that her door was wide open. That's not like Diana at all. When I knocked and she didn't answer, I let myself in, and I found her like this."

I felt like screaming in rage and horror. Another woman in my immediate neighborhood dead! Who was doing this to us? Was Cassandra guilty? "When?" I asked again. I spotted a cordless phone faceup on the coffee table and picked it up.

"Just now." She studied my face. "Why? Surely you don't think *I* did this, do you?"

"No," I said automatically, dialing 911. "I just wonder how the dog got loose. Somebody had to have let Bugle out recently."

"I did. By mistake. He darted out when I let myself in. I was afraid he'd get hit by a car and wound up chasing him halfway through the neighborhood, before I gave up and doubled back to check on Diana . . . and found her like this."

The dispatcher answered while Cassandra was talking, and I struggled with the lump in my throat as I said, "My name is Erin Gilbert. I need to report a murder."

My police interview was lengthy and draining. Afterward I canceled my appointments for the day and went home. By then the neighborhood was in a major upheaval at the news of a second murder, this time to one of its longtime residents. Our phone rang incessantly: neighbors sought Audrey's reassurances that everything was going to be all right. I needed her to get off the phone and talk with me.

As I waited for her to complete this latest call so that I could suggest we turn off the ringer, the doorbell rang. I dragged myself to the foyer to answer. It was Lisa Findley. She was hugging herself and shifting her weight from foot to foot and immediately said, "Hi, um, Erin? I, um, I just kind of wondered if . . . What's going on next door? There's, like, all sorts of police cars there and stuff."

"Is your mom home?"

"No, she's in Denver or someplace, but she'll be back soon. I just got back home from an overnight at a friend's. Her mom was kind of worried about leaving me alone, so she drove me here, instead." She pointed behind her with her thumb. "I told her I'd come over here and find out what's happened."

I peered past Lisa's shoulder. There was a metallic-blue minivan with its engine idling in front of the house. The woman driver had hunched down to watch us through the passenger window. A girl in the back-seat was also staring at us. The woman met my gaze and rolled down the window. Feeling drained to the point of numbness, I pretended not to understand that she wanted me to come speak to her and, instead, gave her an okay sign.

"Come inside, Lisa."

She stepped into the foyer and waited while I shut the door behind her. "Something bad happened to Diana?" she asked me.

I winced, wishing I didn't have to answer. Was Francine going to accuse me of overstepping my bounds if I told Lisa the truth? "Yes, I'm afraid so. She's dead."

"Was she murdered?"

"I don't know," I said, skirting the issue a little.

She pouted and crossed her arms, looking decidedly younger than her twelve years. "Bet she was. Bet there's a killer on the loose."

"Or else Diana died of natural causes." With a pillow over her face. It was possible.

Lisa crossed her arms tightly and stared at the floor. "I was mean to her," she said in a near whisper.

"To Diana?"

"And Willow. I was mean to both of them." She was trembling.

I'd made a stupid mistake; I should have spoken to her friend's mother, allowed them to keep Lisa with them until Francine returned. "We all say things we regret, Lisa."

She reached for the doorknob. "My mom's gonna freak if I'm missing when she gets home and sees all the police and junk next door."

"Why don't we write her a note telling her that you're over here?"

Lisa chewed on her lower lip, not answering. Audrey came into the foyer and said gently, "Hello, Lisa. It's a good idea to leave your mother a note. Let me get a pen and piece of paper for you."

Lisa insisted on taking the note to her house herself, but agreed to let me accompany her. We took the long way there, around the block. She hadn't said an unnecessary word, and her steps now were dragging, as though she wanted to delay our arrival. Her every movement suggested to me that some major pronouncement was building up in her like a teakettle before it whistles. Now I sorely wished I'd brought Audrey with us. If Lisa was on the verge of admitting she'd seen Willow's killer's face, I wanted to let Audrey be in charge.

"I overheard a huge argument between my parents," Lisa muttered abruptly when we reached her front walk. "Two years ago. My dad's not really my dad."

"Oh, Lisa," I said sadly.

"After that, my father moved out right away."

"I'm so sorry. Your . . . mother knows you overheard the argument, doesn't she?"

She shook her head.

I cursed in silence. I should have encouraged the girl to stay with her friend at a time like this, when a traumatic event had taken place right next to her home. Meanwhile, I didn't have the slightest idea of how to respond to such a painful confession. Not knowing what else to say, I opted to make a painful confession of my own. "I was adopted. When I was almost two years old. Then my adoptive father left my mother when I was twelve."

"My age." She hesitated. "Has your mom remarried?"

"No." In her current mood, I didn't want to reveal that my mother had died.

"*Mine* will. She wants to marry a real creep. She's known him for a long time. Now he's back in town all of a sudden."

She had to be referring to Hugh Black. "You don't like him, obviously."

She grimaced. "He's the worst."

"But your mom's in love with him?"

"I guess. Mom told me that she's known him since she was a kid, but he moves around a lot. And that he's finally come back for her."

Uh-oh. Now I was worried that Audrey's ex could be Lisa's biological father. I felt a little nauseated. Directly in front of us, the backdrop of the foothills was marred by the police yellow tape that stretched across Diana's entire front yard. A neon-yellow plastic reminder of how ugly things could become in a beautiful place.

Lisa said shyly as we started up her walkway, "Now that Willow's dead, you're the only adult I can really talk to."

"Thanks, but your mom seems like a fairly good listener."

She rolled her eyes and said nothing.

Francine's car sped into the driveway and screeched to a stop. She emerged from the car. She was once again dressed to the nines, wearing an elegant green dress and heels. "I'm so glad to see you, sweetie. I just heard about . . . what happened to Diana. I rushed right home."

"I'm fine," Lisa said flatly, apparently impervious to her mother's concern.

I explained, "She only just now got home from her friend's house and came over to find out what all the commotion was about next door. We were about to leave you a note."

"Thanks, Erin." Though she forced a smile, Francine's gaze was piercing as she met my eyes. "I don't know what we'd do without you."

At home that night, I stared out the kitchen window at the Findleys' house while waiting for my tea water to boil. How had everything gone so dreadfully wrong so fast?

Suddenly there was a faint image of a girl in white on the roof. My heart started pounding. In the blink of an eye she was gone, and this time, there was no thinking that I'd seen a ghost impersonator. Either I'd dozed off for an instant and dreamt the image, or I'd actually seen the ghost of Abby Chambers. I continued to watch the house, trying to see if the vision would return. I was so exhausted that it *was* possible I'd momentarily fallen asleep on my feet.

"What are you looking at?"

Audrey's unexpected voice made me jump. Feeling my face flush, I turned to face her.

"I was just looking out the window."

Audrey crossed her arms and arched an eyebrow. "You've been staring, not looking."

"I was watching for . . . a ghost. Cassandra told me that she'd seen one a couple of times. Just now, I thought I saw her myself."

Audrey didn't chuckle, or even smile. She merely looked out the window herself. "Maybe you *did*."

Suddenly I realized that I'd never actually asked Audrey about Abby Chambers's ghost. "Have you ever seen Abby yourself?"

She sighed. "Twice. Though not for almost three

years now. After I inadvertently saw Hugh and Francine embracing one night, I've made it a policy *not* to look at her house." The teakettle whistled, and Audrey turned off the burner and poured steaming water in the royal-blue-and-turquoise-checkered mug I'd set on the counter.

"But you definitely saw the ghost?"

"Both times I convinced myself it was a figment of my imagination . . . a reflection on the glass . . . steam from my coffee mug." She gave me a sad smile. "Eventually I decided it wasn't important. There's more than enough horror in life to scare oneself silly. Just look at what's happened here in the past couple of weeks. What's a ghost on a neighbor's roof in comparison?"

Francine called me Sunday night to tell me that the windows were going to be installed the next day. I was there to greet the work crew at seven a.m. Afterward, I drove to my office, needing to put the finishing touches on my presentation board for a client's bedroom. Sullivan stopped by my office not fifteen minutes later.

His gaze was smoldering as he climbed my stairs, but he said casually, "Aha. You're still alive."

"You heard about Diana Durst, I take it."

"You know, Gilbert, you don't seem to grasp this concept of working together. You didn't even call to tell me someone else in your neighborhood had been murdered. The whole point of the exercise is to *watch out* for one another."

He really meant he'd be watching out for *me,* not that I would be able to return the favor, but I let the remark slide. "Sorry."

He dropped into the antique leather smoking chair I'd recently acquired for my office—which was not to say that I allowed anyone to actually smoke in it. "What have you learned?"

"That my client's husband is slightly color-blind if he keeps insisting that this plum drapery fabric will go with burgundy walls."

"*About the murders,* Gilbert."

I shut the portfolio, satisfied with the swatches I'd selected and fastened on the board. "As a matter of fact, if you've got an hour free, you can help me."

He spread his arms. "I'm all yours."

Oh? I rose and grabbed my purse, trying to refocus.

"What's the game plan?" he asked.

"They have old CHS yearbooks at the Crestview Historical Library. We're going to see if we can find anything out about Bob Stanley and Ralph Appleby . . . and Abby Chambers."

I filled Sullivan in on yesterday's conversation with Ralph as we walked the five blocks to the library; with parking at a premium in downtown Crestview, it's most practical to walk short distances. Once there, we searched through the yearbooks from forty years earlier and soon found a picture of Abby Chambers in the freshman class. The photograph was the same one Ralph had used to create her portraits. She was a nice-looking girl—very young, huge smile, bright eyes.

I thumbed through to the photographs of the higher grade levels and discovered that Ralph and Bob were juniors when Abby was a freshman. Sullivan was drumming his fingers, so I said, "Could you look through the next yearbook and see if both Ralph and Bob are still at CHS?"

"Didn't Ralph say he dropped out?"

"Yes, but I want to double-check."

A minute or two later, while I was flipping through the yearbook in search of some telltale cameo photograph of the three of them, Sullivan reported, "Only Bob Stanley is listed."

"So Ralph must have . . ." I let my voice fade as I stared at a familiar face in the senior class, one year ahead of Ralph and Bob's graduating class. "Look at this, Sullivan," I said, pointing.

"Hugh Black," he said. He took the yearbook from my grasp.

"Strange that Ralph never mentioned Hugh being in high school with him and Abby Chambers."

He flipped to the back, and we looked up Hugh's name in the index, which listed his memberships. "It was a large school, though. They weren't even in the same graduating class. And, according to this, Hugh was a major jock."

"Was he on the football team?" I asked, not-too-politely snatching the book away from him in the process.

"Yeah. A linebacker."

"One of Bob's bodyguard buddies, maybe. Ralph

obviously had a crush on Abby and is certain that Bob killed her. Maybe he thinks Hugh helped."

"Right. Ralph's got a motive if Stanley gets murdered, and possibly for hating Audrey's ex-husband. Too bad Willow McAndrews and Diana Durst are the ones who wound up getting killed."

"I know." I rubbed my forehead. "I don't think I'm ever going to forget seeing Cassandra kneeling by Diana's body, holding that heart-shaped pillow."

Sullivan stared at me. "Was it pink satin?"

"Yes. How did you know that?"

"Diana keeps a box of them in her attic. Saw 'em there when I was designing her house. She says she gives them to her clients as housewarming presents. She must have given Cassandra Stanley one when she moved into the neighborhood, because I saw one in the Stanleys' linen closet just last week."

chapter 18

The sky was a crystal-clear azure as we left the library and walked back toward my office. We discussed the possibility that Cassandra had killed Willow because of some connection to her daughter's fatal car accident, but I didn't want to believe that. The woman had lost her only child; she deserved the trappings of a happy second marriage. Sullivan agreed that, despite her eccentricities, he liked Cassandra. "I think we're on the right track . . . that Bob, Hugh, or

Ralph killed Willow and Diana. Because they uncovered something about Abby's death," he said.

"Maybe so. The first time we were able to go up on the roof, I saw Willow stash something she found underneath the floorboards in her pocket."

"It could have been something she dropped herself when she was masquerading as the ghost of Abby the night before."

"Or it could have been something incriminating that Ralph planted."

Sullivan replied, "Does seem odd that Ralph's up there for a couple hours replacing the boards, doesn't ever spot this . . . whatever . . . then Willow's up there for some five minutes and finds it."

"Exactly." A flagstone of the red sandstone sidewalk was uneven and I took care not to trip on the edge in my heels, envisioning myself doing a face-plant in Sullivan's presence. "And Ralph wants to convince anyone who'll listen that Bob Stanley killed Abby. Even so, that'd be pretty stupid. I mean . . . Ralph's suddenly trying to entrap someone for a murder-ruled-suicide that took place forty years ago?"

"Yeah, but remember: it was the first time since Abby's death that the roof was accessible."

"True," I muttered. "Or maybe Ralph accidentally dropped some memento of Abby's from when *he* killed her, and Willow started blackmailing him, then Diana found out so he killed her, too. Willow and Diana could have been working the scam together, for that matter. Diana told me she had recently formed a partnership with Willow. She could have been telling a partial truth."

Steve gave no reply.

"And none of this started until Hugh Black suddenly shows up in town again. He was there that night. And he was conveniently at my house Saturday morning when Cassandra and I found Diana."

"Why was he at your place?"

"Trying to see Audrey. He's still hoping to reunite with her."

"Good luck to the sap," Sullivan said with a chuckle. "She's not going to be fooled by him twice."

"Right." We reached my office, and I paused at the door. "Thanks for going to the library with me."

"No problem. See you later, Gilbert. I'm officially on a prolonged lunch break. I'm going to keep digging."

"Into the murders?"

"No, into the nearest well," he quipped. "I'll let you know what I turn up."

I glanced at my watch. I really, really had some work to do before I met with my client in two hours, but I could always wing it. "Where are you heading first?" I trotted down the sidewalk and caught up with him.

"Hugh seems to be a man of leisure, so he might be home. I want to see what he has to say about his attending Crestview High School the same time as Abby Chambers did."

"Good idea. Also, Hugh has collectibles from World War II."

"You mean those old Uncle Sam posters? What

about them?" Sullivan was squinting a little in the bright sunlight, but that only accentuated his all-too-appealing laugh lines.

"Maybe he's putting them in storage because he doesn't want everyone to know he collects war memorabilia . . . because the dog tag I found actually belongs to *him* and is tied to the murder."

"Or maybe he's just storing them because his tastes have changed," Sullivan countered. "In a liberal town like Crestview, he might not have wanted old war posters placed front and center."

"Yeah, but he practically vaulted across the room to stop me from looking at them. And the dog tag isn't the only piece of war memorabilia I've found. Last week I found a loose baseboard in the tower room and discovered a little plastic Nazi soldier behind it. Someone had hacked it up pretty badly."

We'd reached his van and he opened the passenger door for me. "Weird. Do you still have it?"

I shook my head. "Linda Delgardio was at Willow's funeral, and I gave it to her then."

He rounded the van and got behind the wheel, donning sunglasses. "Meant to go to that myself. I had a job I couldn't get out of. Was the service nice?"

I shrugged. "Her family is devastated. They and Diana Durst were sobbing throughout. It was depressing as hell." I paused, unable to shake free of my suspicions. "My point is, maybe there's a connection. Abby Chambers apparently hides this World War II toy that someone's treated like a voodoo doll, then we find German dog tags hidden someplace else in her room, and all the while Hugh has a collection of war posters he *really* doesn't want us to see."

Sullivan gave me a long look. "Thing is, Gilbert, I was going to tell Hugh that I happened to be in the area and wondered if he'd like to go grab a beer. That won't work if you're with me."

"Why not? You don't think it's believable that I would be thirsty for a beer at . . . eleven-thirty on a Monday morning?"

"Not especially, no."

Admittedly, the idea of a beer at this hour was repulsive. "So we'll claim we're stopping by to see if he's completely satisfied with our work last Sunday."

"He'll say yes, and we'll have wasted a trip."

"At which time I'll draw him into a conversation about World War II collectibles by mentioning the dog tags or the toy soldier . . . and ask if the police have discussed it with him yet. We can watch how he reacts."

He frowned, but then nodded. "Fine, Gilbert. I'll follow your lead on this one." He drove in silence for a minute or two, seemingly lost in thought. "Those miniature plastic soldiers come in packets of a hundred or so. Some kid who lived in the house probably just lost one of 'em."

"But it had been deliberately mutilated . . . stabbed with a pin, with a noose tied around its neck. And there were red spots painted on it to look like blood. It was really creepy."

"So maybe that was part of the kid's game . . . torturing the evil Nazi soldier. Doesn't mean anything, Gilbert. Just violent playacting."

"That's not the way a typical girl plays, though . . . 'Ooh. Let's stick pins into the German soldier!' Sounds more like something a boy would do. . . . Such as a much younger Ralph Appleby or Bob Stanley? They were born and raised in Crestview. Bob was living right across the backyard from Abby during their childhoods."

"Even if that's so, it's got nothing to do with Hugh Black. Or with these murders."

"But we can segue into a discussion of Hugh and Abby's relationships in high school—"

We pulled into the parking lot near Hugh's building. "Let's go over our game plan," Sullivan said as we left the van and headed toward the outside stairs to the second floor. "We're obsessive-compulsive designers making sure our two-hour furniture-arranging job a week ago went well. And we both have a healthy, coincidental curiosity about World War II paraphernalia. *Then* we ask him why he didn't mention that he knew Abby Chambers back in high school. Am I leaving anything out?"

"Would you rather wait for me in the van?" I asked him as I started up the steps.

"Nah. There are worse things I could be doing. Such as knocking on doors of houses with garish paint jobs and saying, 'Say, there. I'm a designer and couldn't help but notice you're color-blind. Wanna hire me?' "

"You don't actually do things like that, do you?" I

rang the doorbell.

"Not yet. But making a phony goodwill call on a one-shot client is also a first, so who knows how low I'll sink?" Sullivan whipped off his sunglasses, and his smirk morphed instantaneously into a dazzling smile as Hugh cracked open the door.

I took the lead. "Hi, Hugh. I was hoping we'd catch you home."

"Erin?" He opened the door fully, even though he was dressed in just a black silk bathrobe. "Did . . . did something happen to Audrey?"

"No. Why, did she call you?"

"No, I just couldn't figure out any other reason you'd be here."

"We're just making a quick . . . goodwill call to make sure you're pleased with your furniture choices and floor plans."

"Oh. Yeah. It's just fine. Thanks."

"Also," Sullivan said as the door started to swing shut, "we wondered if you had any interest in getting a ballpark appraisal for those war posters you were planning to keep in storage. They might be more valuable than you realize, and I know a collector who's always on the lookout."

Very smooth, Sullivan, I said to myself.

"Really?" He opened his door wide and stepped aside. "Maybe you should come in. Make yourselves at home. I'll be right back."

While Hugh went into his bedroom, presumably to get dressed, Sullivan and I eased ourselves into opposite ends of Hugh's camel-colored Ultrasuede sofa; I adored this particular fabric for upholstery. Not only was its hand—the feel against one's skin—luxurious, but it was durable, attractive, and super easy to clean. On the opposite side of the scale, however, there were wear marks in the cheap brown wall-to-wall carpeting, and a shoddy repair job covered a crack in the dingy bone-white wall facing us. Having this sofa, along with his lovely black table set, housed in such a drab interior was tantamount to setting a full-carat diamond in a plastic ring.

Hugh returned, wearing gray slacks and an orange T-shirt. "What kind of figures might we be talking about here?" he asked as he dropped into a yellow-ochre leather recliner.

"No idea," Sullivan replied. "I'm not a collector myself."

"It's remarkable sometimes what can make an item valuable, and what some people collect," I interjected. "For example, I found a plastic German-soldier action figure in Abby's former bedroom, which Steve's client is very interested in looking at. Once the police get through examining it."

Hugh's bland expression never changed.

"Along with the German-soldier dog tag I found behind her closet," I persisted doggedly. Still no reaction.

"We also wanted to ask you about Abby Chambers," Sullivan said.

"Who?"

"A girl you went to high school with in Crestview," I said.

"In Crestview? I don't remember many of my classmates. I was only there for three semesters—the end of my junior year through my senior year. My father was stationed up here for a little over a year, so we all moved up here temporarily."

"Stationed?" Sullivan asked. "You're an Army brat?"

"Air Force, actually. For a while, back in the sixties, they had a small division at the Crestview airport. I even spent a couple semesters at the Academy myself, but it wasn't for me."

"You don't remember Abby?" I said. "That's surprising to me. I would think Francine would have at least mentioned the name to you. She died from a fall off Francine's roof. She supposedly still haunts the place."

"Oh, *that* Abby. Her last name was Chambers, eh? I'd forgotten. She died something like forty years ago, and like I said, I was only living in Crestview for a short period of time. And Francine never mentioned the ghost's last name." His plastered-on expression of confusion made his words totally unconvincing.

"You had to have at least heard about Abby's death, though," Sullivan stated. "Around the school."

"Yeah. Now that you mention it, I do remember hearing about some girl's death, but not at the school. I'd already graduated and moved back to Colorado Springs by then. She was a couple years younger than me, so I'd never even met her."

His explanation was plausible and, because neither Sullivan nor I were police officers, left precious little room for follow-up questions, drat it. "Did you know Ralph Appleby?"

"Vaguely. Odd-looking fellow." He grinned. "Ran into him in the neighborhood recently. Can't believe he lost his hair, too. Like he didn't already have enough problems. He was quite an oddball. Spent all his time in shop class or art class." He shook his head. "Rumor was, he was madly in love with Abby. Painted her portrait and gave it to her for her birthday or Christmas or something. Like a cute girl would ever fall for *him*."

I could sense a shared "Aha" between Sullivan and me. Moments ago Hugh was claiming he didn't know Abby, yet now he knew about a portrait Ralph had painted and had given to her.

"So did you know Bob Stanley in high school?" Sullivan asked.

"Of course." Hugh's grin widened. "Everyone knew who Bob Stanley was."

"Were you friends back then?"

"Kind of." Hugh narrowed his eyes. "We barely bothered to acknowledge the relationship when I wound up living next door to the guy a couple years back." He leaned back and crossed his arms on his chest. "Why the third degree? Did I miss a memo? Are interior decorators serving as police consultants these days?"

"Only when murders hit a little too close to home for comfort," I replied, trying to sound tough, but realizing

I sounded more like someone who'd been watching too many cop shows on TV lately.

Obviously also picking up on the fact that we'd gone about as far as we could, Sullivan raised an eyebrow at me, then said, "Thanks for your time, Mr. Black," and rose from his seat. Reluctantly, I followed suit. "So should I have that collector of old posters get in touch with you?"

"S'pose so. Can't hurt to talk to the guy." He gave me a visual once-over. "I'll be seeing you tomorrow night, Erin."

"You *will?*"

His haughty smile nearly made me shudder. "If you're home when I'm picking up Audrey. She finally agreed to let me take her out for dinner."

I was dumbstruck, but then managed a weak "Thanks for your time."

As we trotted down the stairs, I didn't even care if Hugh could overhear as I grumbled to Sullivan, "There's no way Audrey has suddenly decided she's attracted again to that creep."

"Yet she's going on a date with him."

I stormed across the parking lot toward his van. "She's afraid he's the killer! She told me so the night Willow died. She's setting herself up as a . . . whatever the police call it when they try to catch criminals by disguising themselves as possible victims."

"Decoy?" He unlocked the door for me.

I climbed in, reached across and unlocked his door, and the moment the doors were shut behind us, raged,

"Meanwhile, if he *is* the killer, he's only going to turn around and kill Audrey! I'm not going to let her get away with taking a risk like this! We'll go on a double date with them, if we have to, to keep an eye on them. Clear your schedule tomorrow night, just in case."

"I knew it. The moment the committee appoints you to be my boss on the Stanleys' house, you're forcing me to go on a date with you." He feigned a sigh and shook his head. "This is sexual harassment, Gilbert."

"Very funny." I flicked my wrist in the direction of the exit. "Just drive. I haven't had twelve seconds to prepare for a client meeting that's coming up in less than an hour."

"Enough with the sweet talk, darling," he said, jamming his key in the ignition and giving it an angry twist till the engine started. "I already know how grateful you are to me for trying to help you gather evidence . . . and prevent your becoming another murder victim yourself."

I winced and sank back into my seat, mulling but then dismissing a dozen ways to apologize as we drove in silence back to my office. Ironic that selecting new patterns for my clients was such a big part of my job. I couldn't seem to change my behavioral patterns with Sullivan to save my life.

My client presentation went a little better than expected. Afterward, I picked up the wallpaper for the tower room and brought it over to Francine's house. In a wonderful treat, the windows had indeed been installed—though Ralph would be doing all the finish work on them—so I was finally able to see all of the major architectural elements of the room, except the spiral staircase. The space looked absolutely magnificent.

Francine pleaded with me to hang "just one or two panels" of the paper right now and offered to help. "Even if Ralph winds up having to take it down later, we have that whole extra roll." I'd advised Francine, as I do all my clients, to order an extra single roll of paper and store it, just in case of disaster.

Wallpapering is something that I enjoy and am good at, so the suggestion was tempting, but I said, "It's too likely that the paper will get stained. The ceiling hasn't been painted, let alone the trim, and the floor still has to be sealed, and so on."

She frowned. "Can we at least *open* one roll? You can hold it in place against the wall for me, so I can imagine how it'll look when it's done."

"Of course," I said happily, relieved to see that she was regaining enough enthusiasm for the project that she wanted to envision how glorious the room would be when it was completed.

We took turns holding the wallpaper as high as we could against the wall with the other standing back to admire it. To my delight, the paper was going to be perfect. The pale yellow with white print was exactly the right touch—soul cheering. The ultimate effect would have the warmth of an afternoon picnic on a sunny day.

"You're pleased with it?" I asked her. Even though

she'd already said how much she liked the paper when it had been my turn to display it for her, I'd witnessed her mood swings more than once and hoped her opinions wouldn't waver as frequently.

"I love it," she declared. "And the new staircase will be such an improvement, too, don't you think?"

"Absolutely." I eyed the existing stairs. The rich grain and reddish hues of the new wood steps would be awesome. When my paint crew had finished—not scheduled for another month yet as a final step—the posts would be a luscious ivory, along with all the trim. "Can you picture it? How the floor will match the wood in the stairs? And your grand piano will be positioned directly beneath the crystal chandelier. The whole room will be bathed in sunlight from the arched windows. It will be a grand ballroom, suitable for royalty!"

She laughed a little. "I'm afraid I have too hard a time looking past all the dust and bare, gray drywall to picture it. But I believe you, Erin."

"I'm going to indulge myself and go up on the widow's walk, then examine the room again from the new entrance. That's a great trick of the trade, by the way . . . to enter a room from a different direction than you normally do. Sometimes that can spark some new ideas. Want to join me?"

She shook her head. "I get dizzy up there. But take all the time you want. Get this . . . *Lisa* actually volunteered to make dinner for me tonight. On the condition that I make you wait till she's back from her volleyball day camp at five before I let you get started on redecorating her room."

"I can come back at five." I had planned on finishing up here and then going to my office to get my bills printed and sent, but that could wait till tomorrow. Francine went downstairs, while I went up to the roof. I took the time to examine the widow's walk carefully. As always, Ralph had done a masterful job of replacing the well-aged redwood decking with composite boards. As he'd said, the railing was sturdy, the floor solid.

I felt a pang as I gazed down at Diana's house. I'd forgotten all about her murder while admiring Francine's music room. Even as I watched, a police car pulled up to the curb. Linda Delgardio emerged. Diana had mentioned packing up Willow's things for Willow's parents to take. Diana's whole house would now be subject to the same treatment, to the emptying out and discarding. Maybe Diana had discovered the evidence that Willow had pocketed and Diana too had tried to blackmail its owner. . . .

I returned to the tower room and took a moment to survey the space yet again. I placed the wallpaper rolls in the attic by the door, where I hoped they'd be suitably out of the way, and left Francine's. I walked next door and asked the officer guarding the door if I could speak to Linda.

She emerged a short time later and joined me on the porch. "Hey, Erin. What's up?"

"I know you don't want me to stick my nose into

your investigation, but I was thinking I might be able to help."

She had to fight back a smile. "We're checking and collecting the evidence. If we let friends and neighbors in to look through it, we've broken our chain of evidence and then it's no good to us."

"What if there's some clue that you and your fellow officers are overlooking because it looks so insignificant to anyone who wasn't part of Willow's and Diana's daily lives? Something maybe that Willow found and that, when Diana packed up her things for her parents, she stumbled across? And so they were both killed to keep whatever it is suppressed."

Linda arched an eyebrow and said evenly, "And nobody's going to recognize this clue's significance other than you, right?"

"Basically, yes."

"And that's because . . . ?"

"Because I'm familiar with Diana's home, and it's my job as an interior designer to notice the details that most people tend to miss. I might be able to remember if anything's missing or is placed where it shouldn't be." Also, I sorely wanted to discuss Diana's trove of heart-shaped pillows with Linda.

"Fine. I don't see what harm it'll do, provided I'm with you at all times to make sure you don't touch anything." She got the door for me and said, "Just keep your hands in your pockets and follow me." I meekly stashed my purse on the floor by the front door, then allowed Linda to take me on a slow tour.

The house was exactly how I remembered it. Nary a coaster was out of place. "Shouldn't there have been signs of a struggle? Things knocked over? Something?"

"Maybe the killer used chloroform to knock her out first. We'll know more once the autopsy reports come back."

"It seems to me that if this was a heat-of-the-moment crime, the killer would have grabbed the closest pillow available. What's odd is that I'd never seen the pink satin pillow that was used to suffocate her. Steve Sullivan said she kept them in a box in her attic office. Apparently she gave them out as housewarming presents when she sold clients their homes."

"Erin! You wouldn't know a thing like that unless you've been nosing into this investigation!"

"I just happened to mention the pillow to Sullivan. He told me Cassandra Stanley had one. Since Diana gave them to all her clients, Francine Findley probably has one, as well."

Linda was glowering at me.

"The thing is, though, they'd be wrapped in plastic when they were still in the box from the factory. The one I saw Cassandra holding wasn't wrapped. So . . . maybe Diana also gave one to Willow, and that's the one the killer used."

"Could be," Linda replied, less than loquacious due to her increasing irritation with me. "Notice anything out of place now?"

"Nothing. Unfortunately. But I was wondering . . .

did you find anything unusual in the pockets of Willow's jeans?"

"Her pockets?"

"I saw her pick something up from underneath the old floorboards on the roof a couple of days before she was murdered."

"That's interesting. Did you see this object at all? Could it have been a pin, by any chance?"

"A pin? Like a safety pin?" Willow never would have bothered to retrieve a cheap safety pin, come to think of it. "A brooch, you mean?"

Linda said nothing.

"I'll take that as a no. So it wasn't jewelry. Was it a *man's* pin? From a fraternity or something that she had in her pocket?"

She hesitated. Then she said, "Her pockets were empty, but Air Force wings were fastened inside the waistband of the jeans she was wearing."

"Hugh Black's father was in the Air Force! And Hugh said he went to the Academy for a short time himself!"

"And?" Linda asked, annoyed.

"And maybe he lost the wings pin when he was shoving Abby Chambers off the roof! Willow found it, once the deck up there was removed, figured out whose it was, and tried to blackmail him. Why else would she pin that on the inside of her clothing, unless it had something to do with the murder?"

"Even if that's precisely what happened, the pin doesn't prove anything . . . not even if we trace it back to Hugh Black. Willow would have found it at an unsecured scene, *forty years* after the crime took place. A crime that was ruled a suicide, by the way. We already know Ralph Appleby and Willow McAndrews were up there in the interim. Plus Hugh Black was seeing Francine Findley on the sly. They could have gone up there on a romantic rooftop tryst, and he lost his pin then."

"But why would he have his Air Force pin with him some forty years after he was at the Academy?"

"Maybe he and Francine were role-playing. I don't know. I just know we can't prove the thing was up there all that time."

I sighed. "I guess the German dog tag I found hidden at Francine's house is going to be meaningless, too."

Linda's eyes widened, and I remembered that I'd yet to relay all things related to the closet to her. I gave her a sheepish smile. She said evenly, "Let's go have a chat in my squad car, Erin. Time for you to fill me in on this unauthorized private investigation of yours."

"Dell?" her partner called. "Want to take a quick look at this vase? The description you gave me the other day sounds just like the one I found in the cabinet above the refrigerator."

We both rushed into the kitchen. "Can I see that?" I asked. I held the vase in its clear plastic bag up to the light. A tiny teardrop-shaped bubble was near the rim; I'd noticed it earlier. "Same slight imperfection in the glass. It's mine."

"We already dusted it for prints," Mansfield said.

"Nothing. There were no rubber gloves in her kitchen, so it's unlikely she managed to wash the vase and put it away without leaving fingerprints."

"This is totally weird," I muttered, mostly to myself. "I can't understand why someone took the vase. Not to mention the flower."

"Could have been an impulse, or some sort of a trophy . . . one-upsmanship," Linda replied.

"Women seem to develop crushes on Steve Sullivan all the time. Maybe Diana was so jealous of his giving me a flower that she took the whole thing, vase and all. Unless she assumed it was Audrey's flower, given to her by someone else entirely." Another possibility hit me, and I cried, "*Or,* the killer simply snatched the vase along with the flower because it was quicker that way, and he or she wanted to scare the hell out of me by proving how easy the access to my possessions is. Then the killer tried to stash it at Diana's to frame her, or just to throw us off the trail."

Linda's jaw muscles were working.

"Throw *you* off the trail, I mean."

Linda took the vase from me and handed it back to her partner, then she grabbed my arm firmly and escorted me toward the door. "Before you get distracted with the curious incident of the prodigal vase, let's have a little chat about Francine Findley's closet. Shall we?"

An hour later, Lisa was back from her "day camp" and I was eager to get started on her bedroom. She approved of my finalized plans for her room, and she and her mother asked if we could get to work right away on removing the wallpaper. I'd explained that I needed to quickly check the quality of the walls beneath the numerous layers of wallpaper to ensure none of the plaster needed to be repaired.

"There's a corner that had already peeled loose. I glued it down a couple years ago," Francine said.

"Good. I'll go grab some tools and be right back."

"I'll help you," Lisa volunteered. She came outside to the van with me. "Erin? I, uh, kind of got started on pulling some of the wallpaper off? By the door. Where you can't see it when the door's open."

"Oh, okay." I handed her a bucket and sponge and carried the scraper myself. "I'll have a workman or two come out with a steamer, by the way, to pull all the paper down, but we'll just be working on a small section today."

"The old paper underneath mine is kind of cool, actually," Lisa said.

"Good. Did you show it to your mom yet?" I asked as I held the door for her.

"Not yet."

"Show me *what* yet?" Francine asked.

"The old paper," Lisa replied. "It's neat. Kind of like a picture in a kid's book."

The paper was indeed marvelous, a pattern that I suspected was by a German manufacturer, circa 1940s. Lisa had been right about the children's book illustrations; it was depicting Heidi. "Francine, if you don't mind, I want to try to salvage at least some of this."

"That's fine. But you won't be able to recover enough to get a full wall's worth, will you?"

"No chance. For one thing, it'll be too faded everyplace except here, where the colors have been protected by the open door. I'm just hoping to get a large enough section to frame as a picture or two."

The process was slow and exacting, working with vinegar and warm water to peel the top layers of paper away from the bottom one. Francine grew bored and left, but Lisa kept me company and assisted me. We managed to scrape along the plaster to remove that piece intact. I felt like an archeologist, recovering tiny fossils from beneath a foot of bedrock.

The wall itself was in good shape, but I also wanted to check the section with the peeling paper on the opposite wall. As I carefully made a horizontal slice perpendicular to the loose seam and pulled the wallpaper back, a small piece of white paper slipped a little. Something had been hidden behind this seam. In case this was yet more evidence, I wanted to be alone to get a look at it. Francine had not returned, but Lisa was watching me like a hawk.

Remembering Hugh's trick that Audrey had told me about, I feigned a cough and said, "Lisa? Can you get me a glass of water?"

"Sure," she said, and headed down the stairs.

The moment she left, I snagged the corner of the paper with my fingernail and tugged it out from behind the loose wallpaper seam. It was a small section of a page that had been clipped from an old yearbook. At the center of the clipping was Hugh Black's likeness. A red heart had been drawn around it.

chapter 19

I've forgotten many things about the house I grew up in, but I still remember the wallpaper patterns vividly. So I wallpapered my sons' bedrooms, even though I knew they would inflict some minor damage as they augmented the patterns with pens . . . and pins. I realized that was a small price to pay for fond memories of one's childhood home.

—Audrey Munroe

DOMESTIC BLISS

"What are you doing, Erin?" Audrey asked, looking over my shoulder at the screen of my notebook computer as she entered the dining room. I'd kept the yearbook page hidden in my pocket after leaving the Findleys' house an hour ago.

"I'm researching wallpaper patterns."

"That one's remarkable," she replied, scooting the chair closer and taking a seat beside me.

"It is, isn't it?"

She grinned as she peered at the design on the

screen. "Is that supposed to be Heidi? With the goats and snow-crested mountaintops, and so forth?"

"Precisely. It was first manufactured in Germany, sixty years or so ago. The original pattern was, that is. This one here is a retro pattern."

"How delightful! Where are you going to use it?"

"I'm not, actually. I discussed doing an accent wall in Lisa Findley's room with it, but she felt it was too childish. At twelve, she's at that age when everything's got to be sophisticated and grown-up."

"But Francine asked you to use whimsical wallpaper in her daughter's room even so?"

I shook my head. "Actually, I found the original Heidi paper as I was removing the wallpaper from the room. I'll show you the section I managed to salvage." I flipped open my portfolio, which I'd stashed under the table, and let her examine the piece itself. "Once I uncovered that paper, I just *had* to try and restore at least a small section of it."

"I love it," Audrey murmured, running her fingertips gently over the paper.

"So do I."

She closed my portfolio. "What pattern are you going to put up in the room in its place?"

"I'm not using wallpaper at all. We're applying apricot paint instead."

"What a pity!"

I shrugged. "The color's going to be wonderful in the room; elegant and inviting, with medium-green curtains accented by dainty white pinstripes. I'm framing this one section of paper, though. It's still going to make an exceptional piece for the accent wall, which is going to be a dark red-orange, almost tomato red."

"Sounds lovely. Still, I *do* hope Lisa has had the chance to have wallpaper in her room till now."

"Oh, she has. It's dark blue, with a paisley print. Rather ugly, frankly. Not at all something anyone's going to regret losing. Least of all Lisa herself."

She arched her brow. "Lisa will feel differently when she becomes an adult. Wallpapers make memories. Even the ugly paper. Maybe *especially* the ugly paper."

"She is going to have memories of the blue paisley, I can assure you. Lisa used to gouge holes into the dots of the pattern, behind the door, where she figured her mom wouldn't notice it."

Audrey chuckled. "That's part of the process . . . part of what makes wallpaper so memorable for us in the homes we grow up in. We remember the little acts of vandalism we committed on our wallpaper as vengeance for being wronged by the world outside our bedroom walls. I remember in Michael's room . . . my oldest son . . . we had this nautical wallpaper. It showed the old historical three-mast sailing ships, compasses, those old steering wheels with all the spokes, flags . . . that kind of thing. One night when he was three he didn't want me to read any of his usual books, so I told him some story about sailors and pirates on the high seas, by using the designs on the wallpaper. That became his big bedtime ritual . . . you had to 'read the wall,' as he called it, to him before he'd go to sleep."

"What a wonderful family tradition you established! Thanks, Audrey. I'm going to keep that in mind the next time I'm designing a young child's bedroom. I never had wallpaper in my own childhood homes. But you're completely right about how memorable wallpaper is. Nowadays, they're doing such great things with wallpaper materials."

She patted my shoulder. "You're always so helpful to me on my *Dom-Bliss* segments. It's nice to know that I can be helpful to you in your job from time to time." She snorted. "Although I've got to tell you that, three years ago, when Francine Findley broke up my marriage, I was feeling so spiteful, I'd have liked nothing better than to have convinced Francine to install nautical wallpaper in Lisa's room. You have no idea what an enormous task having to 'read the wall' every night for six straight years of my life came to be. I swear I did backflips the day Michael finally decided he wanted plain old sky-blue walls in his room."

I grinned. "And now he's about to become a parent himself. Did it freak you out last month when he and his wife announced that you were going to become a grandmother soon?"

"Not a bit."

I raised an eyebrow. This was the woman who'd

decided on her last birthday to give herself negative numbers for every birthday from then on.

"The trick is in the pronunciation, my dear. I've known for thirty years now that I am, indeed, a *grand* mother."

chapter 20

While we're on the subject of wallpaper in children's rooms," I told Audrey, "I need to show you what I found hidden underneath the paper I was removing in Lisa's room." I handed the yearbook clipping to her.

Her eyes widened. "My," she exclaimed, "Hugh certainly was a handsome young man. Are you suggesting that it was Abby who drew the heart around his picture?"

"That's what I'm assuming, yes."

"You're sure it wasn't Francine?"

"No, but it's more the type of thing a kid might do, don't you think? Francine's fifteen years or so younger than Hugh is. She couldn't have been much more than a toddler when this picture of Hugh was taken."

She slid the page back toward me. "Hugh never as much as let on that he'd spent any time in high school in Crestview. Let alone that he'd gone to school with his new next-door neighbor."

"You'd already owned this house when you married Hugh, right?"

"For several years," she said with a nod. "I introduced Hugh and Bob when Hugh first moved in and I'm certain they acted like it was the first time they'd met." She eyed the photo again. "In fairness, more than thirty-five years had passed, and I've heard that CHS was a large school, even back then. They might not have even recognized each other."

"Steve Sullivan and I went to see Hugh yesterday, and he told us he did remember Bob. He said something like '*Everybody* knew Bob Stanley.' But that they didn't want to acknowledge that they knew each other."

She arched her brow. "Probably because they did something they weren't proud of in high school. Such as torment poor Abby Chambers."

"According to Ralph, Bob Stanley had a posse of guys from the football team he bribed into acting as his henchmen. I suspect Hugh was one of them. Maybe Abby had a big crush on Hugh and thought Hugh was interested in her for himself."

"While he was actually asking on Bob Stanley's behalf," Audrey said, completing my thought. "Hugh is quite the manipulative narcissist. If it would benefit him in some way, I can see him using Abby's crush on him to trick her into a rendezvous with his wealthy but undersized buddy. But how could any of this be connected to Willow's or Diana's murder?"

I studied Hugh's arrogant smile in the photograph. "Francine could have let something slip about Hugh's relationship with Abby to Diana or Willow that led to their discovering incriminating evidence in Abby's death . . . so that they were a threat to him."

"I suppose that's possible," Audrey said thoughtfully. "And it might be a motive for Francine as well. Maybe she was trying to keep Hugh out of jail by murdering anyone who could prove him guilty of Abby's murder."

I fought back a shudder at the thought of my own client, a mother herself, killing other women just to keep her beau out of prison. How could anyone be that sick? Yet the fact that two women had been murdered in our sleepy little neighborhood was *already* unfathomable.

"By the way, Audrey, Hugh *also* told me that the two of you have a date tomorrow night." I leaned forward and held her gaze. "You're not seriously thinking of going through with it, are you?"

She hesitated. "Yes, but I'll take any and all necessary precautions. Including arming myself with pepper spray."

"No! It's still too risky, Audrey! For all we know, you could be about to go out on a date with a serial killer!"

"If it turns out that I was actually married, however briefly, to a murderer, I'm not going to sit back and let him continue his murderous ways." She rose and headed into the kitchen. "Besides, you have the worst record imaginable for risking your neck to play amateur sleuth, Erin Gilbert, so you're hardly in a position to tell *me* to be cautious."

"But nevertheless, that's what I'm doing. I would

never go so far as to agree to a date with a man I thought was a murderer, just so I could pump him for information."

She spread her arms. "I was married to the man for a couple of months. We had some of the worst fights imaginable. If Hugh didn't kill me then, he is certainly not going to kill me now during our first reconciliatory date."

"At least let me arrange to go on a double-date with you."

"No, that would completely undermine my ability to manipulate the conversation. In which case I'll have wasted an evening of my life to spend with a terrible man I utterly despise."

"I'll make a deal with you, Audrey. You cancel tomorrow night's date, and I will be a guest on your show. On the topic of your choice." She'd pleaded with me ever since we'd first met to appear on her show, but I was terrified of being on television and had repeatedly refused. Even now the thought of what I was suggesting made my heart hammer, but I was desperate to protect my friend.

Audrey gaped at me. After a long pause, she said, "All right, Erin. You win." She grinned at me, which made me even more nervous about my end of the bargain, and repeated, "The topic of my choice, hmm? This will be *fun*. I'm thinking . . . mud baths. Or maybe stomach antacids."

" 'Stomach antacids'? My. That *does* sound like fun."

• • •

The next morning, I called Sullivan and asked him to meet me at my office. The moment he arrived and settled into my smoking chair, I leaned forward against my mahogany desk and said, "We know that the tower room was built in the mid-fifties, not all that long after the war ended. I was up half the night thinking about this, and I'm certain that the beat-up World War II toy soldier is significant. We need to go back to the local library."

He said nothing.

I clicked my tongue, but stood up, slung the strap on my purse over my shoulder, and marched to the door, grabbing my keys so as to lock him inside if he wouldn't join me.

"All right, then. To the library," he muttered, following me down the steps to the glass door.

I locked the door behind us. "Have you changed your mind about teaming up with me?"

"We're a *team?* Feels more like I'm the foot soldier and you're Herr Kapitän."

"You have a better idea for how to find the killer?"

"Not yet. I'm just sure we're wasting our time. We've concentrated on Abby Chambers's death from forty years ago, which wasn't even ruled a murder. Meantime, in the very recent past, two women who share the same house are killed a week apart."

"Just a couple of days ago you were saying we were on the right track with Abby's high school acquaintances!"

"Yeah, but now I'm not so sure. Maybe Diana's and Willow's murders had nothing whatsoever to do with Abby Chambers."

"I'm certain it was Willow posing as Abby on Francine's roof that set off the chain of events that led to the murders. Besides, Linda and her fellow officers are checking into recent motives and incidents. No way are they going to consider that the histories of these houses might hold the key to the whole tragedy. But, hey, Sullivan, you're welcome to poke around into Willow's and Diana's lives. I'm doing this."

We reached the library's front steps, and Sullivan held the door for me. "Might as well join you, since I've walked this far. But I *am* going to start digging into some things on my own."

And I'm sure you'll "waste" far less time than I have, I grumbled to him in silence.

The air was redolent with the scent that all libraries seem to bear—aging paper or binding glue, I wasn't sure which. The same elderly woman who was here during our last visit sat at the librarian's yellow-hued ash desk near the door. With Sullivan trailing me by a couple of steps, I went up to her and asked if they had any books on local connections to the Second World War.

She removed her glasses and started to polish them with a small lilac-colored flannel cloth. "We did, until very recently."

"Oh?"

"We used to have a wonderful reference book about

the POW camp just fifty miles north of us."

"There was a prisoner-of-war camp here in Colorado?" I was stunned.

"Oh, yes. There were a lot of Germans living and working the farms and ranches in Colorado back then. Most of us were at least somewhat sympathetic to them. The German prisoners were just kids, most of them, after all. Scared. Wanting to get home."

"And the reference book has been misplaced?" I asked.

"Stolen, more likely."

"How long ago did it disappear?" Sullivan asked, stepping forward to stand beside me.

Her face lit up as she looked at him, and she toyed with her gray hair coquettishly. "Oh, it was just a month ago, when school was still in session. That book gets requested a lot when students from Crestview High need to write term papers on the history of Colorado. A couple of pairs of teens were doing reports using that book, and it's never allowed to be checked out. One of them probably stole the book to save himself from having to keep coming in to do his work here."

"Can you get another copy on an interlibrary loan?" Sullivan asked her.

"It could take a while, but I'll do my best."

"I'm sure your best will be all that's necessary and more," he replied with a sexy smile and a wink.

She giggled. I felt like "accidentally" goosing the man. Did he have no pride whatsoever? He didn't need to flirt with the woman; her *job* was to assist library patrons!

Reading the nametag pinned onto the decorative bow of her frilly pink blouse, he said, "Ms. Jones, my name's Steve Sullivan. I'll give you my cell phone number and home phone, and you can contact me when the book comes in. All right?"

"Let me get your information in my computer records, Steve."

Still ladling on the charm, he gave her his numbers and address as she typed and told him that she'd call him "the minute the book arrives." In a considerably less ebullient voice, Sullivan muttered to me, "Might as well go."

"Whatever you say, Steve," I said with forced sweetness. I said sincerely to the librarian, "Thank you for your help, Ms. Jones."

"You're welcome. It was nice meeting you."

"We'll see you again soon." As he held the door for me, he protested, "I was just being nice."

"You were *flirting*."

"She's my grandmother's age! You can't flirt with someone fifty years older than you are!"

"Says who? If that had been a man in his seventies or eighties and our roles had been reversed, would *I* have been flirting, or just being *nice?*"

"No need to make a federal case out of it, Gilbert."

"In other words, I'm right and you're wrong." A thought hit me, and I turned back toward the library door, exclaiming, "We forgot to ask her a really important question."

"Like what? Whether she's got any single granddaughters my age?"

I didn't bother to respond. Instead I strode through the door and over to the librarian. "Hello again. By any chance, were you living in Crestview back at the time of the POW camp?"

"Yes, I was. Though I was just a child." She peered over her reading glasses at me. "Why?"

"Do you happen to remember what happened to the POWs after the war ended?"

"They were all shipped home to Europe."

"Nobody stayed in Colorado?"

She was already peering past my shoulder at Sullivan, who stood near the door. "Only the one escapee."

I glanced triumphantly back at Sullivan.

"Do you know anything about this escapee?" I asked her. "What became of him?"

"Oh, yes. It's been far too long now for me to remember names or addresses or anything of that sort, though. He'd gone on to strike it rich and became quite the model citizen, telling everyone he was from Switzerland. It wasn't for a decade or two until his identity was uncovered. By then, some leaders in the community stood up for the man, and eventually everyone decided to let bygones be bygones."

Switzerland! That was where Ralph had said Abby's father had lived during the war!

"This must have been reported in the newspapers at the time," Sullivan said.

"Oh, I very much doubt that," Ms. Jones replied. "As I recall, nobody wanted to get the authorities involved. I remember my father saying that there was some hush money exchanging hands."

"You don't remember any personal information at all? Whether or not this man had a family?" I pressed.

"I think he and his wife just had the one child. A girl."

Steve and I exchanged glances. It wasn't necessary for us to say aloud what we'd both come to realize: Abby's father hadn't been Jewish as Bob had said, or Swiss as Ralph had claimed; he was an escapee from the German POW camp.

As we walked back to our offices, my brain was filled with images of Abby Chambers being tormented years after the fact when someone discovered that her father wasn't a Swiss patron of the arts, but an escaped German prisoner of war instead.

I reveled in my unspoken "I told you so" to Steve as we parted and went to our separate clients' homes, mine in the foothills.

My clients raved about my design. Feeling as if I was on a roll, I went home for lunch and made a mental note to make sure that Audrey had canceled tonight's date with Hugh.

The phone was ringing as I opened the door. The caller immediately cried, "Erin, thank God you finally got home!"

"Francine? What's wrong?"

"Lisa is missing. She was supposed to stay in the

house, but she's nowhere to be found."

"Is her bike still around?"

"Yes, but I specifically told her to stay inside."

"She's probably nearby. I'll look for her. I'm sure there's nothing to worry about."

"Probably not, but this is so frightening, with two women dying. I can take the worst that fate has to mete out, but . . . only just so long as my daughter emerges unscathed."

"I'll find her," I promised rashly.

I spotted Lisa the moment I charged out the back door. She was sitting on the ground in the back corner of our yard by Audrey's carriage-house-cum-garage. Curious as to why she'd obviously ignored her frantic mother calling her name, I sneaked up on her. When I was just a few steps away, she heard my footfalls and turned. "What are you doing?" I asked.

She hid a piece of paper behind her back. "Hi, Erin." She'd been digging in the dirt behind a bed of apricot irises. She held up a doll. "I found this. Just now. Buried here, right next to your garage."

The doll had a porcelain head but a plastic body and black nylon hair, and was dressed in a navy blue sailor's dress. I didn't know enough about dolls to tell if this one was an antique. That it had been buried had gone a long way toward making the clothing and the doll's hair look much older—and dirtier—than it might have looked otherwise.

"And what's that you're hiding behind your back?"

"That's private," she snapped.

"Okay. But . . . is it something that could worry your mom if she knew you had it?"

"Only if she's crazy."

"That's not a good enough answer, Lisa. How about if you show it to me? Or would you rather show your mom now when I take you home?"

She curled her lip. "Those are my only choices?"

"Yeah. 'Fraid so."

She sat there glaring up at me without moving.

Finally deciding that I'd waited long enough, I said, "Your mom's worried. I need to tell her you're here."

"It's just an old treasure map," Lisa announced before I could take more than a couple of steps toward her house. She rose and thrust the paper at me.

It was a sheet of notebook paper, folded up to make it as small as possible. The drawing was crude, with just a few trees and the alley between our houses shown, along with the garage itself and an X to identify where to dig. She was right: it did look like a treasure map. I'd once staged a treasure hunt in my own days as a babysitter.

"Did Willow draw this map for you?"

She nodded. "We were going to go on a treasure hunt the next time she came over, but . . ." She let her voice trail away.

"And you just remembered it now?"

She shook her head. "I had to find the map first. She'd hidden it in the ice cream container in our freezer. I haven't been eating ice cream, 'cuz it was something special she and I would do together."

"Do you know where she got the doll?"

"I think it's just her old doll from when she was a kid. That's what she usually hid, anyway. Stuff that she was giving away."

"Willow did more than one of these treasure hunts for you?"

"All the time. Just around the neighborhood, usually in my yard or Diana's. Erin, I'm sorry I trespassed."

"Oh, don't worry about that, Lisa. Audrcy certainly wouldn't mind your digging a small hole next to her garage. I just think you should've answered when you heard your mom call."

"But Mom's going to get all freaked out about my being in someone else's yard. She always does."

"Let's go now and explain it to her."

"Fine. But it won't do much good."

Lisa hastily refilled the hole. We cut through the backyard; she let me carry the doll, and she returned her spade to their own freestanding garage. Francine greeted her daughter the moment we walked in by saying harshly, "Where have you been? I was shouting your name for a good twenty minutes!"

"I was fine. I was barely over our property line."

"So why didn't you answer me?"

She gave an angry shrug. "You get all upset whenever I'm at Audrey's. I knew you'd never let me go back if you knew I was over there, and I wanted to finish looking for something."

"What do you mean?" Francine paled visibly.

"She was digging up this old doll of Willow's," I

explained. “Willow buried it there for her to find.”

“Where?” she demanded. “In Audrey Munroe’s yard? Whatever for?”

Lisa sighed, rolled her eyes, and clicked her tongue—the teenager’s trifecta—then handed her mother the map.

I again interjected on Lisa’s behalf. “They were doing treasure hunts during her babysitting stints.”

“So can I go to my room now?”

“Go ahead.” Lisa swept out of the room without a glance behind her. “Did Willow ask Audrey’s permission before she buried things in her yard?” Francine asked me.

“I’m not sure,” I replied, “but I sincerely doubt Audrey would have minded. In any case, I think I’m going to take the doll to the police station, just in case it turns out to be evidence.”

“You really think that’s necessary?”

“I know it’s a long shot and probably has nothing to do with Willow’s or Diana’s death, but I just don’t want to make assumptions that impede the investigation.” Heaven knows Linda had made that clear enough to me yesterday, although I was still ignoring her stay-out-of-this directive.

“What could a filthy old doll have to do with anything?” she sniped at me.

“Maybe something valuable is hidden inside the doll. Something so valuable that some heartless, gutless maniac has killed two people in order—” I finally took note of the slack-jawed look of terror on

Francine's face and broke off abruptly.

"Oh my God," she said. "Is Lisa in jeopardy herself, now that she dug the darned thing up?"

"No, of course not. Like I said, it's extremely unlikely. That was all just . . . incoherent ramblings on my part."

She gestured for me to leave. "Definitely, take it to the police. And let me know if there's anything more we need to do. In fact, let me go speak to my daughter right this very minute. I'll gather up any and all treasure maps she got from Willow, and you can give those to the police, too."

I brought the doll and half a dozen maps to the police station. Linda wasn't there, but Officer Mansfield, Linda's partner, was. As I handed everything over to him, he explained that Linda had a dental appointment and would be back soon.

"I know some people collect old dolls," Mansfield told me. "You're some kind of designer, right? Does this look like a valuable collector's item to you, or anything?"

"No, it just looks like a twenty-dollar, ten-year-old doll. I wouldn't think twice about it, except that it was hidden in our yard by the murder victim, Willow McAndrews, shortly before her death."

He nodded. "We might want to send someone out with a metal detector to see if there's anything more substantive buried there. We'll see."

"I also found out something that might be really

important about Abby Chambers."

"What's that?" Mansfield asked.

"Her father was an escapee from the POW camp in northern Colorado. Apparently he made good and had a lot of support and so he was never turned in to the authorities. I think it was his dog tag I found hidden in a gap behind the closet in the tower room of the Findleys' house. There's a two-by-four between two studs back there where someone wrote 'Leave me alone or die,' and it was hidden in a hole someone drilled in the board."

"Ah," he said with a nod, but he looked confused. He apparently wasn't following my thread.

I persisted. "Remember the mutilated plastic model of a German soldier that I gave Linda at Willow's funeral? I think someone gave Abby that toy as a cruel prank, to tease her about her father's checkered past, and that somehow led to her death. And so maybe the two murders in the house next door are also tied to Abby."

"I see," he muttered with a noncommittal nod. He gave me a smile. "Thanks for bringing in the doll."

My last appointment of the day was to give a much-needed facelift to the great room of a squabbling couple. They couldn't agree on a single thing and each kept urging me to tell the other that he or she had "no taste" (his words) or "all the judgment of a three-year-old" (her words). I was late getting home and was in a lousy mood when I finally got there. Audrey was upstairs, and Hildi was, too, leaving me a glorious period of solitude in the kitchen. I delighted in the crisp, full flavor of Audrey's chardonnay as I scanned the paper. The news reports on Diana's "homicide" and Willow's "suspicious death" were rehashing stale information, and stated that the police were "pursuing several leads." Today's paper, however, ran a long and touching obituary for Diana Durst, citing that funeral services would be held Thursday afternoon.

The doorbell rang, and Audrey called down the stairs that she'd get it, but I called back on my way to the foyer, "That's okay. I'm closer."

It was Hugh Black, bearing his arrogant smile and a single red rose that looked as though he'd picked it up from the supermarket on his way here. Had Audrey forgotten to call and cancel their date? Perplexed, I said, "Evening, Hugh. Can I help you?"

"Yes. You can get Audrey for—" He beamed as he looked over my shoulder. "Ah. Hello, Audrey." He held out the rose to her as she descended the stairway. "My last flowers for you were short-lived, so I only brought one this time."

"How sweet!" she exclaimed. She accepted the rose from him and deftly plucked the bud off its stem, giving me hope that, despite her stunning black-and-white evening gown, she was going to do something appropriate with his offering, such as grind it beneath the toe of her fuchsia Manolo Blahnik slingback. To my horror, she dropped the stem onto the table and tucked the rose into the lapel of his black jacket while he continued to beam at her like a lovesick puppy.

I'd watched this too-chummy scene play out as though it were a slow-motion car wreck, but now I gathered my wits and said with a smile that no doubt looked as phony as a cardboard fireplace, "Audrey, I need to get your opinion on some room designs I've got spread out on the kitchen counter. It's *really* important."

"Oh, that's all right, dear. I studied your design last night. I gave it careful consideration and decided that I would only be getting in the way of your creative process if I were to interject *my* ideas into *your* plans. After all, you're a grown woman. You're not going to do anything stupid, and it's simply more efficient to work alone."

"But we already made a deal that we were in this one together!"

"I had my fingers crossed at the time, so our deal wasn't valid. I won't be long. Hugh knows I have to be in Denver to tape my show early in the morning."

Through clenched teeth I replied, "Yes, I was planning to drop in on your show one day, but I've changed my mind."

"Whenever you change it back again, you'll be greeted with open arms, Erin. Have a pleasant evening." She let Hugh escort her out the door.

Short of tackling my willful landlady and dragging her back into the house, there was nothing I could do. Livid, I cursed up a storm.

I made dinner for myself and railed at Hildi from

time to time about how impossible Audrey was. I called Linda at home, and she told me that, yes, Mansfield had told her about my bringing in the doll, but that there was nothing hidden inside it. Although she was patient and kind as always, I could not fail to sense that I was teetering on the edge of becoming a major nuisance to my police friend.

In desperate need of distraction, I decided to redecorate for the umpteenth time. Audrey treated her parlor, living room, and den as though they were an enormous junk drawer. I shuffled the positions of the chairs, area rugs, and end tables to form conversation nooks, and I made her regal fireplaces the focal point of the rooms. All the while, I checked out the front window periodically for her return. After about two hours, a horrendous sight greeted me on the front porch, one that left me feeling slightly ill.

Audrey was in Hugh's arms, and he was kissing her passionately.

chapter 21

When Audrey stepped through the French doors and into the parlor a minute later, I promptly stopped my pacing and cried, "Have you lost your mind?" Not the warmest of greetings, but it did get right to the point.

She hooked the strap of her purse on the back of the wing chair, either not noticing or not caring that it had migrated from the den and into a much more harmonized setting in the parlor. "You were spying on me just now."

"Yes. And I want to know why you think it's acceptable for you to be making out with a man you told me you suspect has murdered three people!"

She sank gracefully into the chair. Studying her manicure, she replied, "You'll make a fine mother someday, Erin. It already sounds as though you're speaking to your daughter."

"The very thought of a child of mine dating a murderer makes me want to join a convent, Audrey!"

She chuckled. She settled back into the mauve-and-magenta floral damask, folded her hands in her lap, and lifted her chin as she regarded me, looking uncannily like Hildi in her self-satisfied grin and mannerisms. "Trust me, Erin. It was worth forcing myself to neck with that vile man. That was what was required for me to trap him."

Hopeful despite the likelihood that this was just another of Audrey's hyperbolic pronouncements, I perched on the edge of the brown leather ottoman, which I'd arranged to double as a coffee table. "Fill me in," I demanded.

"I collected some rather incriminating evidence." She reached into her purse. "I borrowed his wallet and searched through it in the ladies' room, then slipped it back into his jacket pocket."

"You pinched something out of Hugh's wallet? Audrey, what if he finds out it's missing?"

"Oh, I'm safe. He'll be behind bars before he even notices. He had these things tucked between other photos and cards in his billfold, and he's too egotistical to suspect I had ulterior motives for dating him. Hence our passionate good-night kiss."

I rose and took the items from her, then dropped back onto the ottoman. One was a photograph of Willow McAndrews, identical to the one Ralph Appleby was using to carve his portrait of her. The other was some sort of identification card for the Air Force Academy dated forty years ago. Bizarre as it was for Hugh to hold on to his ID card all these years, it didn't seem to be actual evidence to me.

"I don't get it, Audrey. Explain how either of these things incriminates Hugh."

"A good prosecutor will be all over him for carrying around the photograph of a victim he's been claiming he didn't know from Adam. Especially when you see the inscription on the back."

I read aloud, *"To the man of my dreams. I'm so glad we found each other! Love, Willow."* I frowned. "Granted, that looks bad, but it wasn't signed to him personally. Willow was enough of a flirt to have signed a dozen pictures this way and give them to every man she knew. It wouldn't surprise me if she gave one to Steve Sullivan as well. For that matter, Willow might have meant to give it to someone else but lost it at Francine's, and Hugh took it."

"Highly unlikely. However, the fact that Hugh has been spending so much time at Francine's does make it possible that *she* is actually the murderer," Audrey said. "If she looked in his wallet and spotted that picture, she might have lost control. Maybe she decided to kill off the competition."

"And murdered Diana as well?"

She tilted her head. "Hugh has quite the wandering eye, believe me. He could have been hitting on all of us at once. He'd have enjoyed that immensely . . . sleeping with two women in the same house and not letting either woman know about the other."

"You're proving my point. You've named a second suspect based on Hugh's supposedly incriminating evidence." I glanced at the second item. "What does his ID card from the Air Force Academy prove?"

"Notice the dates."

The card was for a summer session forty years ago.

"He didn't have any other old ID cards in his wallet, but he did keep that one," Audrey continued. "Why? He attended the Academy for just two years before dropping out, yet the only card he kept is for a summer session when Abby was murdered. What do you want to bet it's a macho memento of how he rid himself of Abby?"

"Again, Audrey, that proves nothing. In fact, if the ID and Willow's photo *were* in any way incriminating, wouldn't he have gotten rid of them?"

"Unless he forgot he had them." She pursed her lips, then said, "Maybe they don't prove he killed them, but they strongly *imply* that he did. Erin, during dinner he told me that he spent the summer after he graduated high school in the Mediterranean. But he didn't. He was *here,* in Colorado, attending the Air Force Academy. The ID card proves that. If he's innocent of Abby's murder, why would he lie about his whereabouts?"

"The two of you were discussing a summer vacation that took place four decades ago. Maybe he vacationed in the Mediterranean *prior* to his stint in the Academy. Besides, even if the police *would* originally have considered these things incriminating, they *aren't* now, because they're no longer *in* his wallet."

Audrey rose and snatched the picture and ID card from me. "Honestly, Erin! You are such a cynic! I'm telling you straight out who the killer is. I feel it in my bones."

Exasperated, I fired back, "And yet moments ago, you told me Francine could have killed Willow and Diana in a jealous rage."

"Maybe she did. But *Hugh* is still very likely guilty of Abby's murder. Francine was only six years old at the time and living in a whole different town. She couldn't have killed Abby."

"Which reminds me . . . Lisa mentioned the other day that her mom's boyfriend—and she must have meant Hugh—had known her mom for many years. Do you know if that's true?"

"Yes, actually. I asked him about that tonight, when we were discussing the 'other woman.' He was, of course, busily assuring me things were long since over with Francine. Knowing Hugh, he is probably with her right this very minute, telling *her* how he and I are past history." She shook her head, then continued, "He said Francine had a schoolgirl crush on him clear back when they were in the same neighborhood in Colorado Springs, before he spent his late teen years here in Crestview. It turns out Hugh was Francine's *babysitter* when she was little. Then decades later, the babysitter she's hired for her own child is murdered. How is that for a coincidence?"

I had an appointment at Francine's first thing the next morning. She seemed distracted and agitated, obviously feigning attention as I showed her and Lisa the materials for Lisa's room that I had purchased on her behest. The moment Lisa left the room, she shut the door and asked, "How is Audrey doing these days, Erin?"

"Just fine. Why?"

"I've heard her name mentioned a few times lately, within my circle of friends outside the neighborhood."

"In what context?"

"Oh, that she's dating someone. And that it's maybe getting serious."

I kept my expression blank.

"Do you have some sort of agreement where you know you'll get the boot if she remarries?"

"We've never discussed that, no."

"You probably *would* get kicked out, though, don't you think? If Audrey were to remarry?"

"I honestly haven't thought about it, Francine."

"Maybe you should ask her, then. About the rumors, and what she's got in mind."

I held her gaze, incredulous that she was being this transparent. I put the samples aside. "Francine, I don't for a minute believe that Audrey will ever take Hugh back. Frankly, she's too good for him. And so are *you*."

She stiffened. "I don't think you know Hugh Black well enough to stand in judgment, Erin. I've loved the man for much longer than Audrey has. If she ever really did love him, which I doubt."

"So he's a good man? And you love him?"

She nodded.

"Then why were you hunting for his Air Force cadet pin on your roof, back when this all began?"

She gaped at me. "Pardon?"

"That's obviously what you were doing. And I think that's why you were so reluctant to have Ralph open up the access to the roof. Because you knew there was evidence there that could incriminate Hugh Black in a murder from many years ago."

She made no attempt to disguise her shock. "How did you know about his pin? Did he tell you?"

"The police found it hidden in Willow's clothing."

She trembled and closed her eyes, her lips now pursed so firmly, they were white. She rose and began to pace. "It's not what you think."

I stayed put but kept a wary eye on her every movement. If she was in on three murders with her lover, there was no telling what she might do next.

"A month or so ago, Hugh was . . . here for a visit.

This was just after I'd hired you, and you'd suggested removing the wall and restoring the staircase. That night, we . . . got a bit carried away. We had such an amazing time that, after our date, he came back and planted a rosebush in my yard, just because he saw that the rose was called American Beauty and . . ." Her voice grew thick with emotion and faded. She cleared her throat. "Later, we climbed onto the roof with a ladder, but it wasn't tall enough, so Hugh broke a pane and knocked out the boards."

"Whose idea was that? To go onto the roof, I mean?"

She blushed. "I don't remember. We were intoxicated. It's lucky we didn't fall down and break our—" She stopped, embarrassed at the connection to Willow's death, then continued quietly, "He realized afterward that he'd lost his pin."

"Why would he have had his cadet pin with him?"

Her cheeks grew even redder. "If you must know, it was . . . this silly game we enjoyed . . . just a way of reviving old memories from when I knew him years before . . . when I was a little girl and used to see him in his uniform. Anyway, a couple of days after our date, he called me and told me that he'd lost his cadet pin up there between the boards, and his fingers were too thick to retrieve it. He'd since realized that it would look bad if anybody discovered his old Air Force pin up there, because of Abby's suspicious death. I couldn't find it . . . and that's why I needed to keep the roof access sealed."

"And yet you changed your mind. Why?"

She grimaced. "When you told me about seeing Willow on my roof that one night, I put a few things together . . . and overreacted. Hugh had been ogling Willow from the moment he first saw her. I was certain he'd also convinced *her* to do his dirty work and search for the pin. Then Diana told me that she'd . . . heard a rumor that Hugh had contacted Audrey again. So he happened to come to my door at exactly the wrong time, and I reacted in the heat of the moment and told you to open up the roof access."

"Was this just after we'd found the threat written on the wallpaper?" I wondered if Hugh had written that to further ensure Francine wouldn't remove the wall.

"Yes. I asked him if he'd sent Willow searching for his pin on my roof. He denied it, but I could see in his eyes that he was lying, and it made me so angry, I lost my head for a while. I figured, the heck with protecting the louse . . . I'd open up the roof again."

"*Was* that why Willow was on the roof? Was she looking for Hugh's pin on his behest?"

Through a tight jaw, Francine answered, "Not on Hugh's, as it turned out, but on Diana's."

"But . . . how could *Diana* have known about Hugh's lost pin?"

"She didn't. But after she came over here all bubbling about the ghost and asking if you'd seen it, too, I went over to her house. I asked just what *else* she'd seen while spying on me from her attic window. She admitted she'd seen Hugh and me . . . embracing on the roof, and that afterward she'd seen me up there searching for something. So she sent Willow, disguised as Abby Chambers, up on my roof to investigate. Killing two birds at once, as it were." Francine sighed again and said sheepishly, "I told Diana that it was a diamond earring, but that I'd finally found it." She brushed back her auburn hair. A full-carat diamond glinted from her earlobe.

My stomach knotted. "Francine, Willow *did* find Hugh's Air Force pin. And she had it hidden in her clothing on the night she was pushed off your roof. I think Willow went onto your roof that night to meet the killer. If she was blackmailing Hugh about the pin, he could have lured her up there, telling her that's where he'd put her payoff money, or something."

She shook her head. "No. Hugh would never kill anybody. He was framed. The killer planted that pin on her and then threw her off my roof. I'm certain of it."

"But Hugh was here that night! When you were probably supposed to be meeting him someplace."

"We'd miscommunicated and he went to the wrong place. He came here briefly to find me. He only got here just after the tragedy."

"But he—"

"Hugh did not murder anyone, Erin," she interrupted harshly. "He's an incorrigible flirt, and I admit that's infuriated me more than once. But he's not a murderer. I'd stake my life on it. My daughter's life, even."

chapter 22

Still reeling, I drove directly to the police station after leaving Francine's and relayed the whole conversation to Linda and her partner. Although they listened and took notes, Linda merely said, "Thanks, Erin. We're keeping an eye on Mr. Black." She exchanged glances with her partner, then added kindly, "Come on. I'll walk you out."

When we reached the lobby, she stopped. She said, "I know how hard this has hit you, with two people you know dying violently so close to your home. But we *will* get the killer, Erin. You've got to trust me on that."

I forced a smile and nodded. She held the door for me and gave me a friendly wink. "And, hey, once we do? I promise, you'll be the first person I call with the good news."

Still stewing too much to be creative, I went to my office and dug into my bookkeeping. After an hour or so, Sullivan charged up my stairs and, not even slightly out of breath, ordered, "Take a look at this." He spread four photocopied pages from a newspaper across my desk. Before I could as much as get my eyes on the captions, he said, "They're articles I've dug up about the death of Cassandra's daughter. In a nutshell, Willow McAndrews was suspended from school the day of the one-car traffic accident that claimed Cassandra's daughter's life. Willow had broken into her parents' liquor cabinet and brought vodka to school in a pair of water bottles. One of which she gave to her ex-boyfriend, who shared it with Katelyn Adams. Those two ditched the rest of their classes that day, and promptly got into the car accident that killed them both."

"And Katelyn Adams is Cassandra's daughter?"

"Correct. Check the obituary. The odds of there being a second Katelyn-Cassandra daughter-mother scenario are pretty long."

A single glance verified Sullivan's statement. Katelyn's photograph was proof enough that she was Cassandra's daughter; the physical resemblance was unmistakable.

My thoughts raced. Could Cassandra Stanley be the murderer? "This would give Cassandra a motive for killing Willow. But not for killing Diana."

Steve jammed his hands into the back pockets of his jeans. "Diana found Willow's body. It was her scream that we heard. For all we know, Diana could have seen the whole thing. Maybe she was blackmailing Cassandra in exchange for her silence."

That was plausible. With my heart racing, I skimmed the articles. "I hope it's not Cassandra. She's already had so much pain in her life, losing her only daughter. It would be doubly heartbreaking if that tragedy drove her to murder."

"When you think about it, Gilbert, there isn't going to be a happy ending, no matter who the killer is."

"True, but . . . I'd feel a little better knowing the killer wasn't someone I like."

• • •

When I went home that evening, I couldn't get my concerns about Cassandra out of my head. I kept an eye on their house and spotted her pacing past the window in the library. There was no sign of Bob, and his car was not in its usual place in the driveway.

Impulsively, I decided to try to chat with her and rang their doorbell. Cassandra didn't even ask the purpose of my visit. Instead, she immediately said, "Come in, Erin. I sensed you were going to come over. It's perfect timing. Bob's at a baseball game in Denver." She looked as though she hadn't slept in days.

"Is everything all right?"

"Not really." With a sigh, she led the way into her living room and we both sat down on her sofa. I glanced at the front window opposite us, where the bay window with its comfy built-in seat would have been, had my original plans gone into effect. This room would have been so much nicer that way, less weighty and claustrophobic.

"Erin, there's something terrible going on. I'm getting the worst possible readings from the Other Side."

"What kind of 'readings'?"

She shook her head and wouldn't answer. "I'm thinking maybe I'd feel better if I moved out . . . left Bob before things get any worse."

"The two of you are fighting?"

She shut her eyes. I noticed that her hands were trembling. "I can't take the pressure anymore. Last night, my daughter Katie told me that Hugh killed Willow and Abby. That he pushed them both off the roof. She wouldn't tell me who killed Diana . . . yet she *implied* it was Bob!"

That was the kind of evidence that convicted the "witches" in Salem. Even so, it was painful to see how stressed out she was and my heart ached for her. And I wasn't willing to dismiss her story out of hand. "You didn't tell Bob about this, did you?"

She opened her eyes and met my gaze. In a near whisper, she said, "I couldn't. I'm afraid of what he'll do."

"A brief vacation from the neighborhood might be an excellent idea. You look pretty stressed out—"

"That's because I *am,*" she interrupted. "Try being mellow when your deceased daughter is telling you your husband might be a murderer!"

Maybe Cassandra had snapped, perhaps under the pressure of knowing that she'd killed Willow and Diana herself. I scooted to the very edge of my seat, fully prepared to run for my life if necessary. "Cassandra, did you ever talk with Willow about your feelings over her relationship with your daughter? And about how it was Willow who supplied Katelyn and the driver with the alcohol that day?"

To my surprise Cassandra merely sighed. "I sensed that you knew about that, too." She looked utterly defeated. "Erin, I know how it must look to you . . . as though I'm totally whacko. But I'm not. My visitations from the Other Side are real. As for Willow—she didn't even recognize me when Diana brought her into my shop to apply for the job. *I* recognized *her* immediately, of course, but I'd since changed my last name to Stanley, and Willow almost never hung out at our house with Katie, so she'd only seen me two or three times. One day at work, I asked her straight out if she knew I was Katie Adams's mom. Willow looked like she'd have a heart attack on the spot. She asked if I hated her, and I told her truthfully that I had at first, but that anger and hatred eat up a person's soul. My conversations with Katie in the past few years taught me that. Hiring Willow helped me to realize I truly had moved past my anger.

"Even right after the accident, while still totally enraged at Willow for giving that alcohol to Katie, part of me always knew that she didn't force my daughter to get into that car with a drunk driver. Katie made that terrible and tragic choice all on her own." She sounded sincere.

I said, "You must have felt horribly betrayed when Willow stole money from you."

"Yes, but . . . that's why I fired her. And Diana reimbursed me, probably as guilt money for hiring Willow against my better judgment. Diana had begged me to."

"Did you or Willow tell Diana about Willow's connection to the accident?"

"Willow. Diana took a perverse pleasure in watching the two of us together. Diana had her good points, and I truly miss her, but underneath all that perkiness, she was the type of person who needed to put others down in order to build herself up."

"Why was it so important to Diana that Willow be hired? Do you know?"

"With no job, Willow had no rent money for Diana." Again, she searched my eyes. She took a halting breath. "I didn't kill Willow, Erin. But now Katelyn assures me that my husband *did*."

"I'm so sorry," I said, not knowing how else I could possibly respond.

Her eyes filled with tears. "Lately I haven't been carrying my weight at the store. My employees are working overtime." She sighed again. "But you're right. I've got to get away from his house, to pull myself together. I'm going to tell Bob that I'm visiting my sister in the Springs. Then I'll check into a hotel and decompress." She pulled me into a hug. "Thanks, Erin. You're a lifesaver."

Early the next morning, Audrey left for Denver, and I lingered in our kitchen, sipping a cup of Earl Grey tea as I read the newspaper. Once again, the articles on the murders were rehashes of what had already been reported in previous editions. I heard some raised voices and looked out the back door. Francine and Bob were standing toe-to-toe, just inside the corner of Bob's property line. Bob, his face red, was snarling, ". . . You really should keep a closer eye on her!"

Lisa must have done something to annoy Bob. I dashed out the door in case they needed a mediator.

"Well, Bob, this really isn't—" Francine broke off when she noticed me heading toward them.

"What's the matter?" I asked.

Francine gave me one of her tight smiles. "Bob seems to think that Lisa's little game of treasure hunting is endangering her safety."

"That's because it is," he insisted. "She's sneaking around onto other people's property at all hours of the night. She could be attacked by a dog. Or shot by an overly anxious homeowner who mistakes her for a prowler."

"That's just silly," Francine sniffed. "It's not as though we have packs of wild dogs roaming the streets. The only dog in the immediate vicinity is Bugle, and he's been adopted by a sibling of Diana's."

Puzzled, I said to Francine, "I thought Lisa had already given you the treasure maps."

"She has, but apparently . . ." Francine gestured at Cassandra's flower bed. "Look what she did last night!"

Incredulous, I scanned Cassandra's large garden. Its soil was now uneven, the flowers hastily replanted onto its miniature peaks and valleys as if in an afterthought, and the remnants of a dirt pile had flattened a sizable portion of the lawn. "That . . . looks to me like an awfully big area for one twelve-year-old girl to dig up in a single night. Unless she had a backhoe at her disposal."

"Lisa can be surprisingly enterprising when she wants to be," Francine said with a mild chuckle.

"She admitted she'd done all this digging?" I asked, puzzled.

"Francine hasn't had the chance to ask her yet," Bob put in. "I only just now discovered this mess and called Francine over to come see for herself."

"I'll go speak with Lisa now," Francine said. "She won't repeat this kind of outrageous behavior."

"Unless the *real* culprit was the man I spotted digging up your yard that night I called you," Bob said to her.

She blushed. "I explained about that."

He snorted. "Sure. You told me he was planting a rosebush for you in pitch-blackness at two a.m."

She stepped over the short decorative fence to return to her own yard and said over her shoulder, "It was a romantic gesture. Anyway, Bob, I'll talk to my daughter and have her come apologize."

We watched her leave. Our eyes met. Bob chuckled, shaking his head. In conspiratorial tones, he asked, "What kind of a 'romantic' goes digging in his girlfriend's yard at two a.m.?"

"It *is* unusual." I no longer trusted Bob enough to tell him that the "man" he'd seen was Hugh Black, his high school classmate.

"Well, if I were her, I'd tell him I expected my boyfriends to act like *men.*" He gave my arm a squeeze and added jokingly, "Not golden retrievers."

My hunch was that Hugh had been looking for incriminating evidence in Francine's yard and had planted the rosebush as a ruse. But if something implicated Hugh in Abby's murder, why wait all these years? Could he have seen an old treasure map that

Willow had drawn that showed something buried in Cassandra's garden?

Bob, I realized, was watching me with unusual intensity. Embarrassed at having been caught with my mind wandering, I asked, "How's Cassandra doing?"

"Fine. She's in Colorado Springs at her sister's place for a couple of days. The murders have rattled her. They've affected all of us, but Cassandra thinks she has conversations with the dead, so she's really shaken up. The poor thing really needed a vacation."

"Can't say that I blame her."

"Neither do I," Bob said, glaring at me as though I'd said something offensive. He turned away from me as if in disgust. "But I can sure see how *you* wouldn't blame her. She told me how it was all your idea."

Cassandra had made me the fall guy to her husband.

Feeling as though everyone in the neighborhood hated me, I said good-bye and left for work. I drove to an art store near the campus and purchased the supplies so that I could frame the small section of old wallpaper I'd extracted from Lisa's bedroom, then headed to my office to start in on the project.

First I very carefully created an oval-shaped cardboard stencil so that I could crop the wallpaper to its best effect; if I botched this task and cropped too closely, there would be no second chances; this one section was all that I'd managed to retrieve.

I'd selected an off-white linen paper for the background board for its rough, gunny-sack-like texture and deliberately used a light hand as I glued the Heidi cutout to that background, giving the desired effect of a wallpaper decoupage on an artist's blank canvas. To use the yellowing of the paper to its best advantage, I chose a mat that was naturally the same hue as the darkest section of the once-white background, and I used a second mat board as an accent that featured the same muted-by-time ruby red of the pattern, found on Heidi's dress, the flowers, and the trim on the house in the background.

When the task was complete, I sat and admired the completed picture in its dark wood frame that matched Heidi's hair, picturing it against the rich, rusty red that faced Lisa's bed. It would have looked wonderful in my own bedroom as well, but this was hardly the first time I'd lusted after something I'd acquired for one of my clients.

My door opened. Someone entered and began to climb the steps. Hastily, I flipped the picture to face the wall behind me and sat down at my desk. I could tell by the heavy footfalls that it was a man, and paused to watch the stairs, hoping it would be a new, wealthy walk-in client or maybe even Steve Sullivan.

To my deep disappointment and alarm, it was Hugh Black. It was all I could do not to grimace at the sight of his pompous, wall-to-wall grin as he approached.

"Good morning, Erin. I hoped to find you here. I dropped by Audrey's and discovered that you weren't home."

Mustering a pleasant voice, I replied, "Yes, and here I am. What's up, Hugh?"

"I'm looking for some advice from a woman."

"Sure thing." It was no use. I could not be pleasant to the man, not after being told by Audrey that he was her prime suspect. I needed to encourage him to leave. "I'd rethink that shirt, for starters. The big white cuffs and collar matched with those pinstripes just don't work for me."

Undaunted by my blatant rudeness, he slipped into the leather chair across from me. "Audrey's admitted that she misses me. She wants to give our marriage a second try."

Too alarmed to fake nonchalance, I cried, "She did? In so many words?"

"Not in so many words, no."

"Exactly what words did she use, then?"

His brow furrowed. "She wants to give me a second chance. My dilemma is that Francine, on the other hand, would say yes in a heartbeat if I popped the question to her. Even though Audrey's considerably older, I came back to Crestview because I realized she's the one I want to spend my golden years with, not Francine." He chuckled and searched my eyes. "The thing is, I don't want to put all my eggs in one basket, and yet Audrey is such a tough egg to crack."

The only responses that came to mind were of the four-letter variety. Calculating that if Hugh came at me, I could smash his head with the heavy glass-and-steel frame, I rose, lifted the picture, and propped it up on my desk so that he could see it. "Does this look familiar to you?"

He arched an eyebrow, but showed no surprise or unease. "A little. It's wallpaper, isn't it? And you've framed it?"

The man was a veritable rocket scientist. "Yes. Francine's going to hang it in her house."

Hugh snapped his fingers. "That's it! That's where I saw it before—in Francine's house, back when the Chamberses owned the place. It was in their guest room."

"Right. The room that's currently Lisa's bedroom." I tightened my grip on the frame, ready to swing it at his face if he made the slightest threatening motion. "So you were in Abby's house when the Chambers family still owned it. Even though you told me a few days ago that you didn't know her."

He hesitated, then replied, "Actually, yes, I did know Abby. But not well. Over the years, I'd forgotten all about her. I was only in her house once for some school project or something. The wallpaper touched off a memory . . . stuck with me, for some reason."

"It's fascinating, some of the things that turn up in my job. Such as when I remove old pieces of wallpaper. As a matter of fact, when I removed this very wallpaper, I managed to find some evidence that could help solve Abby Chambers's murder."

His expression remained blank. "Really? What did you find?"

"The police will want to tell you that themselves." Which reminded me: I'd yet to share that particular item with the police. Afraid that Hugh might call my bluff, I lied. "A couple of officers are on the way here to speak to me right now, in fact. Maybe you'd like to wait and ask them."

His face flushed, and he stared at me for what felt like an interminable time. Finally he said in a simmering voice, "I'm not guilty. I didn't kill Abby. Or anyone else, for that matter."

"Good, because there's no way either Audrey or Francine deserves to be romantically involved with a murderer."

He looked again at the wallpaper, blinked, then rose.

"My advice, Hugh, is to stay away from both women. Audrey's too smart to be fooled twice. Francine has a young daughter to raise. And if you were a gentleman, you would stop leading her on."

He listened in silence, not moving a muscle, then he smiled down at me. "Thank you, Erin. You've told me precisely what I came here to find out." He turned and walked to the stairs and left without another word.

chapter 23

Hugh's parting words had me spooked—and regretful. Once again, my ego had interfered with my judgment; I'd assumed that I was outsmarting the man, but he could have staged this whole conversation to find out if I suspected him, thereby revealing that Audrey had shown me the items she'd taken from his wallet. If so, I had indeed told him everything he needed to know. I had to warn Audrey.

My heart pounding, I grabbed the phone. Audrey was in the middle of taping, the receptionist at the television station informed me. She refused to call her to the phone. I left a message that she "might be right about Hugh, so avoid him at all costs today," and asked that she please call me before she left Denver.

Then I called Linda Delgardio and gave her the full story about Audrey's sneaking the photograph and ID card from Hugh's wallet, my finding the hidden year-book clipping, and my conversation with Hugh just now. She listened without comment, but I could sense her anger in the crackling silence that followed my confession. I felt a pang of guilt. She was right to be angry. I should have told Linda last night about Audrey's date with Hugh. Linda probably felt that I'd encouraged Audrey to rifle through Hugh's billfold. I added, "A two-hour drive from the Air Force Academy is not an alibi for Abby Chambers's death. And I know for a fact that Hugh was in the immediate vicinity during both Diana's and Willow's murders."

Still, Linda said nothing.

"I'm worried about Audrey, Linda. If he *is* guilty, and he feels like he's getting hemmed in or something, I'm really scared that he'll go after her next."

"We'll keep an eye on her," Linda said harshly. She paused. "This is the type of thing that happens when civilians meddle with police investigations."

"In other words, 'I told you so.' Mea culpa. I appreciate your restraint in not telling me that straight out. Thanks."

"You're welcome, Erin. You owe me a consultation on my living room when we arrest the killer, you realize. It'll be high time we returned professional favors."

"Will do. And, if it'll make you feel better, I'll allow you to ignore all my suggestions and professional expertise the same way I've ignored most of yours."

She laughed. "Deal. Now, here's my last suggestion, which I'm *begging* you to follow: Stay away from this investigation, Erin. From here on out. No matter what."

"Fine."

"Are you listening to me?"

"Yes." *Although, surely it would be harmless enough to get a quick look at Bob's yearbook, which could prove to be insightful.*

"We'll bring in Hugh Black for questioning again, and if he's the guy, we'll arrest him."

"Great. *Thank* you."

"Meanwhile, you can start thinking about what to do with my undersized den and oversized television set."

"I thought you said it was the living room you needed help with."

"That too. I'm running you a tab."

I hung up and sank my head into my hands, desperate to quiet my rising panic. Had I foolishly endangered Audrey? Or had we been living next door to a murderer all this time? Was my home ever going to feel safe again?

I mulled over the possibility of driving to Audrey's studio and insisting we both stay in a Denver hotel for a couple of days. Knowing Audrey, she'd refuse to let Hugh oust her from her home, even temporarily. Besides, there was no guarantee that the police would arrest Hugh any time soon.

I needed to get a look at Bob Stanley's yearbook from his junior year. Hugh's and Abby's farewell notes to Bob could contain enlightening information about his relationships with them at the time of Abby's death. Furthermore, if the section of the page containing Hugh's senior picture had actually been removed from *Bob's* yearbook, that would go a long way toward clearing Hugh; Bob could have drawn the heart around Hugh's picture and hidden it behind the loose wallpaper to frame Hugh. After all, Bob knew I was remodeling that room and that I would find the picture.

Cassandra might know where Bob's yearbook was now located. I grabbed my cell phone and looked up the number for her cell phone. Then I hesitated. Out loud, I fretted, "Which will totally tip my hand if *she's* the killer." Cassandra could have planted the picture just as easily as Bob. In which case, as long as I made it clear I merely wanted to see if the book contained evidence to use against Hugh Black, she'd simply give me a brush-off, and I'd notify Linda to get the yearbook. A perfect plan.

I dialed, then rubbed my aching forehead as I listened to the phone ring. Once Linda found out about this, my "running tab" with her would include redesigning her entire house. And a relative's as well.

Cassandra answered with a cheerful "Hello." I knew I shouldn't be interrupting her much-needed respite but persevered. "Hi, Cassandra. It's Erin Gilbert. I need your help."

"Absolutely, Erin," she said kindly. "What do you need?"

"I need to take a look at Bob's yearbook from his junior year . . . when Hugh Black was a senior at Crestview High. I think Hugh Black is the murderer, and I'm hoping to get some additional information from the signatures from your husband's classmates."

"Oh, Erin, I can't help you, dear. I loaned the yearbook to Francine a few days ago. Apparently Hugh Black's birthday is coming up. Francine wanted to photocopy the pictures of him back then and make up a poster for him."

"Francine has Bob's yearbook?" I gripped the edge of the desk to keep myself from pounding on it in frustration. Now there was the possibility that *Francine* framed Hugh out of spite when she learned he was pursuing Audrey again.

"Yes, but surely she's done with it by now. I'll just ask her to return it to me right now. I'm already on my way home and will be there in another minute or two. Do you want me to call you when I have it?"

"Sure. That'd be great." I scanned my surroundings.

Lovely and welcoming as this room was, I'd feel less—exposed—at home. Right now, I seriously craved the sensuous comforts of curling up on my favorite velvet sofa, with my cat and my angora afghan. "Call my cell, Cassandra, I'm leaving here soon."

We exchanged good-byes and hung up. I wondered if Francine would be home. Surely we'd see her at Diana's funeral. Because Francine had dodged Willow's funeral, I doubted she'd see fit to bring Lisa to Diana's funeral this afternoon.

That reminded me of an entry in my daily planner I'd made a couple of weeks ago, when I'd been fitting my work schedule around hers. I snatched the planner out of my purse to verify. "Oh, great," I grumbled aloud. Francine was taking Lisa to a concert in Denver that started in less than an hour. She'd have already left home.

I wasted several minutes on pointless searches on the Internet, trying in vain to get more information on Hugh Black and Robert Stanley. I finally gave up and decided to leave. My cell phone rang as I locked up. With no preamble, Audrey said, "I got your message, and I'm leaving right now for home."

"Me too. Have you heard from Hugh today?"

"In a manner of speaking. He sent flowers to the studio. Get this: they're mango calla lilies. Just like the one that was crushed and stuffed in the envelope."

I unlocked my van and replied, "Maybe he spotted

Steve's, assumed it was yours, and figured he'd get you something he knew you liked."

"Or maybe it's a pattern with him that indicates his smarmy intentions."

"Right. I'm hoping I can get some evidence from Bob's yearbook . . . eventually. Cassandra said she loaned it to Francine, but I just now realized she and Lisa are going to be in Denver this afternoon."

"Maybe Cassandra will use her key and let herself in."

"The Stanleys have a key to the Findleys' house?" Francine was so aloof that it never occurred to me that she might have given a key to a neighbor for use in an emergency.

"Yes. It slipped my mind till now, but a couple of months ago, when I was visiting with Bob, Lisa had lost her key and gotten locked out. We both walked her home, and I remember that Bob let her in."

"That means the Stanleys have had private access to her house all this time!"

"So it does. Unfortunately." She sighed. "Well, my dear, I'll see you in an hour or so. Bye."

I muttered, "Bye. Drive carefully," and hung up. I started the engine and made the short drive to my house. Our neighborhood looked as picturesque as ever—quiet and peaceful. Somehow that seemed wrong. It would have almost been a comfort if my surroundings were in as much turmoil as were my emotions. I parked and headed up the walkway, then stopped and looked at Bob's house, where all was quiet. Could he himself have dug up Cassandra's garden last night because he'd somehow gotten the notion that incriminating evidence was buried there? Was it possible that he could have been behind everything—three murders, the Air Force pin, the picture behind the wallpaper, the falling chandelier, the death threats?

Learning that he had a key to Francine's was making me paranoid.

The house was still as I let myself inside; Hildi was no doubt fast asleep, her black fur soaking up the warmth of a sunbeam someplace. I crossed the foyer, went straight to the phone in the parlor, and dialed the number for our message system. The first message was: *"Hey there, gorgeous lady. It's me. I hope you like my flowers. Beautiful flowers for a beautiful lady."* I shuddered. Hugh had obviously called my private line when he'd meant to call Audrey's.

A second message said, *"Erin? It's Cassandra."* Her voice was tense. *"I think I may have seen Hildi on Francine's roof just now."*

Hildi? On somebody's roof? Cassandra had to have spotted someone else's cat; Hildi would never do that in a million years!

"You might want to check, just in . . . Oh. You told me to call your cell phone. Sorry. I'll go look up that number in—"

Someone pounded on the front door, ignoring the doorbell. I hung up the phone, glanced out the sidelight, and threw the door open. It was Bob, out of breath and alarmed. "Erin. Do you have a key for Francine's house? She's not home, and I've got to get into her house!"

"Yes, but—"

"It's Cassandra. She's on the widow's walk. I've got to get her down!"

"Call nine-one-one right now, and I'll—"

"I already did! They'll be here any second. But she's my wife! I need to talk her down.

"She's hallucinating!" Bob cried, as I rifled through my purse for Francine's key. "She thinks she's Abby or Willow or something. She was at our house a little while ago, talking all crazy. Then she took our copy of Francine's keys and locked herself inside."

Poor Cassandra! As my fingers closed around Francine's key, I steered him toward the kitchen to take the shortcut. "Let's go. My key will get us in through the back door."

Bob grabbed my arm. "She could be dangerous. It'd be best if you wait here."

"No. I wouldn't feel right about doing that."

We raced out the back door toward Francine's house. I scanned the roofline as I ran up to the house. "She doesn't seem to be up there now."

"Thank God," Bob said, as I fumbled to put the key in the lock. "Maybe she's gotten control of herself and has come downstairs."

We burst into the kitchen. Bob dashed to the staircase and called, "Cassandra, honey? Are you all right?"

The house was silent.

"Oh, dear Lord," Bob groaned, sounding on the verge of tears. "We're too late. I'll bet she's driven off someplace. I'm scared for her. I think she killed Willow and Diana."

"Did she confess?"

"Not exactly. But she did say she— It's all my fault, Erin. She was trying to protect me. Trying to save me from getting sent to jail for Abby's murder."

"*You* killed Abby?" I exclaimed.

Gripping the banister, he shook his head. "I didn't kill her, but I was on the roof with her when she jumped."

"Abby jumped?"

He nodded, tears in his eyes. He raked back his thinning gray hair. "Thanks to me. I bullied her . . . called her dad a Nazi. See, I'd been doing a class report on the POW camp in Colorado. Went up there myself and interviewed a former guard. He told me about this one escapee. I figured out it was Abby's father. I . . . harassed her about it. On her birthday, she called me. Told me to come over to her house and meet her on the roof. I was so stupid. I thought she was going to let me kiss her." He winced and explained sheepishly, "Like Ralph's said all along, I was a jerk back in school. I really thought I could pressure her into . . . dating me."

He balled his fists. "Her suicide was Abby's revenge. She made it look like I was guilty of murdering her. She told me she'd hidden clues where I'd never find them. That she'd hidden this . . . awful toy soldier I'd goaded her with and a stupid, nasty note I'd written to her. Along with a signed note from *her* that said 'Bob Stanley murdered me.' Then she jumped from the roof. Afterward, I searched her room, but I was too rattled. I couldn't find a thing."

"*I* found the toy soldier that you gave her."

Bob winced and searched my eyes, his own bloodshot and despairing. "That's what I was afraid of. So you found her note, too?"

"There wasn't a note." Trying to decide if I believed him, I studied his frightened features. "You're the one who tore down my wallpaper samples and wrote a threat on them? To stop the remodel? So nobody would find an incriminating note from forty years ago?"

"What was I supposed to do?" Bob asked tightly. "There's no statute of limitations on murder. Abby was a really disturbed girl. I made things worse for her, because . . . I could. Just like I did to Ralph Appleby. Harassed him mercilessly." He searched my eyes, then said softly, "But I've changed, Erin. I swear to God, I'm not the same person as the bitter, spoiled brat I was back then. Turned my life around. But, yeah, when I couldn't stop the remodel, I just faked some evidence of my own."

"So, the dog tag that Abby's father probably wore. Did you plant that?"

"Yeah. And I . . . tried to make Hugh look guilty of killing Abby. So I bought an Air Force pin, climbed up there, and crammed it between the boards. Then I . . . realized I couldn't live with myself if I'd framed an innocent man. So I warned Hugh not to let anyone mess with the roof, or the police were going to wind up assuming that he was guilty of something he didn't do."

"Maybe Cassandra's still here," I said. *And maybe Cassandra didn't murder anyone. Maybe she was suicidal from having just now realized her husband had murdered our two neighbors.*

"What in hell's keeping the police?" Bob said as he grabbed Francine's phone. "I'd better call nine-one-one again. Maybe they picked her up already, or something."

I'd left my cell phone at home! Damn it! If Bob was lying to me, he'd never let me rip the phone out of his hands to call 911 myself.

"I'm going to look for Cassandra," I told him, and trotted up the stairs, my heart pounding. I dearly wished I could wait for the police—escape to my own house, lock myself safely inside, and let them deal with this horror. But if Cassandra *was* suicidal, every second was precious, and we'd wasted too much time already.

"Cassandra?" I called as I entered the room.

I heard a noise, turned, and saw Cassandra standing in the open closet. She looked stricken. "Bob's lying, Erin. Last week *I* found the note he wrote to Abby. He said he was going to kill her if she didn't have sex with him. And I found Abby's note, too." Sobbing, she managed to say, "My daughter is right. Bob's guilty."

"Bob says he harassed Abby, but that she jumped."

She shook her head. "Oh, Erin, I believed that story,

too. That's why I tried so hard to protect him." She brushed past me and gestured at the yearbook on the floor near the door. "But he continued trying to frame Hugh afterward. He never told me about the missing page from his yearbook. Right after I loaned her the book, Francine called me and said it was missing. If only I'd put two and two—"

"She's lying to you," Bob snarled, suddenly in the doorway. He slammed the door and stood in front of it. "The police are on the way, Cassandra. We have to put a stop to this! I'm turning you in."

Cassandra gasped, but shook her head. "One time he even called Willow 'Abby.' Willow's treasure hunts to Lisa were a threat to him. He never knew where Abby had hidden the evidence. Then Willow made the mistake of mentioning to us she'd found an old note of Abby's. She must have meant the childish note Abby'd written on the board in the closet crawl space. But Bob thought that Willow was hinting that she intended to blackmail him. So he conned me into helping him search for Abby's notes. And he killed Willow."

"None of that's true!" Bob insisted. "*She* killed Willow. Because of her daughter." He was beginning to perspire profusely; he wiped his forehead with the sleeve of his ratty-looking sweatshirt. "I begged Diana to boot Willow out, so that my wife didn't have her daughter's killer under her nose. Diana just laughed at me."

He looked at his wife. "She's always hearing voices. All this nonsense about ghosts . . . it's just her psychosis. She could never forgive Willow. Willow's boyfriend had dumped her for Katelyn. So Willow convinced them to meet her out in the boonies, got them both drunk, then took off. They felt they had no choice but for one of them to drive home in that condition."

"No, no, no. He's making this up." Cassandra was rocking herself and covering her ears. Maybe Bob was telling the truth, I thought. The woman really did look insane.

"Diana had a thing for me for years. She hated Cassandra for winning my heart. I made the mistake of telling her all about Willow, so Diana tracked her down . . . found out she was here at CU, and convinced her to rent a room from her for a pittance. All just so she could torture Cassandra." He said in a choked voice, "I don't blame Cassandra for killing either of them. They got what they deserved."

"You bastard!" Cassandra shrieked. "It's all lies!"

"Cassie, you need help, sweetheart. This has to stop now. It's time to turn yourself in."

My brain was in a whirl. I didn't know which of them to believe.

"Stop it, Bob!" she screamed, stomping her foot. "No more lies! This won't work!" She gulped for air and fired her husband a hateful look. "I'm telling the police where I hid the notes! So just . . . stay away from me! Both of you!"

At that, she darted up the stairs and onto the roof.

"We can't let her be up there alone, Erin. She . . .

confessed to me. She said she'd jump off the roof and kill herself before she'd go to prison for murdering Willow and Diana." He grabbed my shoulders. Tears filled his eyes. "When she hears those police sirens, she'll jump! I just know it!"

I nodded. Regardless of which of them was telling the truth, I didn't have any doubt that Cassandra was crazed enough to kill herself. "We need to get her down. She can't fight both of us off at once."

I said a quick prayer and climbed onto the roof. A stiff breeze whipped my hair into my eyes. Just as I swept it out of the way, Cassandra let out a guttural scream and barreled into me, knocking me down.

"Cassandra! What—"

She charged at me again as I tried to rise, knocking me backward. I gripped the railing at the edge of the roof and stared at her in shock. Her face was red, her eyes wild.

"I'm not going to jail! Willow took everything from me! Everything! And Diana . . . she helped her do it! I tried so hard to forgive, but . . . Those bitches *deserved* to die!"

chapter 24

As she once again tried to ram me over the railing, I braced myself and stepped into her, cracking my elbow into her temple. She staggered backward, whimpering.

Where the hell was Bob? "Help me!" I cried.

"He *can't,*" Cassandra taunted. "He'll go to jail himself. He murdered Abby. The notes proved it."

Bob was suddenly standing behind me. "Sorry, Erin," he muttered meekly. "I wanted no part of this . . . but you're the only one who knows that I ever had a yearbook from my junior year. That's where we got Hugh's picture, so we could frame him."

"But that wouldn't have proven anything!" I cried in desperation. "You could have just said someone stole it from you!"

"The fingerprints would have proven otherwise," Cassandra said, sounding chillingly sane. "So this is our only way out."

"But you can—"

"No. They'll search the dump," Bob interrupted. His voice was cold. "Once the police know I had a yearbook where the photograph of Hugh could have come from, it's all over. We shredded everything with a signature . . . but we just threw the rest in a Dumpster."

"But . . ." I let my voice fade, all hope of reasoning my way out of this trap abandoning me. Their fingerprints—and not Ralph's or Francine's—would be all over the yearbook. They couldn't make it look like someone else had used Bob's yearbook to frame Hugh, so I had to die.

My heart sank. No wonder the police hadn't arrived. They'd never been called. Bob had set me up. He and Cassandra had staged the dramatic finger-pointing to convince me that Cassandra was suicidal. "The police will never buy that I fell trying to rescue my cat," I argued frantically.

Cassandra charged at me. As we both fell to the floor, she scrambled on top of me, clawing at my eyes. I grabbed a handful of her hair and tried to push her off me.

With the strength born of desperation, I thrust the heel of my hand into her nose.

Yelping with pain, Cassandra cupped her nose with her hand. I grabbed her wrist, wrenched her arm behind her back, and dug my knees into the small of her back.

"Bob!" Cassandra screeched. "Grab her!"

"No, I—" he said.

"Remember, I still have those notes! She dies, or we're both going to jail!"

Bob let out a furious roar. He grabbed me under the arms and wrenched me away from his wife.

"No, Bob! Don't!" I scrambled to my feet, desperately hoping I could somehow dodge past him and run down the stairs.

He attacked with chilling speed and strength. I was sent flying backward and landed hard. My breath was knocked out as he fell on top of me. The back of my head cracked against the wood deck, and my vision went gray.

Bob had risen, but now he was lunging at me again, gripping a piece of scrap wood from the banisters. He bore down on me, trying to press the board against my windpipe to choke me against the floor.

Terrified, I struggled to save myself, grabbing the wood near his hands and pushing back with all my might. He was too strong. I was fighting a losing battle. I could barely breathe. He shifted his position, swinging his knee up and over me. All his weight was now bearing down on my neck. My throat felt clamped shut, the pain unendurable.

I kneed him in the groin. Bob groaned, and his crushing pressure on my neck lessened. I managed to suck in a lungful of air and cracked him in the jaw as I scrambled out from under him.

Suddenly there was a dark blur of motion, and as I got up, I realized that help had somehow arrived and someone else was now battling Bob. Within seconds, Sullivan had flattened him onto the decking.

Just beyond the men's sprawled bodies, Cassandra, sobbing, her face covered in blood, was staggering toward us. She was looking past me. Her fingers were shaped like rakes and were aimed at Sullivan's face.

I dived. As I slammed into Cassandra's knees, she collapsed into wracking sobs. Though I was still gasping for air, I pinned her down.

Police sirens wailed. I'd never heard a more welcome sound in my life.

I risked a glance at Steve. He was managing to keep a tight grip on Bob, despite Bob's flailing efforts to free himself.

For an instant, our eyes met. "Audrey called," Steve told me. "Said you were probably coming here for Bob's yearbook. I saw you from the street."

"And you called nine-one-one," I said, wheezing.

Minutes later, Linda Delgardio raced up the stairs. "Police!" she yelled, her gun drawn.

Before my brain could get a handle on anything, her partner was slapping handcuffs onto Bob Stanley.

Linda took quick stock of the situation. Giving my arm a reassuring squeeze, she turned her attention to Cassandra and handcuffed her.

Despite all efforts to stop myself, I burst into tears. I cried because this was finally over. And I cried, too, with immeasurable sadness for Abby, Willow, and Diana, and for Cassandra, as well.

chapter 25

I've heard it said that if you want someone to like you, ask him to do a big favor for you. How lovely to think that whenever you truly need a helping hand, you're also deepening a relationship!

—Audrey Munroe

DOMESTIC BLISS

I felt a pair of eyes on me as I finished touching up the ceiling trim in Audrey's dining room, but didn't allow myself to get distracted. Although this ceiling already featured a mild cove—a curvature where the walls met the ceiling—I'd decided to emphasize it with the subtle gradation from darker to lighter peach-tinted hues. I'd also installed cove molding, which, with its subtle lines and shadows, enhanced the effect.

If there was any advantage at all to being relegated to working only on this one surface in this one room, it was that I'd honed my already perfectionist tendencies to a fine edge. There was not the slightest blemish in this ceiling, so when future houseguests puzzled about how a live-in designer could tolerate mismatched furniture and wallpaper on half of a wall, I could at least point out my ceiling design with pride. Satisfied, I descended the stepladder and massaged the crick in my neck.

"Fabulous job, Erin!" Audrey stood watching from the kitchen doorway. "Did I tell you how much I like the work you're doing?"

"A couple of times, yes." I returned my tiny paintbrush to its tray. "Back when you were saying you wanted to be the one to help me get the appliqué installed."

"And I intend to do so shortly."

"Good, because it's all painted and ready to go, but I absolutely have to have an extra pair of hands to hold it in place as the glue dries. Otherwise, it's going to be a nightmare for me. The edges are so fragile, they'll crack off if you as much as tap it with a fingernail."

"I promise you, I've no intention of deserting you.

I'm hoping you'll restore the ceiling in the parlor next."

At that, I couldn't help but glare at her. "This isn't an attempt to placate me, is it? You're not planning on just letting me do the ceilings and nothing else from here on out, are you?"

"Heavens, Erin! You make me sound manipulative."

"Well? You *are*."

"I realize that." She put her hands on her hips and arched an eyebrow. "I'm also short. That doesn't mean you have my permission to call me Shorty and pat me on top of the head."

I fought back a smile. "Duly noted. I promise to resist the temptation to pat you on the head. All bets are off with the nickname Shorty, though."

She smiled a little at my sarcasm and set her purse down. "You really should have come with me to the homeowners' association meeting, Erin. I got caught up on all the latest. A young couple with a three-year-old daughter now have Diana's house under contract. And that quiet couple who live kitty-corner to Francine are going to assume Bob Stanley's position on the board. Also, Bob's cousin, I think it is, has arranged to put the Stanleys' house up for sale next week, *after* your friend Mr. Sullivan has the chance to complete his work. Ralph's offered to donate his services, because he's so relieved that Bob is finally going to serve time. Last but not least, Francine gave Hugh the heave-ho, and Lisa, of all people, introduced her to the divorced dad of a friend of hers. So far, all four of them are getting along famously. Everyone says that you did a fabulous job on Francine's remodel, by the way. But the historic-homes tour, of course, has officially been canceled for this year."

In the three weeks that had passed since the arrests, we'd learned that two months ago, Bob had panicked and confessed to Cassandra about having murdered Abby. The sight of Hugh Black innocently planting the rosebush in Francine's yard had been the instigator that set the Stanleys onto their heinous path; Bob assumed that Hugh had a clue directing him where to look for the incriminating letters from forty years ago. Cassandra vowed to "use her powers" to find the incriminating evidence. Although she eventually succeeded, it was too late. By then, she'd murdered twice, having gotten it into her head that Willow—the bane of Cassandra's existence—and later Diana, had discovered the notes before *she* could. Desperate to escape prosecution himself, Bob tried to cover for his wife and to scare me away from Francine's house. All the while he was frantically searching Cassandra's garden for Abby's letters, which his wife had hidden from him.

But I didn't want to talk about the victims now, let alone the murderers, so I said, "That reminds me. We never heard a peep from that clandestine committee of the association, after the initial decision to put Sullivan and me in charge of approving each other's designs."

She replied breezily, "No news is good news, so the silence must mean they liked the results."

"Did you ever find out who was on the committee?"

"Oh, it's better to let that question go unanswered, dear. As you found out for yourself, it's not always wise to peer into people's closets."

"True." I collected the brushes I needed to clean. "I'm just curious if there was anyone on the committee, other than you yourself."

Audrey at least had the decency to freeze for a moment, and then to meet my gaze. "You don't actually expect me to answer that question, do you?"

"If your entire purpose was to get me and Steve Sullivan together, it didn't work. We're right where we were when this whole thing started—professional rivals." I gestured at the medallion. "So, are you ready to give me a hand installing your ceiling's centerpiece? Otherwise, all that's left to do is to clean the paintbrushes and pans."

She gave a quick glance at her watch, which invariably spelled trouble for me. "Let me take care of the cleanup for you right now. It's the least that I can do to thank you for the marvelous job you've done."

"You don't need to—"

"I insist." Gathering everything, she headed for the

laundry room in the basement. The doorbell rang, and she said casually, "Can you get that? It's my stand-in helper this evening."

"What are you talking about?"

"I'm not tall enough to help you, so I've asked a tall person over to help us." She winked at me as she shut the basement door behind her.

"And here Sullivan is now," I grumbled to myself as I headed to the foyer. Audrey could shove Sullivan and me together as often as she wanted, but we were still going to remain incompatible. Period. End of story.

"Hey, Gilbert." He was wearing a really attractive silk shirt—in a mango color. It reminded me of the calla lily he'd given me on our "first official date." That brought back an image of the smashed flower that Bob had turned into a death threat; I would probably never know why he or Cassandra had stashed the vase at Diana's, and that unanswered question would likely haunt me like a missed spot of wall paint. "Audrey says you need a tall guy. Will I do?"

I laughed, which sounded alarmingly like a giggle. "Sure, Sullivan. You're plenty tall. Come on in." I hesitated at the threshold of the parlor. "Watch your head on the doorways."

He chuckled and asked, "What did you have in mind for us this evening?"

"Installing a ceiling medallion. Then we can install the chandelier. And maybe even move the furniture back into place."

"Remind me never to hire you as an entertainment coordinator," he muttered.

Once again, my spirits sagged. We stepped into the dining room, the protective plastic on the flooring noisy as we crossed the room. Sullivan's attention was now focused exclusively on the ceiling. I expected him to make a crack about my fancying myself as a Michelangelo, but all he said was a sincere-sounding "Nice."

Our eyes met, and I hastily averted mine. *Oh, crumb! I hate this! Sullivan's just here as a favor to Audrey, but my heart's getting all fluttery and stupid again!*

"The medallion's on the kitchen counter," I said, not masking the irritation in my voice.

"Okay," he said dully. "Let's get this over with, then." He pivoted and strode into the kitchen.

Feeling horrible, I followed. He cast a bored glance at the magnificent medallion and stood there, waiting for me.

"So, Audrey tells me you're going to finish the work at the Stanleys' house," I ventured. "I'm really glad that you're going to get paid for the full job."

"Yeah, always a good thing to get paid." He wandered over to the back door, saying, "I heard Ralph and your crew finished Lisa's room, and that both rooms were a major success. Congratulations."

"Thanks." I rubbed my forehead miserably, trying

to decide if I should apologize for being so snippy.

He stood staring out the back door at Francine Findley's house. "I thought Lisa was visiting her dad," he said, still fascinated with the house.

"She is."

"Then who's that on the widow's walk?"

The widow's walk was empty, and the lovely windows in the tower room were all dark. "I don't see anybody."

He peered out the panes over my shoulder. "She's gone now. It was a young woman with red hair. She was wearing a long white nightgown."

I clicked my tongue and turned away, finally figuring out what this was all about. "Quit teasing me, Sullivan."

"I'm not! I really . . ." He stopped, gave another long glance out the window at Francine's house, then said carefully, "Sorry. Shouldn't have poked fun."

Stung, I yelled, "No, you shouldn't have! It's hardly a joking matter! That flipping 'haunted' room cost three young women their lives! Every night now, I'm afraid to look out my own bedroom window because I feel so awful. That room was supposed to be my tour de force! All it is now to me is an unhappy ending. The last thing in the world that I need right now is for you to mock me about the whole—"

I gasped in surprise as Sullivan took me in his arms and pulled me into a kiss. Instinctively, I tried to push him away. And then, almost instantly I knew I really didn't want him to stop. Instead, I gave in to an even stronger instinct. I kissed him back.

I might just need to rethink my statement about this being an unhappy ending for me. . . .

Center Point Publishing
600 Brooks Road • PO Box 1
Thorndike ME 04986-0001 USA

(207) 568-3717

US & Canada:
1 800 929-9108